Into The Shadows: Assassination Corps

Michael Brady

WALDORF PUBLISHING

Published by Waldorf Publishing
2140 Hall Johnson Road
#102-345
Grapevine, Texas 76051
www.WaldorfPublishing.com

Into The Shadows:
Assassination Corps
Book Two

ISBN: 978-1-64136-856-8
Library of Congress Control Number: 2018933218

For the men and women who participated in Operation Gold, a joint CIA-SIS operation during the Cold War.

Senua Island, Riau Islands Archipelago, Indonesia, June 2, 2018, 9:08 PM

Into the shadows he jumped. Free falling at a rate of nearly two hundred miles per hour, Michael Brennan executed his rapid descent toward the remote island. The sky was clear and filled with bright stars, but the clouds below meant his approach could be tricky. The MC-130J Commando II aircraft he just hurdled from began a slow banking right turn and headed home to an undisclosed airfield in Malaysia. Its crew, a team of elite special operators and one contractor, wondered what the professional spy's objective was. His unassuming and serious nature left little doubt he was entering a treacherous place.

A mere minute into his dive and hurling toward the earth's surface at terminal velocity, he checked his altimeter. Three thousand feet to the landing zone. Getting close he thought. His contact, a local contractor for CIA since 2009, had been reliable, at least per the file. A few moments later, the automatic activation device deployed his parachute. Thank God, Michael thought to himself. While at Fort Benning, Georgia conducting initial airborne training in 1990, Michael's main parachute failed. With only moments to pull his reserve, instincts drew his right hand to the release handle, which he pulled just in time to land safely on the drop zone. A few seconds longer and he would have been dead the moment his body hit the orange Georgia dirt. Since then, parachute drops made the professional spy nervous despite many advancements in parachute technology.

Though a veteran of nearly twenty solo jumps while at CIA, the thrill of skydiving never really left its mark on the non-official cover intelligence officer. He didn't mind the risks associated with skydiving and that failure would mean a certain death, it just never gave him the excitement others had for the task. His jumps typically meant one thing: he would soon be on his own operating in foreign lands with few friends and trusted allies.

Michael scanned the horizon and searched the darkness below for signs from his contact as he prepared for the night landing. The one thing Michael enjoyed most of any drop was the silence surrounding him after canopy deployment. In the air, there was no sound. It was peaceful and majestic. Michael slowly drifted down toward the island and purple flashing lights emanating from the beaches meant one thing: Operation Ocean Jewel was nearing its final stage.

Operation Ocean Jewel, a joint intelligence operation between CIA and Indonesia's National Intelligence Agency, Badan Intelijen Negara, commonly referred to as BIN, began two years ago, and spearheaded by BIN operatives. The operation was designed to identify and recruit a high-level Chinese naval officer operating in the South China Sea. Therefore, Indonesian operatives spent much of their time in Hong Kong and various naval ports in southern China, including Longpo, Zhanjiang, and Hainan Island. There, Chinese naval forces, known as the People's Liberation Army Navy, were stationed and would patrol the South China Sea or train with willing foreign navies such as Russia or Iran.

Michael would represent CIA at tonight's remote meeting and eventually become the asset's handler if both agreed. Most of his efforts would be directed at collecting technical data on Chinese naval acquisition radars, disposition of land based short-range ballistic missiles directed at Taiwan, and a host of other requirements the asset would have knowledge of. After only two short years, Indonesian intelligence found an officer whose resume was ideal. Coerced into the meeting by BIN agents, the officer felt uneasy but had few options.

He was filmed having sex with a man in Hong Kong while on an earned vacation. He could never continue his career as a naval officer if that information were disclosed. Hearing of these details weeks earlier made Michael cautious. Assets who are coerced rarely provide useful long-term information used for intelligence analysis. He hoped this stranger would be different and the two could develop a relationship based on trust and respect well into the future.

Heading Indonesia's intelligence agency was Lieutenant General Joko Gunawan, a career military intelligence officer who spent time in the United States. Joko was an idealist and believed in democracy and the rule of law. This made him an ideal candidate for CIA and his willingness to help them was evident the moment they approached him. In 1982, while attending the US Army Infantry Officer Advanced Course located in Fort Benning, Georgia, he was approached by a CIA recruiter who gave a guest lecture on counter-insurgency operations. Within weeks, Gunawan was recruited and would become a long-time source in the region. Gunawan was trusted implicitly by CIA and most of Indonesia's political parties. He was generally considered honest and the international community believed his track record on human rights was acceptable for his latest assignment.

Michael gently glided toward the coastline and soon landed on the forgiving shore just mere yards from the Indonesian operative. The contact would escort him to the meeting with their new Chinese source. The beaches surrounding the uninhabited and exotic island of Senua were pristine and one of the thousands of islands within the Riau archipelago, located between Borneo and Malaysia. Loosening his harness, Michael removed the parachute, rolled it up and approached his contact.

"Mr. Brennan, welcome to Indonesia. I'm Angga. I will

take you to the Pantai Kencana hotel in Ranai."

"Thanks, Angga. How long will the trip take us?"

"Less than an hour with the boat we're using. A colleague will meet us onshore and take you to meet the asset."

"Excellent. Let's get moving," said Michael.

The two men spent the next fifty-five minutes slowly navigating across the South China Sea. Conditions were not ideal as three-foot swells rocked the small boat from side to side.

"How long has he been at the resort?" asked Michael.

"He arrived this afternoon. He is officially on vacation and will be there for two days," said Angga.

"No wonder I had to get here on such short notice. Is he alone?"

"Yes. He is unmarried and has no family."

"Are you sure he can be trusted?"

"At this point, we are confident he will provide information. He has much to lose."

"That's what I'm afraid of. He may take unnecessary risks if we push him too hard," said Michael.

"True, but he aspires to reach the highest ranks in the Chinese Navy. He is an ambitious man."

Michael smiled and said, "that may be to our advantage."

The two men arrived at the hotel's marina and were greeted by their BIN operative, a veteran of the agency named Kuwat. Michael liked his serious demeanor and firm handshake. It was a cool evening with fierce winds blowing off the rolling waters and Michael wondered when the rain would come.

The three men stepped onto the dock, lined with soft yellow lights. Up ahead was the Pantai Kencana. Michael scanned the area and quickly noticed the number of tourists still gathered around the pool. People were relaxed, friendly and enjoying the amenities. A popular form of Indonesian music, Jaipongan, could be heard throughout the venue. Everything looked as it should.

Within minutes, Michael and Kuwat walked through the resort's lobby and up to the second floor. Angga remained at the marina where he would wait for Michael. Turning right after climbing the staircase, the two men found their way to the front door and met their new source. The executive suite was adorned with traditional Indonesian art and flora. Turquoise walls gave the room a soothing appearance indicative of the Riau Island archipelago and its mostly unspoiled waters. The career naval officer greeted them warmly and appeared anxious to begin talking.

"Sir, it's an honor to see you again. I've brought a representative from the United States per our discussion. This is Michael."

"Hello, Michael. Kuwat says it's an honor to meet me. Do you feel the same way?"

"No, sir. I do not. However, you have valuable information we seek."

Michael remained respectful which Chinese culture had demanded for centuries. However, he wasn't going to lie to the man. The compromised officer would have seen right through it anyway. Michael wasn't impressed with a man forced to disclose sensitive military information to save his reputation, despite his potential long-term value. The man immediately took a liking to Michael. A career naval officer in the People's Republic of China, he valued men who spoke directly and honestly.

"Straight and to the point. Just like most of the Americans I've met," said the naval officer with a slightly derisive look on his face.

"Sir, what do you have for us?" asked Michael.

MI6 Headquarters, along the Thames River, London, England, June 3, 1:05 PM

"Sir, Mr. Dearlove is on the phone. Are you available?" asked Teresa Holland.

"Patch him through, Teresa."

"Alex, I have an update for you regarding our operation in Hong Kong. Can I stop by this afternoon and bring you up to speed?"

"Of course, John. I have no obligations this afternoon, but you must consider a cup of Earl Grey tea."

The brew, a favorite of Alex and other top brass at MI6, included a citrus flavor and extracted from the sweet-smelling fruit, the bergamot orange.

Alex Sawers, chief of the Secret Intelligence Service, commonly known as MI6, had been at the helm of SIS since June 2016. Sawers was also known as 'C' inside the spy agency. The first chief of SIS was the legendary Mansfield Cumming. Since then, all chiefs were designated 'C' in his honor.

Sawers, a talented and gifted operative, had the skills needed to guide MI6's transition into the cyber age. Alex, having served for several years as an officer with the Royal Scots, entered service with SIS in 1991. One of his first assignments included Geneva, Switzerland, where he spent much of his time cultivating relationships with rising political stars of the Swiss Parliament. His operational cover was that of an employee with Barclays, one of the largest banks in the United Kingdom. Geneva, known for its superior banking system, provided Alex endless recruiting opportunities as politicians were often seen at fundraising events and social gatherings searching for contributions. He would not disappoint his superiors back in London.

The post allowed Sawers the opportunity to see first-hand how software was being designed to protect bank transfers and customer identification long before cyber security became a multi-billion-dollar business. Immediately after his assignment, he requested a tour within MI6's technical division to further augment his knowledge of protecting critical information networks. Sawers, a visionary, saw the power of information technology and its vulnerabilities. Prior to assuming his duties as 'C', he was considered one of the most technically skilled operatives in MI6 and highly respected by leaders at the Government Communication's Headquarters. The Foreign Secretary's decision to place him at the helm of SIS was met with little resistance in the British intelligence community.

John Dearlove, responsible for managing his operatives throughout East Asia, arrived along the Thames river at 3:45 PM. John, a career SIS intelligence officer, spent most of his time in Hong Kong building a large contingent of sources and assets. Some assets traced their origins to World War II. British SIS had an extensive history of long-term asset development, equally rivaling Israeli Mossad. MI6's approach to human intelligence collection was in stark contrast to America's Central Intelligence Agency, which placed a heavy premium on short-term results. In a few minutes, John would enter Alex's office.

"John, how are you, old boy?" asked Sawers.

"Excellent, Alex. I'm sorry to trouble you this afternoon but I have an update from Hong Kong," said Dearlove.

"What is the news, John? You have me a bit worried."

"Our man there is Brian Wu. He's been performing admirably for us since the end of last year. He's missed his reporting window for five days now. I'm concerned the Chinese have him, or he's gone dark," said John.

"I'm familiar with Brian's work. His credentials are impeccable, John. Thought he was deeply entrenched with the South China Morning Post as a reporter? I doubt Chinese counter-intelligence picked him up in Hong Kong."

"I agree, Alex. But this is highly unusual for any of our operatives. We've heard nothing. His cover has not been blown, at least as far as I can tell. He's just gone silent."

"What do you need from me, John?" asked Alex in a very serious and concerned manner.

"You know what I want, Alex. I need to get there immediately."

"You want authorization to find him?"

"I do, Alex. I trained and prepared him for the assignment. I owe it to him to personally go there and find him. I know his wife and children well, it's personal for me."

"You know I don't like my deputies crawling around the globe when situations arise. I need you here, John. We are due in the Foreign Secretary's office next week to discuss our budgets for next year. And personal issues cloud our judgment, John. No, my dear friend, I don't think so," said 'C.'

"Dammit, Alex. You're the politician in this room, do not feed me that nonsense. You will not miss me. You will get the money we need with or without me. I want to leave tonight. Alex, he's one of my top officers working overseas and I need to find out what the hell is going on."

Sawers sat back in his chair and thought for a moment. John Dearlove was a close colleague and probably one of the most gifted intelligence officers in SIS. The intense operations he planned and executed were clearly supported by metrics and treasured by the Foreign Secretary. Dearlove was a long-term collector and his efforts ensured highly reliable intelligence was generated from inside Hong Kong and other locations along the Chinese mainland. Whether the long-time operative knew it or not, Sawers' success was dependent on John's work. Alex suspected he knew, thereby explaining John's unusual behavior.

"Isn't it a bit premature to go looking for him, John?" asked Alex.

"He's missed five days. I can understand one, maybe two, but not five. Something's gone awry and I need to know why he has stopped reporting per our protocols. I'm sorry Alex, but this is not negotiable."

Alex stared into John's eyes. He knew the man was dead serious. There wasn't much to stop John Dearlove from getting to Hong Kong one way or another. 'C' gave in.

"I want updates each morning. Call my cell and check in with me. You do what you must to keep your department up to speed. But I expect daily updates until the matter is resolved. Understood?"

"Yes. Thank you, Alex," said John.

John Dearlove would quickly exit Sawers' office. As always, both men wondered if it would be the last time.

Korla Missile Test Complex, Xinjiang province, Western China, June 3, 10:43 AM

"Sir, all pre-flight tests have been conducted. We are ready to proceed."

"Excellent. Begin the final countdown sequence. The Director is arriving at any moment. The test must be flawless. Funding depends on it, Li."

"We all understand, sir."

Approximately fifteen minutes later, a motorcade of four white Mercedes GLS SUVs arrived at Korla. Exiting the second vehicle was General Zhang Guozhi, Director for the General Armaments Department of the People's Liberation Army. A career military officer, Chinese Communist Party favorite, and close friend to President Xi Jinping, General Zhang was an efficient and competent officer who regularly exceeded expectations. He was affable, steadfast and had few enemies. Rumors in Beijing had him becoming a member of the Political Bureau of the Central Committee at the next scheduled National Party Congress meeting in 2022. Today's missile test would reaffirm his reputation within the party as a rising star and one of Beijing's most influential leaders.

Chi Jun greeted General Zhang. Though confident, he appeared visibly uneasy. One of the brightest minds to graduate from The University of Science and Technology of China in Hefei, Chi's career was remarkably bland. He often felt unappreciated and underpaid. He was, after all, the reason today's test would even come to fruition. If successful, China would have the irrefutable capability to counter the United States' supremacy in space. He, along with General Zhang, knew the Americans would be watching today's test and a successful launch would send shock waves through the

American intelligence community and its allies. There was much to lose on both sides.

The two men, flanked by a group of scientists and military officers, made their way to the control center. General Zhang looked at the digital clock above the massive one-hundred-inch display. Three minutes and forty-five seconds remained until launch. The dozens of launch specialists were glued to their consoles where final checks were performed and reported to the mission director. A sense of anxiety and optimism filled the room as it always had in the past.

Several minutes later, the order to ignite engines was given. Soon after, the Dong-Neng-3 exoatmospheric vehicle began climbing. The direct-ascent designed missile would enter low earth orbit in minutes, then ultimately make its way to high earth orbit to approximately twenty-three thousand miles above the earth. The target, a US spy satellite recently launched from Vandenberg Air Force base in California, had an imagery interpretability rating scale of nine. This allowed US spy agencies to visually identify bolts and screws on Chinese missile components. However, the missile, if successful, would miss the spy satellite by at least three miles. Demonstrating the capability was enough to send the Americans a clear message---China's ability to knock out US spy satellites in high earth orbit was real.

Telemetry data began appearing on the screen. Everything looked positive. The Dong-Neng-3 was moving at a speed of 2.7 kilometers per second along its longitudinal axis. Its south-easterly trajectory and that of the American spy satellite were on display. General Zhang still maintained a stern yet optimistic look on his face. The Communist Party will be pleased, he thought to himself. But first, stage one separation had to occur flawlessly.

Approximately one-hundred and seventy-three seconds

into flight, the four boosters dropped away from the five-me-ter core stage.

"Booster separation from core stage complete," said one of the specialists.

"Understood. Next separation in one-hundred-twelve seconds," said the flight director.

General Zhang remained delighted and smiled. The test was proceeding perfectly as planned.

Four minutes into the flight, the missile approached its next stage. In forty-five seconds, the payload fairing would separate at an altitude of approximately one-hundred and fif-ty kilometers above the earth. Immediately upon separation, two YF-77 engines would deliver the missile into a parking orbit. From there, the missile would coast for approximately two hours until its final stage.

The lull would allow the general an opportunity to eat an early meal with his trusted advisors. Peking Duck, Zhang's favorite meal, was on the menu. Its origin traced back to the Yuan dynasty when Mongol emperors ruled China. Tradi-tionally served in three stages, the first stage included skin dipped in sugar and garlic sauce. Zhang had a sweet tooth and therefore required additional servings of the powdered white substance.

Zhang returned to the operations center just in time.

A few minutes later, Chi turned to General Zhang as the missile test was nearing its conclusion.

"Sir, we will fire the enhanced YZ-2 engine in approxi-mately one minute. From there, the missile will move to its transfer orbit and pass by the American spy satellite."

"I wonder what the Americans are thinking now?" asked Zhang.

"They are probably in disbelief, sir," said Chi.

"Possibly. But they won't see the final boost for some

time. Once they review the telemetry data, they will then know the power of our missile program. I worry what President Trump may do once he is briefed. He is unpredictable. That makes him dangerous."

"President Xi will be ready for whatever response the Americans have, sir."

"Yes, he will be, Chi. You can be certain of that," proclaimed Zhang.

Pantai Kencana hotel, Ranai, Indonesia, June 3, 10:55 PM

Michael continued listening intensely and taking notes when important. It was clear the Chinese naval officer had intimate knowledge of Chinese military capabilities along its southern coastline. Analysts at CIA, DIA, and others throughout the intelligence community would soon have a treasure trove of technical details that would likely keep them busy for months. Michael learned the types of fuel used to propel ballistic missiles aimed at Taiwan. He also learned of probable targets and the launch procedures, along with the types of armaments found in specific missile types.

About forty-five minutes into the meeting, Michael began wondering why the naval officer was divulging so much information. He didn't need to do it this early. The man could have simply offered a small bit of data to gain the trust of Indonesian intelligence and CIA. Requirements could have been levied on him over time.

Since the officer had no intention of defecting nor was he asking for anything in return, Michael became increasingly cautious. Something didn't feel right.

"Sir, you have given us a considerable amount of information this evening. Why are you providing us with so much?" asked Michael.

"Michael, I think it's best to tell you everything now. I cannot afford to risk meeting you again in the future. I do not get much vacation time and we are constantly monitored by Chinese intelligence."

The officer was referring to the Ministry of State Security, China's intelligence and security agency whose headquarters were in Beijing. Formed in 1993, several bureaus resided within the organization, including its immense counter-intelligence apparatus.

"Sir, you do realize we will be asking you for more information in the future, don't you?"

"How can I possibly tell you anymore, Michael. This is everything I'm likely to know in the future. The information I gave corresponds to the newest technologies in our armed forces."

"Sir, I'm not sure you understand what is going on here. My job is to build a relationship with you for the long-term. In exchange for information, we will refrain from sharing your personal shortfalls with your superiors. I don't like it, but this is how it's done sometimes."

"So, I am supposed to be at your beckoning for the foreseeable future?"

"Unfortunately, yes, sir. However, I'd like you to think of this arrangement as a partnership."

"Partnerships require both sides giving. What are you giving me, Michael?"

"Your freedom. Your life. I will never ask you something you cannot provide. And I will rarely call on you. Go back to the fleet, live your life, continue your career, and we'll be in touch when necessary. I can promise it will not be often. I will not put you at risk."

The officer leaned back in his chair. Frustrated and bewildered, he knew his options were limited. His career was no longer his to control.

"Okay, Michael. How will we communicate?"

"Leave that to me, sir. I do have one more question."

"Go ahead."

"Who was the man you were with in Hong Kong and how long have you known him?" asked Michael.

"Why do you need that?" asked the officer.

"Call it a professional curiosity, sir."

"His name is Wu Heng. I have known him for several months."

Michael was pleasantly surprised he answered the question and decided to press on with more.

"That's a common name in Hong Kong. Where does he live?"

"He has an apartment in the Central district. It's the Sha-ma Central apartment complex. Seventh floor, 710."

"Does he know he was filmed?"

"I told him."

"What was his response?"

"That's four questions, Michael. You said one."

The officer continued and clearly understood he was not in control. He had to answer Michael's questions.

"He was unhappy about it. He wants it kept quiet. He has much to lose like me."

"What does he do for a living?" asked Michael.

"He works for a bank, but I do not know which one."

"He never mentioned it?"

"No."

Correct, thought Michael to himself. The Indonesian file indicated this was a gap.

"Alright, sir. I think I have enough for now."

Michael handed the naval officer a business card with only a single telephone number.

"Memorize the number. If you ever need to reach me, call the number and ask for me by name. Flush the card down the toilet when you're done."

"What is your last name, Michael?"

"Just Michael, sir."

Michael shook the officer's hand and left with his Indonesian colleague. He rejoined Angga after slowly working his way back to the marina.

"How did it go, Michael?"

"Good, Angga. I need to get to Jakarta right away."

"We can pick you up in the morning. Let me work the flight specifics, Michael."

Angga and Michael left the dock aboard the small boat as a light rain began overhead. The quick sail to a nearby marina would only take the two men twenty-five minutes.

Michael wondered if the rain was an omen.

Tongchang-ri region, along the Chinese border, North Korea, June 4, 2:30 PM

"The supreme leader will soon be happy, Jung," said Min.

"Yes, sir."

"He will be here in a few minutes. Are we ready for his orders?"

"Yes. The rocket is fueled and ready to go."

"Today's test is historic, Jung. We cannot make any mistakes. Our lives are on the line."

"We will not fail our supreme leader."

Min walked away and prayed he and his team would not disappoint their leader. Recent tests of the new Intercontinental Ballistic Missile had failed due to poorly constructed heat resistant material surrounding the rocket's engines. Their supreme leader was becoming increasingly angry with the team and his patience was wearing thin. Min did not want to be another casualty in the country's burgeoning missile program.

Soon thereafter, North Korea's supreme leader arrived. He was flanked by Nam Ji-woo, the senior deputy director of the Worker's Party of Korea and General Kwon, Commander of the North Korea People's Army Strategic Forces. Behind them were a few bodyguards, and the district commander, along with his staff. Kim Jong-un was only the third leader of North Korea since his grandfather founded the communist state in 1948 soon after World War II.

Kim was named the leader of the Democratic People's Republic of Korea in 2011 soon after his father died of natural causes. A young and ambitious man, Kim had to quickly reinforce to the regime he would be the country's undisputed leader. Reports from outside the country indicated Kim had purged many older members of the government, including those of his family. His methods of killing off rivals were brutal and reportedly included a pack of wild dogs viciously attacking his victim. Another method, a rumored favorite of the young leader, included using anti-aircraft guns to execute five military officers. Within a few short years, Kim's reputation among the country's elite was solidified and no challengers to his rule existed.

Since his ascendancy, Kim's primary focus had been the development of a nuclear-tipped intercontinental ballistic missile capable of reaching the United States. Today, his dream would be one step closer to being realized. If not, more bodies could pile up, further reinforcing his cruel reputation. Failure was no longer an option for Min and his army of engineers.

Several minutes later, Min welcomed the supreme leader inside the command center. His hands were sweaty, and his heart raced. He looked visibly nervous, a far cry from his demeanor just moments ago.

"Supreme leader. We await your orders to fire the missile. Whenever you are ready, sir," said Min.

The young leader walked into the room and found his way to the empty console. He then leaned forward to the microphone and simply said, "Today we make history. Today the world will come to know the true power of the Korean people. Today is the day that America will wish had never come. Today is the day the world will finally respect us as a great power............. Fire."

Rising from an underground silo, the missile began ascending toward the skies above. Traveling eastward, the ICBM reached low earth orbit in minutes and continued toward its destination, four hundred kilometers off the western coast of Hawaii. A new threat to the United States became alarmingly apparent.

United States Embassy, Jakarta, Indonesia, 3 Jun, 3:35 PM

Michael's trip to Soekarno-Hatta International Airport, twenty miles northwest of central Jakarta was over. Indonesian intelligence used the Hawker 900 XP jet, built by British Aerospace, to transport the American spymaster. Michael thought the aircraft was pleasant while the flight gave him time to update Langley and coordinate for this afternoon's visit. Awaiting him on the ground were Sebastian Leiter and Joe Cartwright, both junior operatives with CIA and stationed at the United States Embassy.

"Welcome to Jakarta, Michael. I'm Sebastian Leiter. This is Joe Cartwright."

"Thanks, Sebastian. This is my first trip to Jakarta. How long is the ride to the Embassy?"

"It should take us about forty-five minutes depending on traffic."

"Damn. It smells here. What's that stench?" asked Michael.

"Industrial pollution. The city is awash in it. You get used to it."

"Okay. If you say so. Reminds me of some New York City subway stations. Let's get moving fellas."

"It's much worse here. Wait till you see some of the rivers as we go through town," said Sebastian.

The three men left the airport and traveled along the toll road for several miles as they approached central Jakarta. To Michael's north, he could see the Java Sea lined with fishing boats and pollution. A haze was evident several miles off the coast indicating air pollution. As they made their way into the city, the rivers were brown and carrying plastic bottles, plastic bags, and other miscellaneous junk. Jakarta was a mess, thought Michael to himself.

About thirty minutes had passed and the three men found themselves entering the embassy. As they climbed the stairs, marines were seen mulling about along with a group of civilian employees made up of mostly local Indonesians. Waiting for Michael was Linda Hunt, the chief of station for CIA in Jakarta.

"Michael, welcome to Jakarta. How was your flight?"

"Great. The Indonesians have taken good care of me for the last twenty-four hours or so."

Linda Hunt, CIA's second female to serve as a Chief of Station in the Asia region was a seasoned professional. Single and focused on her career, her ability to develop assets throughout her assignments in southeast Asia were legendary. She recruited several politicians in Taiwan and was thought to have made an executive assistant in the Philippines executive branch a long-time source. Other assets included bankers and CEOs of major tech companies. Linda was the consummate core collector whose ability to connect with her targets was uncanny. She created lasting friendships where information flowed freely from her sources. The career operative had earned the post she currently occupied and rumors in Langley suggested she was on a short list to lead the Directorate of Operations when the assignment came open.

"How much information did you get?" asked Linda.

"Plenty. He gave us a lot of technical data. I was surprised how easily he divulged the intelligence."

"He had no options, Michael."

"Probably so. However, I would have expected him to hold back a bit. Maybe use some information as leverage if he needed it in the future."

"He's a career naval officer. He doesn't think like a collector," said Linda.

"True, but I'd like to travel to Hong Kong to verify some parts of his story. I want to be absolutely sure of who I'm dealing with here."

"Makes sense to me. You need transport or planning to fly commercial?" asked Linda.

"Commercial is the plan. I'm in no hurry and would rather enter Hong Kong inconspicuously, if at all possible."

"Do you want to stay here or find a hotel downtown?"

"I'll stay downtown. It'll give me the chance to learn a bit about Jakarta. I've never been here before," said Michael.

Linda understood what he meant. Michael was new to the southeast Asia region and clearly looking for potential targets he could turn into sources in the future. They ranged from local taxi drivers to hotel staff. A career core collector is always looking to develop assets when possible. A short stay for Michael would do just that. After all, he did not know for sure how long he would be operating in Indonesia and sources in Jakarta appeared endless.

"How long will you be staying?" asked Linda.

"Probably a few days at most. I'd like to be in Hong Kong before next weekend."

Michael handed Linda his notes from the previous evening.

"There's a lot of technical information in there. I'm sure the MASINT analysts will have a field day. Most of the requirements I received were answered. We got lucky to get such a high-ranking source in the Chinese Navy."

MASINT, a new collection discipline formed in the late 1980s within the Defense Intelligence Agency stood for measurements and signatures intelligence.

"Sometimes, luck is all we need, Michael. What parts of his story concerns you?" asked Linda.

"First, I want to know who the man in Hong Kong is. The

file said he was a banker. I want to verify that first. Second, I want to know who he knows and who he associates himself with. If the Indonesians found out, there may be others."

"Chinese intelligence?" asked Linda.

"Maybe. There's no way to know right now. I'd rather rule out any possibilities and be sure the man in Hong Kong is who our naval officer says."

"Why not have Langley check it out, Michael? They may have already confirmed the intel."

"I'm going to do just that. But I want to personally verify the report with our personnel in Hong Kong. I'm in no rush and will not contact him again unless I am absolutely sure of who I'm dealing with."

"It will take weeks, if not longer, to verify this data and adjust any previous assessments, if at all," said Linda.

"I'm sure the technical analysts will be in heaven. I'll be in touch if I need anything, Linda."

"Please do, Michael. Good seeing you again and take care of yourself."

Michael exited Linda's office where Sebastian waited.

"Sebastian, can you recommend any hotels in the area?"

"Sure, Michael. There are plenty. Looking for something near the water or closer to downtown?"

"Wherever I can get away from that damn smell."

"Okay. You might want to consider the Mandarin Oriental hotel. It's where many prominent business executives stay and is considered the finest location in Jakarta. The hotel has easy access to the financial and diplomatic district."

"Thanks, Sebastian. I'll check it out. It was good meeting you. See you around."

Michael left the embassy and would arrive at the Mandarin Oriental hotel in minutes. His secondary objective in Indonesia was underway.

Dragon Eye nightclub, Hong Kong,
June 4, 2018, 9:50 PM

John Dearlove arrived at the Dragon Eye nightclub. In the country for only three hours, he went to work right away. John already placed two phone calls to sources in the city who might know the whereabouts of Brian Wu. The Dragon Eye would be his first stop of the evening.

Arriving at the front entrance flanked by security guards, Dearlove wore a black Alexander McQueen business suit. He purchased it many years ago to commemorate his fifteenth year of service for SIS. The store's revered location along Savile Row, Britain's premier destination for handcrafted men's clothing, welcomed the career "executive." Rounding out the sophisticated operative's attire was a pink tie he often wore to honor his mother who died of breast cancer. Dearlove looked the part of a highly successful banker in Hong Kong and would be welcomed by the staff, as he always was, before his departure to London.

Dragon Eye, whose doors opened in 2002, and consistently rated as one of Hong Kong's hottest nightclubs, was legendary in style as it was by its world-famous visitors. The interior included luxurious sofas, red phoenix lamps and even a birdcage on the club's terrace. Frequented by international soccer players, top deejays and models alike, most guests had to wait hours before being invited in. Not John Dearlove.

"Mr. Dearlove, welcome back, sir. When did you arrive in town?" asked the security guard.

"Hey Mak, this afternoon. Have you seen Brian this evening?" asked John.

"No. I haven't seen Brian for a while, actually. Are you expecting him tonight?"

John smiled and said, "I am chap. He owes me a drink."

Dearlove reached into his pocket and handed the bouncer three hundred Hong Kong dollars. Tonight's cover charge was only one hundred and fifty dollars, but John always paid more. Despite having been a regular patron of the club and never having to wait, he always tipped the staff generously to keep up his appearance as a senior banking executive. The role suited him perfectly.

John was accustomed to wealth from an early age. His family fortune was made in the shipping industry decades ago when his father created the London Freighters shipping company. Raised to assume the family business, John decided on another career path. While growing up in the suburbs of London, John's fascination with intelligence collection began in secondary education where he learned of the Secret Service Bureau which was established in July 1909. Their operations during World War I were legendary and included the 'La Dame Blanche' network of spies in German-occupied Belgium. He became instantly hooked at the prospect of serving his country and operating in the shadows as a clandestine operative.

John's clash with his father occurred in his first year at Cambridge University where he was enrolled as an undergraduate in the prestigious Land Economy program. Pressured to enroll, John succumbed rather than risk disappointment from his father. However, several months later he would change his major to the Asian and Middle Eastern Studies program. John's desire to eventually serve within the SIS ranks compelled him to make the change. He thought the department, along with his study of the Chinese language, would make him an ideal candidate for recruitment. He made the right choice though relations with his father soured and never recovered.

John scanned the dance floor. All around him were beautiful people, including the staff while loud techno music pumped throughout the club. He made his way to the bar where he ordered his usual whiskey.

"Hi, John. Heard you left for London several months ago. What brings you back?" asked the bartender.

"Hi, Carmen. I'm helping close a real estate transaction for the bank. I'm supposed to meet Brian tonight. Have you seen him?" asked John.

"Not for a few weeks. Did he leave town on business?"

"Yes, but he should be back by now. Is Tommy and his crew in the VIP lounge?"

"Almost every night, John. Are you looking for product?"

"Ha, I won't tell. See you around, Carmen."

John left the bar and worked his way to the VIP lounge. Security officers were everywhere, along with a contingent of Tommy's personal bodyguards. No one challenged John as he approached Tommy's table surrounded by attractive young women and a couple of associates. The table emptied except for John and Tommy, one of Hong Kong's largest cocaine distributors since 2013.

"John, what are you doing back in Hong Kong?" asked Tommy.

"Looking for Brian. Have you seen him?"

"Now why would I tell you that, John."

"I'm in no mood, Tommy. If you know something, you need to tell me now."

Tommy leaned back and said, "I haven't seen him in weeks."

"If I find out you're lying to me, your operation will be eliminated swiftly. Do we have an understanding?"

"You've got quite a pair on you, John. You come into

the club threatening me with my boys around. I'm not that same kid you helped years ago," said Tommy.

Tommy's rise through the ranks of the Hong Kong Triads began as a cocaine distributor in 2005. While working in the Financial district, John recruited the young man known to many as a brash street thug with ambitions to be Hong Kong's leading drug kingpin. In exchange for Tommy's information, John provided the dealer with cash to challenge Triad leadership when the opportunity arose. One of Dearlove's assignments included recruiting assets capable of providing information on a wide range of economic, diplomatic and military developments. Narcotics trafficking was of no concern to the bold operative. Since then, Tommy provided Dearlove routine information on the organization and high profile customers.

"Tommy, let's be clear for a moment. Brian is a friend of mine. You want me to send some digital recordings of our conversations to your associates?" asked John.

"Screw you, John. I can make anything sound authentic using today's technology. I could create a recording of you admitting to crimes if I wanted. Don't try and scare me."

John chuckled and said, "Last chance, Tommy. Where is Brian?"

"I don't know. Now get the hell out of here. I want to party with my beautiful new friends."

John was surprised by Tommy's brashness. The kid had come a long way, and he may not have known, he thought to himself. Dearlove stared into Tommy's eyes for a moment, stood up and returned to the main dance floor. Several minutes later, John exited the Dragon Eye and headed for the eastern district. His next stop would be a visit to the Sun Yee On group, a competitor to the Triads. John thought to himself, where was Brian Wu?

White House Situation Room, Washington, D.C., June 4, 8:00 AM

"Good morning, everyone," said the President who appeared annoyed. Just back from a weekend trip to Camp David, the President was eager to get this morning's briefing out of the way.

Camp David, the Presidential retreat built from 1935 until 1938, and located in the Catoctin Mountain Park in Maryland, had welcomed Presidents and their staffs since its inception. President Franklin D. Roosevelt famously called the mountain retreat the *Shangri-La* and hosted Sir Winston Churchill in 1943 to discuss ongoing operations and strategy during World War II.

The small crowd assembled inside the White House situation room included the National Security Advisor, the Director of National Intelligence, the Director of the Defense Intelligence Agency and the Director of the Central Intelligence Agency. This morning's brief would be given by Oliver Tanner, at the direction of Steven Coats, the President's Director of National Intelligence.

"Sir, I'm Oliver Tanner, an intelligence analyst with the Defense Intelligence Agency. Yesterday morning, the Chinese launched an anti-satellite missile into high earth orbit. As you can see from the telemetry data displayed on the screen, it came within several miles of one of our satellites. The satellite, which was launched from Vandenberg Air Force base in California, is one of our newest surveillance satellites with multiple capabilities. The Chinese have sent us a clear message."

"And what might that be, Oliver?" asked the President who immediately understood the ramifications.

"They have the capability to engage our satellites operating at the highest orbits we use. They want us to know they can knock out our space-based capabilities."

The President moved forward and stared into the analyst's eyes.

"How do we know they didn't just miss?" asked the President.

"We don't, sir. However, I'm confident it was a warning and a demonstration of their improved anti-satellite program. There would have been no reason to engage our satellite now."

The President was pleased with the man's response. He despised alarmists throughout the intelligence community who consistently espoused assessments contrary to his own worldview.

"Are you sure?" asked the Commander in Chief.

"I'm very confident with my assessment, sir. The Chinese have absolutely no reason to attack one of our satellites. It would be highly provocative on their part. It would also be a strategic miscalculation not to expect a swift response," said Oliver.

That was debatable, thought the President to himself. Nonetheless, he pressed the analyst.

"Okay, Oliver. So how many of these missiles do they have?" asked the President.

"It's unclear, sir. The test was successful, so they will likely replicate the engines and design to modify existing models. At this point, it's safe to assume there will be dozens in the Chinese inventory before the end of the year."

"Dozens? How did you arrive at that number?" asked the President.

"Sir, it's merely an educated guess at this point. I have no data to suggest work has begun to replicate the missile's design. It's just too early after the launch. The Chinese have other anti-satellite programs including space-based lasers. I think they will put more research and development into those programs than the traditional kinetic approach."

"If they fired a dozen of these missiles, what would be the impact to us?" asked the President.

Steven Coats chimed in.

"Mr. President, it would depend on what satellites they target. They have no way of knowing the capabilities of each of our high earth orbit satellites, however, if they were successful in knocking out a dozen or so…we would have significant intelligence gaps," said the Director of National Intelligence.

"What impact would it have to our operations in the region?" asked the President.

"Significant, sir. We would lose the ability to keep our commanders informed during any heightened tensions or conventional military engagements. It would be a significant blow especially if they combined the attack against our communication satellites which are much lower."

The President turned to his CIA director.

"Nikki, any recommendations on how to proceed from here?" asked the President.

"At this point, sir, we need more intelligence. And we need it fast."

"Can CIA get that kind of information inside China?"

"Yes, sir, we can. It will take some time, but I could make it a high priority requirement."

"How much time?"

"I cannot speculate, sir. It will likely take months, and probably much longer. The type of information we need will be compartmentalized. The Chinese will limit the number of people with direct knowledge of the test and the missile's performance. We may need to get help from the British.

They have been in the region for a long time."

The President turned back to Oliver.

"Thank you very much, Oliver. Is there anything else?"

"No sir, that's all I have for you now."

The President thanked the group and promptly left. The DNI turned to Nikki.

"Nikki, you really think we can get the intelligence in a few months?" asked Coats.

"Doubtful, Steve. Our human intelligence capabilities are limited in China. As you know, their counter-intelligence apparatus is enormous. It's damn hard to recruit people there."

"What do you have in mind, Nikki?"

"We'll need to get someone inside right away. Someone who the Chinese don't have on their radar. We may have to contract it out. I have some ideas."

"Okay, let's get on it. The President is going to want an update soon. I'm going to put today's subject into the President's daily briefing and keep it there until we get more information."

Nikki departed the White House and would soon return to Langley. She called Doug Weatherbee, the Director of the Operation's Directorate.

"Doug, I just left the White House. Need to see you in my office in thirty minutes."

"Sure, what's going on, Nikki?"

"We need to get someone inside China to answer questions the President just threw at me. It needs to be someone with no ties to China and no one in the diplomatic corps. We need an outsider."

"Okay. See you soon," said Doug.

Doug hung up and gazed out toward the Virginia sky. His decision would be an easy one.

Urumqi, Xinjiang Province, China, June 2, 8:45 PM

High atop the fifty-nine-story skyscraper of the China CITIC Bank Mansion, formerly known as the Zhong Tiang Plaza, members of the China Assassination Corps convened. The group was founded in Hong Kong in 1910 until it willingly ceased operations in 1912 after the triumph of the Xinhai Revolution. Long forgotten from history books and nearly erased from Hong Kong legend, the group had been reactivated by its new charismatic leader, Liu Zhun.

The China Assassination Corps had emerged during the last years of the Qing dynasty. The group only had twelve confirmed members and their few successes were dwarfed by their public failures. Deeply rooted in anarchist ideology, the group's goal was to remove the Aisin Gioro imperial clan, which had ruled China since 1644. Liu's goal was much more ambitious.

Attending tonight's meeting were only five individuals. They included Liu Zhun, General Zhang Guozhi and two of his assistants from the Peoples Liberation Army, and a trusted associate from Hong Kong. Each man had their own motivation for joining the resurrected group, however, their goals were similar.

"General Zhang. Will tomorrow's missile test yield positive results?" asked Liu.

"The test should go as planned. My engineers at the facility indicate the test will be successful. With good fortune, the Americans will observe the test and our leadership in Beijing will be pleased."

"Will Beijing request another test soon?"

"I assume so. However, if not, I will. It's my program and there will be a second test next month. Only this time, we'll actually hit something. First, we have to be sure it works."

"How will you override the guidance system and get the missile to hit its target?" asked Liu.

"Leave that to me, Zhun. I have someone on the inside who will guide the missile when the time comes."

"What will be the target?" asked Liu.

"An American spy satellite. I've heard its capabilities are tremendous. Such a loss would likely result in a swift punitive response."

"How can we be sure?"

"We cannot. However, the impact to its strategic collection capabilities and early warning systems would be severe. I do not foresee a scenario where the Americans do not retaliate," said Zhang.

"They surely wouldn't use military force, would they?"

"Not likely. However, they could retaliate by imposing economic sanctions, initiate tariffs, or other measures designed to burden Beijing's economy. Such a scenario would likely include actions from Japan, the Association of Southeast Asian Nations, and other regional states and organizations. It likely won't end the party's leadership but could create conditions for revolt or mass uprisings soon."

"How will you explain the 'accident' to Beijing?"

"A software glitch in the guidance program. The engineer will be eliminated within hours of the accident. He will have committed suicide for his grave error."

"You think Beijing will buy it?"

"I have no doubt, Liu. They trust my loyalty and commitment."

Liu appeared cautiously optimistic and turned to the man from Hong Kong, his first recruit from the sprawling city in 2003.

"Have you developed the plan to take out British intelligence in Hong Kong?"

"I am still working on the details, but we could be ready in a few days. I have five targets in mind. I will make it look like Chinese intelligence. The loss of five operatives will enrage the British."

"Have you already identified the assassins?" asked Liu.

"I have someone who will assist us. He is a narcotics dealer in Hong Kong and won't care who the targets are. He is willing to do the job for a million Hong Kong dollars. The attacks will also occur simultaneously," said Wu.

"Okay, Heng. I will leave the details to you. I will transfer the money to your account when you are ready to pay."

Liu's China Assassination Corps only had a few dozen members, but their influence and capabilities suited the group's mission to end the country's Communist Party and eliminate its ruling elites. China had become a global leader where power was centered around a few individuals while most of its citizens were mired in poverty. The Corps intended to change that.

Liu sat back in his chair and made his final remarks for the evening.

"Thank you, gentlemen. Things are beginning to unfold. Our man in Pyongyang is making progress and will support our efforts there. I should be able to give you an update soon."

Eastern District, Hong Kong, June 4, 11:45 PM

John Dearlove made his way into the Eastern District, home of the Sun Yee On group. Its leader was an older man named Chun. John never determined the man's full name even after an extensive background check was completed over a two-year period. During the investigation, Chun proved useful for SIS and served as a double agent. Chinese intelligence thought Chun was loyal to the mainland while providing intelligence on foreign businessmen. Little did they know, Chun helped SIS identify Chinese counter-intelligence agents operating in Hong Kong. For years, Chun's chameleon-like behavior within both organizations eventually led to his rise as a leading arms dealer.

Dearlove never cared for Chun but he trusted the man's information. He lacked ideology, patriotism, and values. Chun was single, had few friends, and rarely attended social functions. Money seemed to drive the man and if cash flowed into his pocket, reliable information was obtained. Dearlove hadn't spoken to Chun for several years but reports from Brian Wu indicated the relationship with SIS endured.

"Chun, this is John Dearlove. I'm back in Hong Kong and would like to speak with you."

"John, what a surprise. Brian said you returned to London for good. What brings you back?"

"I am looking for Brian. He was supposed to meet me this evening at Dragon Eye. Know where he might be, old boy?"

"Haven't seen him in a couple of months."

John knew Chun was lying. A recent report written by Brian indicated he met with Chun two weeks ago to discuss a suspected Chinese counter-intelligence officer working at the British Consulate-General in Hong Kong. The suspect, a young woman and recent graduate of the University of Hong Kong, had ties with Chun and was working as an administrative assistant in the travel section.

"Okay, Chun. I'd like to stop by and discuss a few things. Will that work for you?"

"Sure, John. I always make time for you. I'll let the boys know you're coming in."

"Great. See you in about thirty minutes."

Dearlove arrived at the front entrance of Chun's home, a large mansion sitting on five acres of prime Hong Kong real estate. At the gate, two men approached John's car. After verifying his identity, one man spoke into his radio and the gate began opening. John made his way toward the manor and spotted several roving security guards walking the perimeter. Nothing had changed since John's last visit, he thought to himself. Even the security cameras were in the same locations as large security lights illuminated the unspoiled property.

A young man greeted the professional spymaster and escorted him into Chun's private study. John knew he would be filmed and expected nothing less.

"Chun, I see you continue to do well for yourself. Still working with the Chinese?"

"Of course, John. How do you think I can afford this house? I provide useful information and they look the other way regarding my business ventures. Like you once did."

"You're getting older my friend. How much longer do you plan on being in this game?"

"Until it ends," said Chun.

"Well, I haven't heard from Brian in quite some time. I fear something has gone wrong. Are you sure you haven't seen him or spoken with him recently?"

"No, John. I would tell you."

"Then why did he report meeting you recently? Something about a female working at the Consulate?" asked Dearlove.

Chun sat back. He was caught in a lie and had to quickly try to pivot away from it.

"How recent, John?"

"Fifteen days ago, Chun. That is what Brian reported to me."

"I have not spoken to Brian for quite some time. It might have been three or four weeks. I do not remember. Why are you so concerned?" asked Chun.

"I just am, Chun. We have reporting procedures. He's missed his window."

"How long?" asked Chun as such information might be valuable in the future. Dearlove was not pleased with Chun's provocative question of SIS procedures.

"Long enough. I need to know what you know, Chun. If I find out you are lying to me I will not hesitate to expose you for the pathetic stool pigeon you are."

Chun was visibly upset with the remark. However, John's leverage over him was cemented years ago and he was vulnerable to being uncovered. Self-preservation kicked in.

Dearlove began probing. His personal relationship with Chun ended years ago and the information he provided to SIS was increasingly becoming less important.

"Has Brian approached you for any contracts recently?"

"He did. I lost it to Tommy's crew."

"What was the contract for?"

"He asked if I could kill five Chinese counter-intelligence agents. I lost the bid."

"Who are the agents?" asked Dearlove.

"I don't know. He said he would provide that information when the time came."

"He knows you work with them. Why would he do that?"

"Money, of course. I offered to do the job for two million Hong Kong dollars."

"How do you know you lost the contract to Tommy?" asked Dearlove.

"Brian told me a few weeks ago. He said the job would go to a competitor. No Triad on the island would do it except Tommy. I'm not sure, but who else could it be?"

John stared into Chun's eyes and became convinced. Chun was getting older and such a windfall of money would allow the man to retain his standard of living for a little while longer.

Dearlove stood up and shook Chun's hand. Both men knew their decades-old relationship was ending. As John departed, the uncertainty surrounding Brian's disappearance made him uneasy. Assuming Chun's information was accurate, Brian was operating as a rogue spy without authorization from London. Dearlove asked himself if this was by design or if he was being coerced. Brian Wu had to be found quickly. Something was awry. John's next stop would be to the one thing in Brian's life that mattered the most, or so thought the career MI6 officer.

Langley, Virginia, CIA Headquarters, June 4, 11:25 AM

"Daniel, it's Doug Weatherbee. Got a few minutes to stop by?"

"Sure, Doug, I'll be there in few minutes."

Doug Weatherbee just returned from his meeting with Nikki Hastings, Director of CIA since April 2017. A favorite of the President, she was a perfect fit for the legendary and controversial spy agency. Hastings was a former intelligence officer in the United States Air Force and stationed at the United States Space Command from its inception in 1986 until her transition to the civilian community shortly after Operation Desert Storm. After the war, she became a state senator for Florida and eventually won the governor's race in 2009. She was also instrumental in helping the President win Florida's twenty-nine electoral votes in a hotly contested Presidential election in 2016. Well respected among Republican operatives within Washington, D.C., her posting was met with little opposition.

Daniel arrived at Doug's corner office within minutes.

"How are things in the Special Activities Division, Daniel?"

"Good. We have several operations ongoing. What's up?"

"I just received a tasking from the Director. She wants specific intelligence from inside China and I need to figure out how to get someone in," said Doug.

"Into the mainland?" asked Daniel with a perplexed look on his face.

"Yes. I just need to get someone inside. But we have to do it discreetly. We are not using official cover officers. I will notify our people in Beijing, but they will have no role in getting the officer into the country."

"How quickly do you want to get someone there?"

"As soon as possible. When I am satisfied with a reliable plan, I will authorize the operation," said Doug. He knew this wasn't going to be easy.

"Do I need to plan for inside the mainland? Or do we have the option of transporting him to the border?"

"Either will work. However, I'm sure it will be safer to deliver the officer along the border."

"Will the officer need to be extracted as well?" asked Daniel.

"No, leave that to me."

"Okay, Doug. China is massive. Any areas you want us to look at?"

"We need to get the officer into the Xinjiang province. Might a good entry point be along the Afghan border?" asked Doug.

Daniel thought for the moment. A veteran of the special operations community, he was all too familiar with Afghanistan.

"He or she could use the Wakhan Corridor. I might be able to put together an operation quickly. But it's going to be expensive. Can you authorize a transfer to special activities?"

The Wakhan Corridor, a geographic region in northeastern Afghanistan, had linked the country with China for centuries. History suggests that even Marco Polo traveled in the rugged mountainous terrain. Today, the region is better known as the route used for delivering Afghan-produced opium into China.

"A transfer will not be a problem, Daniel. This is one of my highest priorities."

"Okay, Doug. Let me put some options together for you. Can I have until tomorrow afternoon?"

"Sure. But let's not drag this out. I know your people are busy, but this is coming from the Director," said Doug.

"I assume my division will have operational control over the mission?"

"Yes, Daniel. The officer will be along for the ride. Your mission is to get the officer in. From there, he will be my responsibility."

"Understand, Doug. See you tomorrow."

Daniel was gone, and Doug shifted his attention to the US Embassy in Beijing. They would be responsible for the evacuation whenever, or if ever, the time came. Michael Brennan would soon be accepting the most dangerous mission of his career.

Shama apartments, Central District, Hong Kong, June 5, 8:40 AM

John Dearlove arrived in the central district of Hong Kong, also home to Brian Wu and his family. Brian was a resident of the Shama central apartments and Dearlove hoped to get some answers. His meeting with Chun the night before was troubling, and Brian's recent behavior had unsettled the SIS operative. Questions were swirling in John's mind, yet he had few answers.

John entered the apartment complex and approached the front desk manager. Lo, a source for John before Brian was ever recruited, eagerly welcomed Dearlove with a firm handshake and smile. Lo's family fled China in 1962 and embraced capitalism found in British Hong Kong. Lo was not a supporter of the Chinese Communist Party and cringed when Hong Kong was transferred to Beijing in 1997. Brian Wu was unaware that Lo was a low-level source for John.

"Lo, it's great to see you again. Can we talk in your office?"

"Of course, John. Follow me."

The two men entered Lo's office and Dearlove did not waste any time.

"Lo, I know it's been quite some time since we spoke. Have you seen Brian Wu recently?"

"No, John. I have not seen him in a few weeks."

"Has anything unusual happened to him or his family?" asked Dearlove.

"Nothing unusual. But his family left months ago, John. Did he not inform you?"

"No. What happened?"

"I don't know. His wife told one of the managers she was returning to the mainland to care for her aging parents.

I think the manager said she was going somewhere in Xin-jiang."

"Did Yan indicate she was coming back?"

"I don't know, John. Is something wrong?"

"Not sure, Lo. When is the last time you saw Brian?' asked Dearlove.

"A few weeks ago. He said he was going to visit her and would be back soon."

"Did he specify a date?"

"No. Just soon."

Dearlove sat back in his seat. Lo was speaking the truth, at least according to what Brian told him. There was no reason to continue the conversation. Lo knew nothing else of importance.

"Okay, Lo. I'm sorry to cut this meeting short. I've got other business to tend to. How is your family?"

"My daughter is almost grown. She will soon be studying in the United States."

"Congratulations, Lo. I will be in touch."

Dearlove exited the Shama central. The situation was becoming clear. Brian and his family were either in trouble or the man was no longer working for SIS.

As Dearlove drove away, he reached for his cell phone and called London.

"Alex, we've got a severe problem."

Mandarin Oriental Hotel, Jakarta, Indonesia,
June 5, 9:50 AM

Michael Brennan returned to his room after eating butter brioche French toast and fresh papaya at the Cinnamon restaurant. Its convenient location next to the hotel's lobby allowed the career CIA operative time to sleep in. As he opened the ruggedized laptop and waited for a secure link with an overhead satellite, his phone began buzzing.

"Doug, how are you, man? I was just about to send an update."

"Michael, whatever it is it has to wait. I've got a new assignment for you."

"I just got here, Doug. The Chinese officer gave us good intel and I'm ready to begin my secondary objective."

"I know. Saw Jakarta's report this morning. Excellent work, Michael, but we've got to put that operation on hold for now," said Doug.

"Okay. I was planning to fly to Hong Kong in a few days to verify some of his story."

"Understand, Michael. However, the Director has authorized an operation in western China."

"Aren't we getting ahead of ourselves, Doug? I just met the man."

"Different operation, Michael. You will receive a file in a couple of hours with instructions. We are still working logistics, but plan on leaving Jakarta as early as this evening. I'm working with our military liaisons on where you're going. From there, you will go into isolation for a few days as an infiltration team prepares to get you inside."

"Who or what is the target, Doug? This is the second time in the last few days I'm jumping through my ass."

"I know but the Chinese launched an anti-satellite missile at one of our satellites. They seem to have missed, but no one is sure if that was by accident or design," said Weatherbee.

"Why are you not using some of your assets in Beijing?" asked Michael.

"The Director wants an outsider. You know the drill, Michael. Chinese counter-intelligence is all over our officers at the Embassy. They will provide you with some local assets on the ground."

"I suppose that's being worked as well?" asked Michael slightly annoyed.

"Yes. We're moving as fast as we can on this, but I won't authorize execution unless we develop a good plan. You could be operating there for quite some time."

"Have you contacted the British? Don't they have more resources in the country than we do?" asked Michael.

"Not yet. I want to see what our guys do first. Right now, I'm more focused on getting you inside. We have much to do Michael. Give me some time. Get some rest and I'll be in touch."

"Doug, I'll feel better working with the British. Request you get them involved."

"Talk soon, Michael."

Michael sat back on the plush leather couch. Short notice operations were often characterized as dangerous with poorly developed intelligence. Assets are often unreliable and risk-taking is commonplace. The possibility of British support appealed to Michael, but the decision would not be his to make.

The professional spy turned his attention to the secure laptop in front him. He wondered if the report was even necessary but pressed on. Details from the last forty-eight hours needed to be documented regardless of how long his new mission would take him away from Indonesia. The monotony of the report would consume him for a while until Langley's instructions arrived.

Two hours later, Michael received the compressed file. Afghanistan would likely be his next stop.

CIA Headquarters, Langley, Virginia, June 5, 4:30 PM

Daniel Ludlum and a team from the Special Activities Division sat around the executive conference table and waited for Doug Weatherbee to arrive. The group included two intelligence analysts, and a liaison from the Air Force Special Operations Command, one of the most elite and versatile units found within the Department of Defense. This afternoon's briefing would be lengthy, thorough, and precise.

"Good afternoon, everyone. Daniel, start when you're ready," said Doug as he sat down.

"Okay, Doug. Our plan is to move your operative from one of our facilities near Kabul to the village of Khandud located in northeastern Afghanistan. It's along the border with Tajikistan in the Wakhan district, next to the Panj river," said Daniel.

Doug maintained a close eye on the map in front of him while Daniel continued to highlight key geographical and historical characteristics of the region. It was moments like this he was thankful for the professionalism, dedication, and courage of the special operations community. They made Doug's planners look like amateurs and their assessment of the region's desolate and brutal terrain would be critical to Michael's insertion.

"Our team will deliver the operative to a group of local Wakhi nomads using a modified CV-22 Osprey helicopter."

"Will you be using refueling aircraft?"

"Yes."

"Who are these Wahki nomads, Daniel?' asked Doug.

"There are about twelve thousand Wahki in the region. Most live a simple existence, but a few earn their living as guides for Afghan opium traders. It's this group that we have worked with in the past and will be relying on to move your officer across the Chinese border," said Daniel.

"How has your division worked with them previously?" asked Doug.

"We used them in our efforts shortly after the 9/11 attacks. They were instrumental in identifying remnant Taliban forces after the Tora Bora campaign. We have no doubt they will assist in this operation. If you approve the plan, our next step will be to contact them and coordinate the specifics."

"Any chance they'll say no?" asked Doug.

"There's always a chance, Doug. However, they have shown no support to the Taliban and they are no fans of the Chinese. The guides we have in mind are motivated by cash. And we will have plenty of it."

"What if they say no, Daniel?"

"Then we will have to get your operative further east toward the border. We won't proceed unless we get their support in the next couple of days."

"Who are you using to get confirmation?"

"Leave that to me, Doug. We have several of these Wahki guides on our payroll and they can be trusted," said Daniel. Daniel's operation in the Wakhan Corridor was part of a special access program and highly compartmentalized. Doug did not have the need to know, at least for now.

"How will these Wahki guides move my officer into China?" asked Doug.

"There is an extensive trail that runs east toward the city of Sarhadd. They will likely use pickup trucks and four-wheelers for most of the trip. They will then move your operative through the Wakhjir Pass and into the town of Tashkurgan, part of the autonomous region in Xinjiang."

The Wakhjir Pass, located along part of the Silk Road, was an ancient system of trade routes, first introduced during the Han dynasty as early as 207 B.C. The network would eventually be used by Chinese, Roman, Arab, Indian and Persian traders, among others. Silk and horses were the primary commodities being traded and eventually led to the development of economic and political relationships between these great civilizations. Some scholars have indicated that Tashkurgan was the location where Chinese traders met their European counterparts.

"How far is it from Sarhadd to the Chinese border?" asked Doug.

"About one hundred kilometers. There is no road beyond Sarhadd. However, our Wahki guides should be able to move him quickly at this time of the year. There is a ninety-mile border fence along the eastern side of the pass inside the Chinese border. Chinese military personnel are stationed there."

"How will the Wahki get my officer around the border guards? I assume they have roving patrols."

"They do, Doug, but they are sparse. Very few people cross the border and Chinese resources are minimal. The Wahki will enter China by bribing local officials there. They've been doing this for quite some time," said Daniel.

"How far will they go?"

"Probably to Dafdar, a village along China National Highway 314. We won't know this until they agree to the transport. We will push for Dafdar. Our analysts are sure they use the village as a distribution point to their Chinese buyers."

"Who are these Chinese buyers?" asked Doug.

"Mostly criminal gangs such as the Triads," said one of the analysts. Doug turned back toward Daniel.

"You think they might be willing to move my officer if we don't have the assets there?"

"Yes. It would certainly cost a substantial amount of

money. Where will your asset go?" asked Daniel.

"The city of Korla in the Xinjiang province. What is the elevation of the terrain along the Wakhjir Pass?" asked Doug.

"About sixteen thousand feet, Doug," said Daniel.

"Do we have the option of using the Osprey to land closer to the border?"

"We thought of that, Doug. The problem is that Chinese radar systems are scanning the region. Dafdar is also claimed by India. The closer we fly to the border the more likely they are to be observed. The risk of detection is too high."

"How long will it take for my operative to get through the Wakhjir Pass?"

"No more than a week, depending on weather conditions," said the liaison from Air Force Special Operations Command. Doug knew Michael was in outstanding physical shape but wondered what the toll on him might be.

"Do the Chinese patrol inside the Pass? I've heard reports some of their military vehicles have been spotted there?" asked Doug.

"It's true, Doug. Open source reporting has confirmed that. However, the Wahki guides are known by Chinese military and they will let them continue until the border."

"How will they explain our operative?"

"They won't need to. Chinese military will not stop the group."

"How can we be sure, Daniel?"

"I can't look you in the eye and guarantee that, Doug. However, I am confident that if they do encounter some Chinese patrols inside the Pass, they will not interfere with the nomads. These incursions by Chinese military are rare. The Wahki will ensure your operative blends in with the group. I believe the risks are acceptable."

Doug sat back in his chair. There were still questions swirling in his mind, but he was confident that Daniel and his team had the beginnings of a workable plan. More details were needed and isolation in Kabul would allow Michael an opportunity to prepare.

"Thank you, Daniel. Let's go with this plan for now. I need confirmation that Dafdar will be the endpoint for my officer. Once I get that, I will give final approval. When will you need my operative in Kabul?"

"In three days. Can you get him there by then?"

"Oh yes, that won't be a problem. We've already alerted him to prepare for movement to Afghanistan," said Doug.

"Who is the officer, Doug? My guys will need to know soon," asked Daniel.

"His name is Michael. Thank you, everyone. That will be all for now."

Daniel and his team exited the conference room and Doug quickly shifted his attention to Michael's suggestion for British support. Michael was probably right, and Doug wondered if he should even get the team from Beijing involved. He had some valuable resources throughout the mainland, but intelligence from within Xinjiang province was extremely limited except some telemetry data acquired by military intelligence during missile tests. Doug returned to his office where a phone call with his counterpart at British SIS would begin in the morning.

Central District, Hong Kong, June 6, 11:10 AM

John Dearlove returned to his hotel. Having spent the last twenty-four hours exhausting several leads, he recalled his conversation with Chun. Chun was probably right that Tommy and his boys were the only Triads crazy enough to accept a contract to kill Chinese counter-intelligence officers. After all, the infusion of that amount of cash would allow him to expand his enterprise and tie up any loose ends.

Dearlove knew he had to speak with Tommy one more time. His behavior at Dragon Eye, coupled with Chun's revelations, left little doubt that Brian's disappearance was linked to Tommy. If Brian offered him the contract, then Brian's tenure at SIS was over. What bothered Dearlove the most was the motive. Why would Brian approach Tommy with such a contract? he thought to himself. Where was he going to get the money? Nothing made sense and then London called.

"John, it's Alex. Are you alone?"

"Yes, Alex. Nothing has changed since we spoke yesterday. Everything leads to Tommy and the Triads."

"I know but I just got off the phone with our friends in Langley. They want to get one of their boys into western China. The Chinese launched an anti-satellite weapon and missed one of their birds in high earth orbit by only a few miles."

"Alex, I don't have time to hold CIA's hands. Can this wait until I figure out what the hell is going on here? We might have to institute a recall for some of our assets. The longer Brian is missing, the more worried I'm becoming that our people are in danger."

"John, I appreciate your concern over this. I am a bit worried too. But we're still only talking a week. We don't know if the intelligence you have is any good. You know some of our officers can go weeks at a time without reporting."

"This is different, Alex. He should have been providing routine updates. There were no new operations ongoing and he wasn't scheduled to travel," said Dearlove.

"The Americans have requested our assistance and I promised to help them, John. Do we have assets in the Xinjiang province?" asked Sawers.

"Yes, we have several. Xinjiang is big. Can you narrow down the map for me, Alex? What do the Yanks want?"

"The operation is in its preliminary stages. They want to get one of their officers into Korla, develop some assets and collect specific technical data on Chinese missiles. They haven't shared more details with me and are simply looking for local support to provide logistics," said Sawers.

"Do they expect to just walk in and have someone hand it over?" asked Dearlove sarcastically, who was becoming a bit annoyed. Supporting CIA now was not his priority, he thought to himself. More Chinese missiles were irrelevant and human assets in Hong Kong were in jeopardy.

"Of course not, John. Stop pissing on the idea. The Prime Minister is also concerned over the launch. It's a matter of time before he tasks me with getting the same intelligence the Americans seek. We might as well get in front of this and work together," said Sawers.

"Okay, Alex. Let me place a call soon and see what I can do. We have some reliable sources working with Chinese military officers in the region. Is the American a male or female?" asked Dearlove.

"Male. Now that's more like it, John. I know you are concerned. For now, focus on Hong Kong and send the information to get this moving. The Americans believe this is going to take some time. Frankly, I agree with them. The more support we get the more likely we'll figure out what the Chinese are up to."

"I want operational control of the collection, Alex. I don't need CIA screwing up and playing cowboy in western China. I've personally recruited several of our sources there," said Dearlove.

"You have it, John. I don't think the Americans will care. They came to us."

A few moments later the conversation ended and Dearlove called his most trusted operative in Urumqi. Mei, the owner of the city's largest brothel had worked for SIS for nearly two decades and was a fierce opponent of the Communist Party of China. Living in the autonomous region of Xinjiang, she provided Dearlove with valuable information on social and economic developments in the region. In addition, she occasionally provided good intelligence on military personnel looking for an escape from the boredom and isolation of their remote postings.

"Mei, it's John. I have a client arriving in the city soon. Please set up a room and plan to entertain him. I'll send you details when he leaves Beijing. He is important to our banking operations and requires special attention," said Dearlove.

John was speaking in code. Mei understood what he meant. John had to be vague due to the probability of Chinese counter-intelligence intercepting the call. It would take weeks for Chinese intelligence officials to listen to their conversation, if at all, but John needed to be careful nonetheless. Chinese intelligence intercepted domestic telephone calls like the National Security Agency inside the United States. Metadata collection was analyzed for any suspicious behavior by individuals who disagreed with Beijing and conveyed anti-government rhetoric. Chinese intelligence spent most of their efforts directed against its own people to maintain a strong central government and internal security was a higher priority for Beijing than overseas collection, though the disparity had tightened in recent years.

"Of course, John. I will take excellent care of him and ensure he is satisfied. I miss you. Will you be visiting me soon?" asked Mei.

"Maybe. I have some business to attend to here in Hong Kong. I'll let you know when I get back for a conference or meeting. The city continues to grow and banking opportunities remain abundant."

"That is good to hear. Any ideas when your client will arrive?" asked Mei.

"Probably in the next week or two. He's working on a large deal in Beijing. I think he's helping to fund a solar project there. I'll let you know for sure when he departs," said John.

"Okay, John. Sounds good. Take care of yourself," said Mei.

John hung up and quickly turned his attention toward Tommy and his crew. Getting logistical support for the American would be easy and Mei's contacts could probably help him. Until London provided further details of the operation, John would focus on Brian.

John Dearlove exited the hotel and began his drive toward the southern district, Tommy's personal residence. On the way, he made a short phone call to a source there.

"Hello, Tan. It's John. Do you know if Tommy is home today?"

Tan was a long-time source in the southern district who owned a small restaurant near Tommy's residence. Tommy often used the restaurant for ordering food and trusted its owner implicitly. Vegetable dumplings and wonton with garlic were Tommy's favorite. John recruited Tan shortly after Tommy's rise in the Triads was complete and took up residence in the southern district; specifically, in the Repulse Bay housing district.

"Hi, John. Yes. He just ordered lunch and we will deliver his food at noon."

"Thank you, Tan. I'll be in touch."

John Dearlove had Tommy in his sights and answers concerning Brian's whereabouts would come shortly. If not, dead bodies would begin piling up in Hong Kong.

China CITIC Bank Mansion, Urumqi, Xinjiang Province, China, June 6, 1:05 PM

Liu Zhun and Wu Heng arrived on the 59th floor. After small pleasantries and a cup of green tea, Wu was prepared to give his leader an update on his operation in Hong Kong. Five British SIS intelligence operatives were to be killed soon.

"I believe we are ready to begin executing our British operatives in Hong Kong as early as tomorrow," said Wu.

"Good. Do you have the transfer information?" asked Liu.

Wu Heng handed his leader a note with the bank account number and routing code. Two million Hong Kong dollars would be transferred within minutes.

"Are you sure the plan will work, Heng?"

"I am certain, Liu. I've provided the five names and their home addresses in the city to our contractor there. Each SIS agent will be killed within minutes of each other."

"What about you, Heng? What does British intelligence think you're doing?"

"They don't. I stopped reporting last week. I've already moved my family back to Toutunhe."

Toutunhe, a city with a population of approximately one hundred and fifty thousand people, was under the administrative jurisdiction of Urumqi city. It was also home to the first carpet industry demonstration park as part of the belt and road initiative launched by Beijing.

"Won't they come looking for you?" asked Zhun.

"They do not know where I am now. I am certain the British will become uneasy after another week. However, it will not matter. They will be losing five assets in Hong Kong and blaming the Chinese."

"How do you know they will blame Chinese intelligence?" asked Zhun.

"The five assets I've chosen are working political and economic requirements for London. They have no ties to the Triads or other criminal organizations on the island. Their contacts only include high-ranking government officials and private sector bankers. The only conclusion they will come to is Chinese intelligence."

"What about the man who recruited you at MI6? Wasn't his name John Dearlove?" asked Zhun.

"John has returned to London to retire. I doubt he will come looking for me at this point in his career. MI6 will certainly come looking for me but they won't know where to look. They have some assets in the region but none that could identify me."

"You better be right, Heng. If they find you here, it could jeopardize our operations in the future."

"Zhun, my goal is the same as yours. I would not jeopardize our mission and I believe in what we are doing. Has General Guozhi returned to his headquarters?" asked Wu.

"He has. He said Beijing is pleased and approved another missile test next month. The loss of British operatives and the American satellite will surely place immediate international pressure on Beijing. And as soon as our man in Pyongyang executes his order, Beijing will be a mess. This will give us an opportunity to destabilize the party."

"What are your plans for me after the operatives in Hong Kong are killed?" asked Wu.

"In due time, Heng. Just go back to Toutunhe and await instructions. I have much work to do and more preparations are needed."

Wu Heng soon departed, and Liu Zhun opened his laptop. He sent a short email to General Zhang Guozhi using a fake account created in Hong Kong.

Mr. Z, we have a potential problem with our operation in Hong Kong. Prepare to dispose of Heng within the week. He may be a liability for our efforts. Kindly reply.

Liu Zhun felt uneasy. His recruit from Hong Kong was the perfect man to join his resurrected Assassination Corps. Young, idealistic and frustrated with China's communist party, Wu's familial ties with the Uyghur autonomous region, made for an easy recruit. He sent the young man to Hong Kong with the hopes of being recruited by British intelligence. His rise within the organization was nothing short of spectacular and beyond any of Zhun's wildest imaginations. However, the prodigy was remarkably sloppy in how he exited Hong Kong. Liu was certain British intelligence would eventually direct their efforts at finding him. Despite being in Toutunhe, western intelligence services had the resources and technology to find him. Their motivation would certainly be strong enough. Wu Heng, also known as Brian Wu, was a liability for the Assassination Corps and his sacrifice would preserve the organization's ability to topple the Chinese government.

A few moments later Liu received the message he was looking for.

Received. Will have associates standing by.

Wu Heng became a marked man.

Repulse Bay, Southern District, Hong Kong, June 6, 1:17 PM

John Dearlove arrived at Repulse Bay, located in the southern district of Hong Kong. With its pristine beaches facing the South China Sea, Repulse Bay was a sunny and plush chic residential area that felt like a resort to the people living there. The odd name is said to have originated because pirates and other thieves used the natural harbor to attack foreign merchant ships in 1841. Eventually, the pirates were repelled by the British Navy and the name had stuck ever since. Tommy's decision to reside in the area was fitting and gave his neighbors the impression he was a successful real estate developer working in the Central District.

John arrived at an intersection several blocks from Tommy's beachside villa. The winds were strong, and the skies were layered with dark clouds. He reached for his cell phone.

"Tommy, it's John. I'd like to speak to you about Brian. Will you be at the club later?"

"John, you tried to make me look bad the other night. We have no further business to discuss. I do not know where Brian is."

"I've heard through my sources you do know where Brian is. In fact, he offered you a contract recently. Is that right, Tommy?" asked Dearlove.

"What the hell are you talking about, John? I know of no such contract. What is this contract that I've supposedly agreed to?"

"I will be at the club at nine o'clock. I expect you to be there." John didn't really think Tommy would show, despite his regular nightly outings at Dragon Eye.

"Forget it, John. Like I said, our relationship is over. Go back to London," said Tommy with a distinct scorn in his voice.

Click. Tommy hung up.

He quickly walked downstairs and alerted his personal bodyguard that he would be staying home for the evening. Additional security for the night would not be necessary.

Dearlove expected the abrupt ending to his phone call. He now had no doubt Tommy would know of Brian's whereabouts. He quickly shifted his attention to the nearby marina. Driving south, he soon entered the Aberdeen Marina Club, a favorite of John's while being stationed on the island. Opened in 1984, the Aberdeen was private and attracted some of the most influential men and women in Hong Kong. John often visited the club and attended functions there to identify prominent individuals for recruitment. Over the years, the master spy developed dozens of close relationships at the club, while successfully recruiting nine individuals that would provide London superb intelligence on Chinese activities, most notably in the banking sector.

John arrived well dressed as he always did. He anticipated Tommy's reaction and was prepared to spend the afternoon at the club until his departure aboard an SIS owned boat, the *Wages of Sin*. John thought the name was clever years ago as part of his cover, a successful options trader, but the name's appeal wore off over the years. Nonetheless, the thirty-foot speedboat would come in handy tonight.

"Anthony, it's John. I need you to meet me at the marina tonight at 8:30. I will be going on a cruise for a few hours. We should be back precisely at 11:30," said Dearlove to one of his most trusted assets.

John and Anthony developed a close personal friendship soon after John recruited the charter boat captain. His talents and skills were useful during several operations throughout the island as they would be tonight.

"Excellent, John. See you in a few hours."

John Dearlove would spend the afternoon playing tennis, enjoying a massage, and making conversation with his favorite bartender. Trevor, an older gentleman, was revered by all the club's patrons, despite his modest income and profession. At 8:20 PM, Dearlove exited the bar and made his way to the marina. Anthony was already preparing the boat and nearly ready to depart. In a few minutes, the men would begin their slow departure toward Tommy's villa. As luck would have it, the waters were calm, and John's approach would be easy.

After John prepared his entry for over an hour, nightfall finally hit Repulse Bay. It was now time for John to use the dinghy and paddle his way toward the rear entry of Tommy's villa. Anthony was operating a micro-drone, a spinoff of the CICADA, known as a Close in Covert Autonomous Disposable Aircraft. London's team of technical wizards at MI6 had improved the capabilities of the CICADA to include video feed for operators within five hundred yards, including night vision capability. Previously only designed to act as a listening post, the micro drone's video feed significantly enhanced human intelligence efforts for its clandestine officers, especially in limited visibility situations.

Tommy always felt safe in Repulse Bay. Crime was nearly nonexistent, and the waters protected his southern flank, so to speak. His role with the Triads was secure and local police were bought and paid for years earlier. At his residence, the tranquility of the waters and upscale community, meant he was safe. Or so he thought.

John Dearlove approached the shoreline with his dinghy on the northern most portion of Tommy's property. It offered him an excellent vantage point to confirm the usual single guard roaming the property.

"Anthony, I'm on the shoreline. Is this thing ready to go?" asked the SIS spy.

"Ready to go, John. Once we fire it up, we have thirty minutes until its batteries run dry," said Anthony.

"Okay, I'm going to hold off until I get inside. Don't need it now. Would rather have it inside in case things get a bit exciting."

"Standing by," said Anthony.

John carefully made his way through the narrow trees and shrubs aligning the eastern and western sections of the property. His first target was now just twenty meters away. Though walking briskly, the man's demeanor indicated he was bored and expected nothing but hearing the nearby ocean waters. Little did he know he was about to lose his life to the British assassin.

The career intelligence operative crouched down to the ground and began observing the man's patterns. There was nothing to indicate he was pacing back and forth or moving in any specific direction. However, John had to be sure he would catch the man when and where he would least expect it. A few minutes later it came.

The man slowly approached John's position and was standing just ten meters away when he turned around. As he reached into his jacket pocket to secure a pack of cigarettes, John's opportunity arrived. John quietly rose from the sand and drew his weapon, a Glock 17 generation four model, which the British Army had been using since 2013. SIS adopted the Austrian made pistol shortly thereafter since many operatives worked alongside regular Army forces in Afghanistan. John preferred the Browning 9mm, but the Glock was just as lethal.

As the man reached for his lighter, he noticed something behind him. Immediately as he began turning, a bullet entered his skull and killed him immediately. John now reached for the man's body before falling to the ground. Placing his arms around the man's back, he dragged the lifeless body into the nearby shrubs. Dearlove briskly moved to the patio and attempted to open the door. Incredibly, it was unsecured, and he could hear the television in a nearby room.

John then removed the micro done and placed it onto his left hand.

"Anthony, I'm inside, fire it up," whispered Dearlove.

Just a few short seconds later, the tiny drone left his hand and began moving toward the nearby room. John remained in place until Anthony provided him an update.

"There are two men inside watching television, John. Tommy is sitting to the left."

"Okay. Did you see the stairs on your left?" asked John.

"Yes, want me to get eyes up there?"

"Yes. I need to know if Tommy has additional security upstairs."

John knew it would take a few minutes for Anthony to get a good look upstairs. In the meantime, he kept the patio door slightly opened and moved carefully across the room. He then moved his body alongside the wall near the opening of the living room. Inside, his targets sat oblivious watching a soccer game. Ironically, the men were watching an English Premier League soccer match between Manchester United and Chelsea.

"John, nothing upstairs. It appears no one else is inside. Just Tommy and one of his crew are in the villa. I'm going to move our toy outside and take a peek in the front," said Anthony.

"Okay. Standing by. Make it quick," directed Dearlove.

Several minutes later Dearlove heard the news he was looking for.

"Clear. No threats remain on the property. I'll keep it hovering over the roof and scan for activity. Good luck, John."

John immediately entered the room and fired a single shot into the man's skull sitting next to Tommy. Tommy turned and looked straight into the barrel of Dearlove's Glock 9mm pistol.

"What the fuck are you doing here, John," shouted Tommy.

Dearlove walked around the sofa and moved a nearby chair in front of Tommy while maintaining his sights squarely on the drug trafficker's chest. John sat down feeling comfortable as he had no immediate threat on the property.

"Okay, Tommy. We are going to talk about Brian. If you tell me everything you know, you might be alive in the morning. Understand?"

Tommy leaned back on the sofa and maintained a defiant look, though his eyes showed fear. He had few choices and decided to be truthful and appeal to John's good nature and their previous partnership.

"When is the last time you spoke to Brian?" asked Dearlove.

"Two weeks ago."

"Did he offer you a contract to kill Chinese counter-intelligence agents?"

"No. He wanted me to kill British operatives working on the island."

"British operatives? Why?" asked Dearlove.

"He's in some group called the assassination corps. He wanted me to join a few months ago but I refused. When he offered the contract, I accepted. How could I refuse a million Hong Kong dollars, John? It was brilliant, and I needed cash."

"The assassination corps dissolved over a hundred years ago, Tommy."

"If you say so, John. I don't really care. They sounded like a bunch of lunatics. I'm a Triad for life. You think the organization is going to let me go?"

"Who are the operatives?" asked Dearlove.

"I received their files this afternoon. They are on my laptop, over there by the desk."

"Have you shared this information with any of your associates?"

"No. I planned to have a meeting with my boys tomorrow."

"Has Brian paid you yet?"

"Yes, the money was deposited in my bank account this afternoon."

"Where did the money originate from?" asked Dearlove.

"A bank from Urumqi, in western China."

"I'm familiar with Urumqi. Is Brian there now?"

"I don't know, John. He said he was returning to the mainland. That's all I know."

John sat back in his chair and thought for a moment. He was sure Tommy was telling the truth as self-preservation kicked in for the Triad. As he stared into Tommy's eyes, a feeling of anger and betrayal befell Dearlove. In the last twenty-four hours, two of his associates had turned on him and his beloved SIS. He took it personally and vengeance was on his mind.

"Do you remember what I told you when I first recruited you, Tommy?"

"Never lie to you, John. Never lie."

Tommy became frightened. The brashness he exhibited a few moments ago was gone.

"Have you been honest with me since I returned?" asked

Dearlove.

"I just was," pleaded Tommy.

"That wasn't the question. Have you been honest with me since I returned to Hong Kong?"

Tommy sighed. "No, John."

John Dearlove immediately squeezed the trigger and a single bullet entered his chest. Then another. Finally, John squeezed a third time and Tommy was dead. Dearlove sat back in his chair and remained emotionless. He never really liked killing but it was a necessary part of the bloody business of espionage. There were winners and losers. Tonight, Tommy lost.

Dearlove got up and immediately secured the laptop and made his way back to the dinghy.

"Anthony, I'm done here. I'll be aboard soon."

John Dearlove never thought he would see the mainland again. His mind raced with thoughts as he pulled on the oars. The hunt for Brian Wu would continue in the morning.

Khandud, Afghanistan, June 9, 10:02 PM

Just outside the remote village of Khandud, the modified CV-22 Osprey, flown by Air Force Special Operations Command, began its slow descent toward the bumpy terrain. The night skies were filled with shining stars and the aircraft's pilot would have an excellent view of the landing zone as he and his crew prepared to deliver Michael Brennan to a group of Wahki nomads. Visibility was excellent, winds were minimal, and radio communications with Wasim, the group's point of contact near the landing zone, had been established. The insertion was proceeding as planned.

"Wasim. We are approaching. How are things on your end?" asked Tom, the special operator leading the mission.

"Clear, Mur. I hear you. Come on in," said Wasim.

Mur, meaning cloud in the Wahki language, was used extensively by Wasim when directing US assets into the region.

"Is the perimeter secure, Wasim?" asked Tom.

"Of course, as always. We are ready."

The CV-22 Osprey began a slow left turn toward the landing zone, a relatively flat piece of ground approximately four kilometers from Khandud. The aircraft, its crew, and passengers were now the most vulnerable they had been since departing Kabul earlier in the evening.

During the team's isolation in Kabul, intelligence provided by the special activities group indicated increased Taliban "chatter" near the village over the previous two weeks. Of course, Michael noticed the disparity in the report to that of CIA analysts, who indicated the area free from the resurgent group. As usual, intelligence assessments in Langley lagged the real-time intelligence collected on the ground in Afghanistan. Michael grew accustomed to these kinds of intelligence gaps in previous assignments and accepted them as part of the intelligence business.

Michael spent most of his time in Kabul studying the Korla military complex, the surrounding geography and memorizing his cover for operating in Urumqi. His request for British support was approved, which included a British passport in case he was ever questioned. He would meet with a brothel owner where he would be provided logistical support including currency, a local operative, and a place to stay. Langley directed only a single intelligence requirement for Michael to answer for however long the operation would be authorized. Additional technical requirements would be levied against the Defense Intelligence Agency and Pacific Command, while other requirements would be answered by London.

CIA needed to determine if the Chinese missile test was designed to engage and destroy the surveillance satellite. Was it a failed test or did the Chinese missile intentionally miss to send Washington a clear message? Michael thought the request probably came from the National Security Council, due to its strategic implications. He believed he could answer the question if he could develop a relationship with any one of many individuals working inside the command center. These would include engineers, communications specialists, and others. However, it would probably take at least three sources to confirm the information which would ensure the reliability of his finding. A sole source would likely not be enough for Washington to rely on for something of this magnitude. After all, Michael's report could lead to a serious and deadly conflict with Beijing. He had to get it right.

As the CV-22 Osprey hovered over the landing zone, its pilot determined the aircraft's power margin was adequate. In higher altitudes and cooler temperatures, margins for error increased as evidenced by the fact that nearly eighty percent of helicopter accidents in Afghanistan were due to pilot error, not tactical enemy air defense artillery systems. Even the slightest wind change at this point could alter the aircraft's power margin to negative, thereby plummeting the aircraft and its crew down from the skies. The pilot, a veteran on his third tour in the region, was a graduate of the High Altitude Army National Guard Aviation Training Site, located west of Denver, Colorado.

Seconds later the aircraft landed safely. Tom and Michael exited the aircraft as the rotary blades continued turning. Tom and his crew would quickly be airborne soon after Michael's delivery to Wasim and his associates.

"Wasim, this is Michael," said Tom.

"It's a pleasure to meet you, Michael. We are ready to begin moving you this evening."

"The pleasure is mine, Wasim. Tom has told me of your efforts here. I look forward to working with you and your men," said Michael.

"We will do our best, Michael."

"Just get me safely across that border, Wasim," said Michael as he smiled.

Tom proceeded to hand Wasim a suitcase filled with one hundred thousand American dollars and turned to Michael.

"I think our work here is done, Michael. Best of luck, man, and stay safe," said Tom with a firm handshake.

"Thank you, Tom. I appreciate the hospitality and ride. Tell your men I'm grateful for their support."

Tom returned to the aircraft within five minutes. As the two large triple bladed propellers began rotating in opposite directions, propulsion from the Rolls Royse Allison AE 1170C turboshaft engine generated the thrust needed for lift. It was time to return to Kabul.

Then suddenly, the CV-22 Osprey was hit with a barrage of small arms fire coming from across the canyon. Bullets ripped throughout the interior and two of Tom's men were hit immediately. Hundreds of rounds were whizzing around and through the aircraft. The Taliban were executing a classic aerial ambush, perfected long ago against the Soviet Union.

"Contact," yelled the pilot.

"Where the hell is it coming from?" asked the co-pilot.

"Damned if I know, I see nothing. Let's get the hell out of here. We're sitting ducks," screamed the pilot.

The pilot then twisted and pulled up the collective, the lever used to control climb and descent, and began ascending rapidly. It was too late. Seconds later, a stinger missile, fired from the bottom of the canyon, struck the underbelly of the aircraft. Almost immediately after rocking the aircraft, a second stinger missile screamed toward the helicopter. Its crew and passengers never had a chance.

After Wasim and Michael heard the gunfire, they quickly moved away from the landing zone, dropped to the ground and could do nothing but watch. The CV-22 Osprey fell nearly a thousand feet to the ground and quickly became consumed in fire. The second stinger had hit three of the aircraft's fuel tanks. As Michael watched the aircraft plummet from view, he knew there would be no survivors. But he had to make sure anyways.

"Wasim, how the hell do I get down there?" asked Michael.

"You don't, Michael. From here, we would have to work our way back toward Khandud, and then move west along a trail into the canyon. It would take us over an hour. We have no climbing gear."

"Not good enough. There could be survivors," said Michael.

"Michael, they were hit with two stingers. They were nearly nine hundred feet above the canyon. It's not possible. I'm sorry. We cannot risk going down there. Who knows how many Taliban there are."

Michael crawled toward the end of the landing zone overlooking the canyon. Below, he could see the flames engulfing the aircraft. He pulled out a night vision scope and scanned the area. There was absolutely no movement around the aircraft which was split in half and shattered into hundreds of pieces. No one could survive that attack, he thought to himself.

Nonetheless, he continued searching for signs of life.

Nothing moved.

A few minutes later, Michael reached into his backpack and pulled out a satellite phone. While in isolation near Kabul, he entered several telephone numbers from the operations center there, including several CIA officers on assignment from Langley. He knew a young man named Jamison, who just recently graduated from "the farm," would be on night shift.

"Jamison, it's Michael. The CV-22 and its crew are lost. Looks like the damn Taliban shot it out of the sky."

"When, Michael?' asked Jamison.

"Just now. Alert the military right away so they can begin recovery operations," said Michael.

"What about Tom?" asked the young operative.

"I'm certain he's gone as well. Two stingers were fired from the nearby canyon. Unsure how many enemy combatants are responsible."

"Will do, Michael. What are your plans?' asked the young operative.

"I will continue with my operation. The Taliban were

shooting at a military aircraft. They have no idea I was aboard. I'll remain here until I see friendly forces secure the area. I don't give a damn if I'm here all night. Now alert the military operations center right away," barked Michael.

Click. Michael turned toward Wasim.

"Has the Taliban ever been this close to Khandud?" asked Michael.

"It's been a very long time," said Wasim, clearly startled by the attack.

"Well, let's hope they don't come up here. Or we're next."

"I think we should go, Michael. The Taliban may have seen us."

"I don't care, Wasim. I'm staying until I know our military forces have secured the area. Make yourself comfortable," barked Michael.

Wasim agreed but was prepared to depart if signs of the Taliban appeared. Michael continued scanning the area for signs of life. Still, nothing moved.

Michael and Wasim remained atop the landing zone for nearly two hours. The silence was deafening and Michael failed to detect any movement. It was as if the attackers simply vanished. Then his phone rang.

"Michael, it's Jamison. Recovery assets are five minutes out. Have you seen any movement?"

"Nothing, man. They were ghosts. I haven't seen a damn thing since the bird went down," said Michael.

"Stand by. Let me send an update to the operations center."

Thirty seconds went by and Jamison spoke.

"Do you see any movement at this point? Anything at all?" asked Jamison.

"Sit tight. Let me check."

Michael scanned the canyon once again. He saw no signs of life nor did he see movement of any kind. Just some scattered fires still burning around the shattered aircraft.

"Nothing, Jamison. Nothing at all. Looks quiet from my vantage point."

"The commander has requested you remain in your position until his crews are safely on the ground and the area is secured. Report anything unusual and I'll relay it in real time."

"Will do," said Michael.

Approximately thirty minutes went by and Jamison spoke.

"Michael, the area is secure. The commander thanks you for standing by."

"Pass along my condolences, Jamison. Have you already alerted Langley?" asked Michael.

"Yes."

"Okay, it's been one hell of a night. Departing the area now."

"Good luck, Michael."

"Thanks."

Click.

Michael turned toward Wasim.

"Let's go, Wasim. Thanks for staying. I know you didn't have to."

The two men, accompanied by one of Wasim's associates, began the slow trek back toward Khandud. Michael Brennan felt uneasy and wondered what other surprises might be on the way. He was alone in the mountains of northeastern Afghanistan, walking with two men he barely knew, while Taliban insurgents just destroyed a CV-22 Osprey aircraft.

What could go wrong? he thought to himself.

Beijing Capital International Airport, Chaoyang District, China, June 10, 11:42 AM

John Dearlove arrived at the Beijing Capital International Airport. Having spent the last few days in near isolation at the British consulate in Hong Kong, he was ready to search for Brian Wu. There, he sent a warning to operatives across the mainland to watch their backs. Brian's most recent photograph was disseminated to numerous sources who were instructed to report his whereabouts immediately. He was to be captured at all costs.

With several pieces of luggage and a slim black leather briefcase, he looked the part of a foreign executive searching for deals. China was jam-packed with western investors scouring the mainland looking to capitalize on a rising middle-class population expected to approach three hundred and fifty million consumers by 2020. He knew Chinese counter-intelligence would be inside the airport, as they always were.

From the moment John first arrived in Beijing, nearly two decades ago, he kept the same routine. He would quickly make his way to the Fairmont Hotel, a five-star rated facility, and call some associates in the banking sector for drinks. The following morning, he would travel to various office buildings around the city. After nearly a dozen trips, John began moving throughout the mainland, always sure to watch his back and look for any undercover surveillance officers from the Ministry of State Security.

In time, John began to travel across the mainland, where he was an effective recruiter. His spotting techniques were legendary within SIS, and his ability to manage long-term assets was equally as impressive. Over time, he would convince Chinese counter-intelligence that he was a senior banking executive from Hong Kong who invested in Chinese start-ups and technology firms. After all, China's meteoric economic rise over the previous two decades was directly attributable to foreign direct investment.

This time, however, he would travel directly to Urumqi. John made a calculated risk that foregoing his usual routine would be acceptable. He had no time to lose.

Sitting alongside the curb, John waited for his ride. The driver, a long-time associate, and trusted source, would be arriving in minutes.

"John, nice to see you," said Chi.

"You as well, Chi. Did you receive my message last night?" asked John.

"Yes. We are driving directly to Urumqi. Why not take a flight, John?"

"Less risk, Chi. Let's make sure we are not followed."

"Of course, John."

Comfortably inside the vehicle, John reached for his cell phone.

"Robert. It's John. How are you, old chap?"

"Excellent. I cannot complain too much. I assume this isn't a personal call?" asked Robert, a long-time career officer for the Government Communications Headquarters, specifically the Composite Signals Organization.

GCHQ, Britain's premier signals intelligence collection agency, would be required to locate Brian's whereabouts in the Xinjiang province. Based in the suburbs of Cheltenham, GCHQ was formed in 1919, shortly after World War I. First known as the Government Code and Cypher School, it became GCHQ in 1946 and located in Bletchley Park. There, British and American code-breakers famously broke the German enigma codes which helped bring an end to World War II.

"No, Robert, I'm afraid not. I need a favor. One of my operatives in Hong Kong has gone missing. In fact, it appears he went rogue. I'm certain he is near Urumqi. Can you direct some of your collection efforts there? I have some phrases you can use to start your queries with. I'd also like you to try and penetrate the closed-circuit television monitors at some of the airports in the province," said Dearlove.

"John, we are a bit overtaxed right now. We're having a devil of a time with domestic terrorism. Most of our analytical efforts are focused on sympathizers and their communications with individuals in hot spots like North Africa and the Middle East. I've never seen pressure from Parliament like this."

"I understand, but my operative has apparently coordinated an attack on our sources in Hong Kong. This could be devastating to our collection efforts there. I need some help, Robert. Please don't ask me to beg. SIS doesn't have the assets to quickly identify the operative's whereabouts. You do. If he's communicating, I'm sure your team can find him more quickly than mine," stated Dearlove.

"All right, John. No promises. Let me see what I can do. In the meantime, send me the phrases we'll use to start our searches and the airports you want us to target. Fair enough?" asked Robert.

"Fair enough. Thank you, Robert. I'll send the information in a few minutes. Can you give me an update tomorrow?" asked Dearlove.

"Of course, John. Watch your back. The Americans recently lost quite a number of their assets."

"I know, thank you, Robert."

John opened the briefcase and reached for his laptop. He sent Robert several phrases and words that his team would begin using to query their technical databases. Phrases including Brian Wu, Wu, Wu Yan, Yan, the assassination corps and others were sent. This would allow Robert's team to narrow down their search in a database that often scooped up billions of pieces of information daily. In addition, his team would attempt to "hack" closed-circuit television cameras at various airports throughout Xinjiang, in case Brian flew in. John didn't think Brian would be this sloppy, but he would try nonetheless.

About an hour into their ride, Chi noticed a vehicle located approximately fifty meters behind them along the bustling G30 Highway. It was the same blue vehicle he saw departing the airport earlier.

"I think we have friends traveling with us, Robert," said Chi as he smiled.

"Unexpected guests? What a surprise. Alright, let them get acquainted with our backside. We're stopping in Taiyuan soon. We will lose them there."

Toutunhe District, Xinjiang Uyghur Autonomous Region, China, June 10, 1:09 PM

Rising above the rocky Xinjiang landscape were dozens of high-rise apartment complexes and government structures. The northern district was a sprawling economic hub dominated by solar wind factories and software centers. Its workers, mostly imported Han laborers from across the mainland, left little doubt that local Uyghur Muslims were being discriminated against.

Many Uyghurs in the district felt their culture was being systematically diluted and turned their frustration toward the Han "oppressors." Han Chinese, China's majority ethnic group, were flooding into the region and Uyghurs were left unemployed. The unfortunate situation led to a wave of terror attacks in central Urumqi that had left at least six people dead and dozens wounded. The Han crackdown was swift, brutal and tensions were rising.

"Heng, I am going to the city for a few hours. I will be back for dinner," said Yan, Wu's wife of nine years.

"Where are you going?" asked Wu.

"I want to visit my uncle in the city. A friend of his was wounded in the attack at the train station," said Yan.

"Okay. Please be safe. The Uyghurs are becoming more aggressive. It won't be long until they try something in our neighborhood," pleaded Wu.

"I am not worried, my love. See you in a few hours."

"Be worried, Yan. It will make you more aware of what's around you," said Wu.

"Oh, stop it. We are not in Hong Kong anymore. We are safe here," said Yan.

Yan closed the door behind her and departed for the bus station, located directly across from the sprawling complex. The bus would take a direct southeastern approach into Urumqi's center square.

Brian sat back on his couch and pondered. Liu's directive to sit tight in Toutunhe weighed on the former SIS officer. From the moment he was first recruited by the assassination corps, Liu had always given him clear direction. Brian never wondered what his next move would be. Why was this different? he thought to himself. Liu would certainly have plans for him after the Hong Kong operation. He figured he could be useful somewhere on the mainland.

Wonder led to boredom and Brian soon fell asleep on the couch. A few hours later he heard a thunderous knock on his front door. Then another. Then another.

Brian approached the door. His hair was frazzled and his eyes were half closed.

"Mr. Wu. I am Kang, your neighbor from across the hall. There was an explosion on a bus this afternoon near Urumqi square. I cannot reach my sister."

"What happened, Kang?" said Wu, a bit more alert.

"I don't know, I saw it on the news and I cannot reach my sister," said Kang frantically.

"Calm down, Kang. Come inside and sit down. I am sure she is alright."

"Have you heard from your wife?" asked Kang.

"No. She is visiting her uncle in the city."

"My sister, Ah Lam, and Yan have become good friends over the past few months. Ah Lam told me earlier this morning she was going into the city with Yan."

Brian's heart skipped a bit. He immediately reached for his cell phone and called Yan.

There was no answer.

Taiyuan, Shanxi Province, China, June 10, 5:57 PM

John and Chi entered Taiyuan, the capital of Shanxi province, a sprawling two thousand five-hundred-year-old metropolis with over four million residents. The city's famous attractions include the Jinci Temple, the Twin-Pagoda Temple, and the Tianlong Shan Stone Caves, where sculptures dating to the Tang Dynasty were on full display.

The two men following John were a problem. He hoped to keep a low profile on the mainland by avoiding public transportation hubs such as airports and railways. The less surveillance from Chinese counter-intelligence, the more quickly John would get to Xinjiang and find Brian. However, Chinese counter-intelligence did not normally follow their targets for six hours along a highway and across provinces. He wondered who else they could be.

"Chi, let's go to the Kempinski Hotel. Pull it up on the GPS," said John.

"Okay, John."

The Kempinski Hotel, a luxurious locale located in the southern section of the city, was built near the Taiyuan National High-Tech Development Zone. John was no stranger to the Grill and Wine restaurant, famous for its authentic French cuisine. The brief pause would allow him and Chi to enjoy an exceptional meal and John the opportunity to weigh his options going forward.

Halfway through their meal, John stood up and told Chi to wait for him.

"Where are you going, John?" asked Chi.

"I'm going to see if our new friends are still with us, Chi."

"Why don't I join you, John?"

"No need, Chi. I'll be back soon."

John returned to the lobby and quickly exited the hotel. He reached inside the jacket pocket and casually pulled out his cell phone. To his left, the blue vehicle sat curbside, along with the two men. John discerned they were not from the Ministry of State Security. Their demeanor, dress, and overly anxious faces gave them away. Chinese counter-intelligence was better than these two amateurs, John thought to himself. But who were they? Time for some answers.

The British operative returned to the restaurant.

"Chi, it's time for us to leave. They're still outside waiting. One of the idiots turned away as I glanced in his direction. We need to find out who these clowns are," said John.

"I doubt Chinese counter-intelligence, John. They wouldn't be this sloppy."

"Agreed. But they are following us. Someone wants to know what we're up to," said Dearlove.

"Then let's find out, shall we," said Chi.

A few minutes later, the hotel's valet delivered their car. Chi slowly departed and soon found the G208 Highway heading south. A short while later, they passed the Yuxin fireworks company, where John spotted a dirt road. Approximately one hundred meters to the east, the dirt road appeared to run into a dead end surrounded by shrubs and scattered trees.

The two men inside the blue car never had a chance.

As Chi turned left onto the trail, John quickly deployed a micro-drone from inside his briefcase, carefully concealed from customs officers at Beijing airport. The drone, known as the HK-100, was similar in size to the PD Black Hornet 100. However, the "hunter killer" 100, created by a team of young specialists from the Science and Technology division, did more than just conduct surveillance.

The HK 100 packed just enough explosive material to

shatter a man's skull, and penetrate an automobile's tire, among other capabilities.

"What the hell are they doing now?" asked the driver.

"I don't know. Should we follow them?" asked the passenger.

"No choice. We have our orders."

John opened his window and out flew the HK 100 as Chi stepped on the gas. He hoped to divert the driver's attention, even if momentarily. It worked as dirt sprayed upward from the vehicle.

"Up ahead, turn right and slam on the brakes, Chi," said John.

John and Chi were now partially hidden in the tree line. Dearlove only needed a few seconds to quickly exit the car and turn his attention to the vehicle, now outside his field of vision. It didn't matter, real-time video feed from the HK 100 showed the vehicle approaching and now just fifty meters from the bend.

And then it came.

John detonated the HK 100, now hovering alongside the driver's window. The explosion shattered the glass and immediately knocked the driver unconscious. A few seconds later, John sprinted toward the car as it came to a complete stop.

John's weapon was raised and squarely pointed at the passenger.

"Get out," yelled Dearlove.

The passenger did as he was instructed.

"What in the bloody hell are you doing? Why are you and your friend following us?" asked Dearlove.

The man just stood there.

"Who are you working for?"

Nothing. John turned to Chi.

"Check the driver's ID. Maybe we'll get some answers," said John.

Chi slowly approached the driver's side. Broken glass was scattered across the seat and on the unconscious driver. There was even a piece of glass lodged in the man's left cheek as blood was slowly oozing from his face and forearm. Chi was surprised the man was even breathing. As he reached into the car he noticed a tattoo, now visible through the shredded clothing.

"Look at this," said Chi.

The inscription on the man's forearm simply read, *assassination corps*.

John turned to the man in front of him.

"Why does he have assassination corps inked into his arm?" asked John.

The man remained quiet and looked a bit more defiant than before. His eyes appeared lifeless as if he knew what was coming. He was prepared for death. And it would come quickly.

"Roll up your shirt," instructed Dearlove.

The passenger had the same inscription.

"Who the hell are you guys? I will not ask again," said Dearlove as he raised his weapon and aimed squarely at the man's forehead.

The young man knew his time was up. He stood to attention and waited for the stranger to decide his fate. Pressed for time and uncomfortable with being off the highway, John had no choice. An encounter with local law enforcement would seriously complicate his mission. He had to get moving.

Dearlove squeezed the trigger and the bullet entered the man's forehead. His body rocked momentarily and then hit the dirt. The man's brief allegiance to the assassination corps was over.

"Chi, take out the driver. We need to get out of here at once," said Dearlove.

A few minutes later, the men returned to highway G208.

"Why were you so quick to eliminate our friends? I figured you would want to talk with one of them more?" asked Chi.

"They were buffoons, Chi. But their tattoos worry me a bit. Have you ever heard of the China Assassination Corps?"

"No, I don't recall so," said Chi.

John was not surprised. China's education system, one of the best in the world, still censored much of its historical past. The short lifespan of the assassination corps was simply left out from China's history books.

"They were a small group of men who got in over their heads. They wanted to end the Aisin Gioro. They were more like anarchists than professional assassins. Don't let the name fool you," said Dearlove.

"What happened to them?" asked Chi.

"Well, after several failed assassination attempts, including an attempt in 1910 against Zaifing, the Prince Regent, many simply vanished. Some members were arrested, while others were hunted down and killed. Legend suggests a few individuals escaped justice, due primarily to the chaos of the revolution in 1911. Either way, they were not professional killers."

While in Hong Kong, John did his research as any professional operative would have done.

"Why are you worried?" asked Chi.

"If one of my operatives is mixed up with them, his skills could be an advantage to the organization, assuming the group has resurfaced."

"What do you suppose are their objectives?"

"I don't know, Chi. If they had been successful in killing five of my operatives, it might have caused tension between London and Beijing. That, by itself, would not have caused alarm. But if other operations are planned, it becomes more complicated."

John stared out the window. A call to an associate in Turpan was forthcoming.

Sarhadd, Badakhshan Province, Afghanistan, June 10, 6:44 PM

The remote and isolated journey from Khandud to Sarhadd, along the Wakhan Corridor, was breathtaking. Flanked by Tajikistan, Pakistan and China, the area known by locals as "the roof of the world," had a tranquility to it. The snow-capped Pamir mountains towered alongside the Wakhan Corridor, where it's majestic landscape was rarely seen by visitors. The province and its inhabitants, ethnic Wahki and Kyrgyz, remained mostly free from Taliban and Al-Qaeda insurgents scourging the rest of Afghanistan. A sense of peace hovered over the harsh terrain while death and despair were commonplace across most of Afghanistan.

Wasim and Michael spent most of the day in their modified Jeep 4x4 navigating the treacherous trail which included rock fields, rivers, and bottomless desert sand. On several occasions, the men were on the edge of a cliff, just meters from certain death. The group also included two of Wasim's closest associates, who drove in front of them.

"Michael, we'll be in Sarhadd in about thirty minutes. There, some of my associates will meet us. We'll get some provisions, yaks, and be on our way."

"How does the weather look, Wasim?" asked Michael.

"Good, but who knows. The mountains will decide. It's very unpredictable here."

"Who are your associates?"

"Friends of mine. We've been doing business here for years. They know the terrain well and will get us into the Wakhjir Pass quickly."

"What do you think happened last night?"

"I don't know, Michael. The Taliban have never been that close to Khandud."

"You think someone might have warned them we were coming?" asked Michael.

"I'm not sure I like the suggestion, Michael. Only myself and a few of my men knew of your arrival," said Wasim.

"Then how do you explain it, Wasim?"

"I cannot. Maybe they were simply moving in the area and got lucky."

"Luck has nothing to do with it, Wasim. One of your men leaked the information. There is no other plausible explanation."

Wasim slammed on the brakes and turned toward Michael.

"It didn't come from us, Michael. I am being paid good money to hold your hand. But don't think for a moment, I won't leave you in Sarhadd. It was not one of my men."

Michael was convinced Wasim was telling the truth and slightly impressed with the man's sudden change in demeanor. The man's fierce loyalty to his men was impressive, despite possibly being naïve. These were, after all, paid CIA assets motivated by money. Michael backed down.

"Okay, Wasim. My apologies. I'm just anxious to get across the border," said Michael.

"Michael, we either trust each other or we don't. You need my men and they need to be paid. It's that simple. The Taliban, Afghan security forces, and others do not pay. Regardless of what you may think of us, we despise the Taliban as much as you."

Michael wondered if that was true. A CV-22 Osprey loaded with nearly a dozen of the finest elite forces in the world lay still shattered near Khandud. He knew most of the Wahki people hated the Taliban, but there were probably a few looking to enrich their lives in the chaos of war.

"I know, Wasim. Tell me a little about Sarhadd. My organization didn't provide much intel."

"The village of Sarhadd, known as Sarhad e Broghil, is an inviting town and the people there are friendly. Women are considered equals to men since they are Ismaili Muslims. You will see most of them wearing red and purple dresses with beautiful ornaments, earrings, and other traditional jewelry," said Wasim.

The tension between the two men had abated.

"Why do they wear red, Wasim? What's the significance?"

"It's their traditional dress. I really don't know why but legend suggests it was because of Russian influence dating back to the Tsars. Others say it's because the Kyrgyz tribes in the seventh century traded with Han Chinese."

"Interesting, tell me more," said Michael.

"Have you heard of the Pamir Knot, Michael?"

"No. Can't say I have, Wasim."

"It's where three mountain ranges, the Hindukush, Karakoram, and Pamir converge and create beautiful u-shaped valleys. This provides fertile land for cultivation and farming. We'll be passing through some of those fields tomorrow."

Then suddenly the lead jeep came to a halt approximately forty meters ahead. Michael noticed both of Wasim's men exiting the vehicle carrying Ak-47 rifles, the most common weapon found throughout Afghanistan.

"What the fuck is this, Wasim?" asked Michael.

Both men began firing but concentrated their efforts on Wasim.

Wasim instinctively placed the vehicle in reverse and depressed the accelerator while Michael reached for his weapon. A few rounds found their way through the windshield but both men remained unscathed.

Wasim's men sprinted toward the jeep.

"Keep moving. Wasim is the target," shouted one of the men.

Michael returned fire as Wasim continued guiding the jeep rearward. The constant bumping and erratic driving ensured Michael's shots missed their intended targets.

"Dammit, there's a tight bend approaching. We are going to have to stop, Michael."

Michael turned and saw they had only twenty meters until the sharp curve. If Wasim was unable to control the jeep, the men would plunge off the cliff to a certain death.

"Brake now, Wasim," yelled Michael.

Michael quickly exited the vehicle and took aim at the man directly forty meters in front of him. The bullet entered the man's stomach and down he went.

The second man stopped and directed his attention at Michael. Their plan was quickly unraveling, and self-preservation kicked in. He sprayed several rounds in Michael's direction. Bullets hit the vehicle and one grazed above Michael's arm. It only took Michael two rounds to bring the man down.

"Wasim, get out. This is the second time in two days that I'm dealing with nonsense. Who the hell were those guys?" asked Michael as he began moving toward the first man he shot.

The man was bleeding rather profusely but still alive. Shortly, he would be dead.

"Baqir and Samim. I don't understand it, I've known both men for over a decade," said Wasim.

"Well, one of them is still alive. Find out what you can before I end his misery."

"Baqir, why have you done such a thing?" asked Wasim.

"I am sorry, Wasim. They have my cousin. They knew

we worked with CIA. It was supposed to be a trade. I am truly sorry, Wasim. Please forgive me."

"Where are they holding your cousin?"

"I don't know, somewhere near Langar."

"Do they know our plans once we reach Sarhadd?" asked Wasim.

"No."

Michael had heard enough. He fired a single bullet into the man's forehead. The man's suffering ended.

"I hope your men in Sarhadd can be trusted, Wasim," said Michael as he walked away.

The two men left the bullet riddled jeep where it rested and walked toward the lead vehicle. Sarhadd was close but the rushed operation was proving more complex than its designers had planned for. Michael's patience was being tested and he hoped that the Wakhan territory would offer him solace.

Urumqi, Xinjiang Province, China, June 10, 7:55 PM

Brian Wu paced briskly as he waited for his turn to speak with the local police. He and hundreds of Han citizens were gathered inside the Xinjiang Medical University yearning for news. Hours before, a suicide bomber attacked a crammed bus within the Urumqi Public Transport Group. Dozens were killed, while nearly seventy people suffered serious injuries. Urumqi was in shock and Beijing's response would be swift.

Yan was a confirmed passenger, but Brian was unsure of her status. He had called her cell phone dozens of times throughout the afternoon.

"Wu Heng," yelled the officer.

"I am Wu Heng. I am looking for my wife, Yan."

"Please come with me, sir."

Brian did not like the policewoman's demeanor or tone. She seemed to lack empathy and that concerned him. He followed and quickly became more anxious. The two individuals soon found themselves in a conference room surrounded by three civilians.

"Mr. Wu. I am sorry to inform you that your wife, Wu Yan, was killed during the attack. Her identity was confirmed an hour ago."

Brian slouched forward and began to sob. One of the individuals, a grief counselor recently assigned to the Hospital, reached for his hand. Brian now sobbed profusely. A few minutes later he gathered his composure and began to speak.

"Who is responsible for this?" asked Brian.

"We do not know but we are certain the individual was a Uyghur Muslim separatist. As you know, they have been more active in Urumqi the last few years," said the policewoman.

"Was she killed instantly, or did she suffer?" asked Brian.

"We found her breathing but her blood loss was severe. She had massive internal injuries. She died shortly after arriving in the emergency room. I am very sorry, Mr. Wu," said the counselor.

"Was she conscious?"

"The paramedics told us she was alert but in shock. I'm sorry I can't be more specific," said the policewoman.

Brian's heart sank further. Yan's last few minutes of life were probably painful and he hoped her state of shock was severe enough to ease the suffering.

"What do we know about this Uyghur separatist?" asked Brian.

"Nothing. We do not know his name," said the policewoman.

"Then how do you know he was a Uyghur? How do you know what his intentions were?"

"Mr. Wu. We have told you enough. The state will determine who the killer was. The state will determine why the killer targeted ethnic Hans. If he was part of a group, the state will determine that as well. We will find justice for you and your family."

"The state should never have allowed this to happen. My children no longer have a mother. This is your fault," said Brian angrily.

The group shrugged off Brian's pungent remarks. His attack on the state could be expected at a time like this. But not for long.

"We understand how you feel, Mr. Wu. We will find out what happened here today. I can assure you of that," said the policewoman.

"How can you possibly know? When can I make arrangements for her funeral?"

"Tomorrow, Wu Heng. One of my officers will visit you when we know what happened. Would you like to spend some time with one of the grief counselors?" asked the policewoman.

"No, thank you. I need to go home and explain this to my children," said Wu.

"Would you like someone from the Hospital to come with you and be present?"

"No. That won't be necessary, but thank you," said Wu.

Brian Wu exited the conference room and soon found himself returning to the lobby. There, people sat awaiting news of family and friends. Some groups of people were frantically speaking on their cell phones, while others just stared across the crowded room and waited for whatever dreadful news would come. Small children played games, clearly oblivious to the horrific act committed hours before. They would remain innocent while a sense of hopelessness and despair consumed the remainder of the lobby's inhabitants.

As Brian approached the exit door to the Hospital, he noticed a man entering the lobby. The man looked like a local Uyghur but wore an expensive business suit. Very few Uyghurs had that kind of money in the region and Wu quickly determined that something was out of place. As far as Brian could tell from local news services, the bus and nearby victims were Han Chinese due to the bus's origin and destination point in Urumqi.

As Brian opened the door, he noticed the man reaching into his jacket pocket. The stranger quickly drew a weapon, a Chinese Type 77 semi-automatic pistol. Used mostly by second-tier People's Liberation Army forces and Chinese police, the 7.62 x 17 mm pistol was still effective.

Brian rushed toward the man and quickly tackled him. As the two men fell to the concrete floor, two shots fired toward the crowd. For a few brief moments, the men struggled until Brian delivered a severe headbutt to the nose of the would-be assassin. Just mere seconds later, two police officers joined in and subdued the mysterious assailant.

After hearing the gun shots, the lobby of the Xinjiang Medical Center became chaotic. Some children were screaming while others cried as they sprinted to the protective arms of their parents. Just about everyone began to wonder how much more they could take.

"You sir, what is your name?" asked one of the police officers.

"I am Wu Heng. I saw him pull out a gun and tried to subdue him."

"We know. You are a brave man. Please come with us so we can get your statement."

"I lost my wife in the bombing and need to get home. My children are asking their grandparents when their father will be home. Can we do this some other time?" asked Wu.

"I am sorry, Mr. Wu. We need to get this done now, but we won't be long."

"Okay," said Brian unenthusiastically.

Brian Wu was reluctant for two reasons. First, he did need to return home and explain the loss of Yan to his children. Secondly, the anonymity he hoped for in Toutonhe would be gone. In a few minutes, Chinese police would have his name and address. It wouldn't be long until the information was shared with the Ministry of State Security.

Thirty minutes passed, and Brian still waited at the nearby police station. He was anxious to return home. He opened the door and approached one of the investigators.

"Sir, may I please go home. My children need me."

"I will find the station commander, sir. Give me a few minutes. We are stretched a bit thin now due to the attacks."

Five minutes later the station commander arrived.

"Mr. Wu. I understand you need to go home and be with your children. We are severely undermanned in this district. Will you be home in the next few days?"

"Yes."

"Then go home and be with your children. I am very sorry for your loss, sir. Thank you for what you did earlier."

"It was nothing. Anyone would have done the same," said Brian.

"My men tell me you handled yourself well. Where did you receive your training?" asked the commander.

"Training? No training. I've seen people do it in the movies. I guess instinct took over."

"Okay, Mr. Wu. One of my officers will come by soon. Please ensure you are home."

"Yes, sir."

Wu returned to his vehicle. A dreaded phone call to the commander of the assassination corps was required. Liu would not be pleased, Brian thought to himself. In time, Wu's fear would come to fruition.

Borak, Afghanistan, Wakhan corridor,
June 10, 11:45 PM

Michael and Wasim arrived at the remote village near Borak. The group included three Wahki nomads that would eventually lead Michael through the Wakhjir Pass. Wasim had used the trio on countless occasions while smuggling opium into western China. For several hours, the group traversed summits and methodically moved through barely visible trails. Donkeys and yaks, packed full of supplies, moved effortlessly through the narrow mountain routes.

Borak was a remote village consisting of just nine stone huts. The group would later use yurts from nomadic Kyrgyz tribes settled in for the summer.

The five men unpacked some of their supplies and prepared for the evening. They would sleep for four hours and continue their trek at four o'clock the following morning.

"Asif, how many times have you crossed the border?" asked Michael.

"Dozens. Once we arrive at the entrance of the Wakhjir Pass, Wasim will pay the border guards. There will be no trouble crossing the border, Michael. We have done this many times. It's how we make our living. And the occasional guest," chuckled Asif.

"How much do you pay them?" asked Michael.

"It depends on how much product we are delivering. They usually take five percent, in cash, of course," said Asif.

"You have the product now?" asked Michael.

"Yes. Why do you think we have so many donkeys?"

"Not my business, Asif. I just need to get across the border."

"It will be okay, Michael. The border guards are more corrupt than we are," said Asif jokingly. The other men joined in a good laugh.

"How long have you been in the CIA?" asked Jamal.

"I don't work for the agency, Jamal. I'm just a contractor."

"What will you be doing in China?" asked Jamal.

"Oh, just delivering a message. Nothing important," said Michael.

"Must be important, huh?" asked Jamal as he turned to Wasim chuckling.

"Not really, Jamal," said Michael.

"Drink your tea, Jamal, and shut up," said Wasim.

"Relax, Wasim. We are just having fun. We don't care what he's doing. We are just trying to make conversation. It's not like we haven't done this before," said Asif.

The group finished their salty yak tea, a favorite of the Wahki inhabitants and soon drifted to sleep for some much-needed rest. The Chinese border was just fifty miles away.

Urumqi, Xinjiang Province, June 10, 8:55 PM

Liu Zhun sat down and stared at the Xinjiang landscape. After a lengthy discussion with Wu, he needed to clear his head and think. Zhun's resurrection of the Assassination Corps began in 2003 and his first recruit was Wu Heng. After nearly a year of constant recruitment, the young Han eagerly joined the revived group.

Zhun spotted Wu at the local university, where the young idealist was studying history and international relations. Wu's fascination with travel and adventure made him an ideal candidate for the Corps. In class, he consistently questioned Beijing's decision to apply communism throughout the country, often to the dismay of many of his professors. He would also challenge the fundamental role of government while arguing that individuals were free to live their lives as they wished.

One day, after a lecture on Britain's decision to transfer ownership of Hong Kong to China in 1997, Zhun invited Wu to join him in the office to discuss the matter further. The two hit it off right away.

"Wu, what do you think the people felt after the "handover" of Hong Kong occurred?"

"Anger and frustration. They had little say over what transpired. First, they had to deal with the British. Then Beijing became their masters. How else could they have felt?" asked Wu.

"Why not optimistic? The handover ended one hundred and fifty-six years of British colonialism. Since most people in Hong Kong are ethnic Chinese, why would they not be ecstatic?" asked Zhun.

"Why would the capitalists on Hong Kong be pleased with the communists in Beijing?"

"Good point, Wu. The two systems run contrary to one

another. How would you change things in Hong Kong?" asked Zhun.

"I would let the people decide what they want to do."

"Okay. And how would you make that happen?"

"I guess I would encourage the people there to protest."

"Do you think that will really change things? Beijing will not give in. What other alternatives are there?" asked Zhun.

"Fight back."

"You mean with violence?" asked Zhun.

"Yes."

Zhun had heard enough and changed the conversation. Wu's advocacy for violence was enough for now. The young man could be molded and manipulated into something else in the future.

"What if you could continue your secondary studies in Hong Kong?"

"Did I upset you, professor Liu?"

"Not at all, Wu. There are times when people must engage in violence to bring about change. I have a good friend at one of the universities in Hong Kong. Are you interested in studying there?"

"I am, professor Liu."

The two would have many similar conversations in the future and their bond grew over the years. Routine correspondence between the men occurred after Wu's arrival in Hong Kong. Zhun even visited with him while attending academic conferences on the island at least twice per year.

As Zhun continued staring out the window, his decision became clear. Wu Heng's service to the Corps was over. General Zhang would be given instructions later that evening.

GCHQ, Cheltenham, England, June 11, 8:05 AM

Robert Wessex returned to his desk and continued to refine his keyword searches. John Dearlove needed his support and Wessex was determined to give it to him. After hours of running queries, he finally found what he was looking for.

An electronic casualties report filed by the Urumqi police department included the name of Wu Yan. The list included all of the confirmed deaths of the previous day's terror attack in the Xinjiang province. Most media outlets outside of China would not learn of the news for at least several months. Chinese state media normally delayed reporting such incidents until all the facts were gathered and approved by Beijing.

"John, it's Robert. I have some information you were looking for."

"Excellent news. What is it?" asked Dearlove.

"One of my queries resulted in Wu Yan. Apparently, the young woman was killed last evening."

"How did she die?"

"She died after an apparent explosion hit the bus she was traveling in."

"Where did the explosion take place?"

"In Urumqi."

"Did the report include her home address or next of kin?"

"No. The report just listed the victims of an apparent attack by Uyghur separatists."

"Where was the report sent to, Robert?" asked Dearlove.

"It appears to have gone directly to the Ministry of Public Safety."

"Did the report list her date of birth or other specific

information?"

"Only a victims list, John. I'll try correlating the data with other technical sources. Our intercept capabilities in Xinjiang are not as robust as you may think."

"Who or what was the source of the data?" asked Dearlove.

"It appears the source came from HUMINT."

"Okay, Robert. Can you keep digging?"

"I will do what I can, John. May I ask why this is so important to you?"

"It's now clear one of my officers has gone rogue. I'm cleaning up the mess."

"Understand, John. I'll do what I can. Watch your backside."

"Thank you, Robert. I will. Contact me when you find something."

Click.

Brian turned to Chi.

"Our hunch was right, Chi. Brian may be near Urumqi."

"Isn't he originally from there?" asked Chi.

"Yes, which is why it doesn't make sense. He knows I know this."

"Why the hell would he hide there? Of all the places on the mainland, and he chooses Urumqi?"

"The question now is for how long? He lost his wife to an apparent terror attack last night. He may flee soon," said Dearlove.

"What about his children?"

"I don't know, Chi. He may take them or leave them with family. If he flees, my bet is that he leaves them with his family. Traveling with children will be logistically difficult and put them in a vulnerable position."

"What do you think he's thinking now?" asked Chi.

"Well, by now he knows we're on to him. He's not scared, but probably worried. If I trained him well, he's considering an exit strategy from Urumqi. After the loss of his wife, he'll think that information won't be released to the public for several weeks or months. This all assumes he's in Urumqi, Chi. He may be elsewhere."

"If he's in Urumqi, how long do we have until he goes on the run?"

"Damn good question, Chi. Maybe two to three weeks?"

"We'll find him, John. His exit from Hong Kong was sloppy. He'll make a mistake soon."

The two men were now driving into Turpan. A meeting with Wang Yong, Xinjiang's largest opium dealer, would soon take place. Wang was known as a "Blue Lantern," the name given to uninitiated members of the Chinese Triads. He had been a Triad associate for nearly a decade and built his reputation on efficiency, secrecy, and reliability.

Turpan, also known as Tulufan, was in the eastern Xinjiang province, approximately one hundred and fifty kilometers southeast of Urumqi. Situated in a mountain basin north of the Turpan Depression, the city's predominantly Uyghur population were employed in the agricultural industry.

John and Chi exited China National Highway 312, and soon entered the Gaochang District. Wang lived in an upscale apartment complex and was known as the district's most successful grape farmer. Only a few senior police officers were aware of his opium business and Wang paid them well for their silence and support.

"Okay, Chi. It's the apartment complex up ahead. Wait for me. I shouldn't be more than twenty minutes," said Dearlove.

Dearlove exited the vehicle and soon found himself at the entrance of the building and buzzed Wang's apartment.

"Yong, it's me."

"Come in, John."

John entered the lobby and quickly made his way to the fifteenth-floor penthouse suite. Wang's business remained lucrative, Dearlove thought to himself.

"So, John. Why the visit?" asked Wang.

"One of my officers is missing. I think he's in Urumqi. I have sources there but I'm quite certain you have more," said Dearlove.

"A missing British SIS officer, John? What kind of mess are you leading me into?"

"No mess, Yong. I simply need to find him."

"Then what, John?"

"Leave that to me, Yong."

"If I help you find this missing officer, I want assurances there will be no blowback on me or my organization."

"There will be none, Yong. I just need help finding him. Whatever happens after that is my concern."

"Is Chinese counter-intelligence involved in this hunt?" asked Wang.

"No. As far as I can tell, they are unaware of his identity."

"Are you sure, John? I've heard they have grown to over one million agents. They are good at catching people like you."

"And you too, Yong. But we're here and not rotting in a prison somewhere."

Wang chuckled a bit.

"Who is the agent, John?"

"His name is Brian Wu. I have his picture here."

"Can you send me this electronically, John? I have a secure server."

"Yes. When can you get this to your people in Urumqi?"

"Immediately. Can you share anything else about him?"

"His wife died in a terror attack last night in Urumqi, but no address was listed in the report. Her name was Wu Yan."

"Then you're in luck. The deputy commander for the Urumqi police is on my payroll. It may take him a few days, but I'm sure we can get her address."

"I'll need that right away, Yong."

"Of course. Anything else?"

"Not for now, Yong. Thank you for the help."

The two men shook hands and Dearlove rejoined Chi who sat parked alongside the apartment building.

"We may have something soon, Chi," said Dearlove.

The two men would be in Urumqi before noon. His first task would be to check on the preparations for his American "guest." The CIA officer had better be good, Dearlove thought to himself.

China Manned Space Engineering Office, Beijing, China, June 11, 10:43 AM

General Zhang Guozhi just wrapped up his speech to the staff and special guests of the China Manned Space Engineering Office. The facility, a special division within the General Armaments Department of the People's Liberation Army, was responsible for the administrative and engineering functions for China's astronaut program. General Zhang outlined a bold vision for China's efforts to colonize Mars before the Americans did, specifically the mythical visionary, Elon Musk.

In addition, China's National Space Administration would now be putting its efforts into deep space exploration and exploiting space for its industrial growth. Zhang briefly described the use of space-based solar power satellites that would eventually beam limitless amounts of energy back to the earth. That energy would have to be paid for, of course, by China's customers. As expected, his audience cheered and clapped and gave him a standing ovation.

After his speech, Zhang requested he and his two military aides be given use of a conference room inside the facility. The staff were all too willing to oblige their commander.

"Feng, I received communications last night from Liu. He has a mission for you. You have been ordered to kill Wu Heng," said General Zhang.

Feng paused for a moment, clearly stunned by the order.

"Wu Heng? Why would Liu give that order? What has Wu done to deserve this?"

"Wu Heng has been compromised. First, his departure from Hong Kong was messy. There's a good chance that British SIS will come looking for him near Urumqi. We can't have that attention now as we ramp up our operations.

Secondly, Wu lost his wife to an unfortunate accident yesterday. Urumqi police have questioned Wu and it's just a matter of time before her name is released to the public. Liu and I believe the British will eventually obtain this information through open sources. I am sorry, but Wu Heng is a liability," said Zhang.

"I thought the corps was family, Guozhi? He may be a victim of bad luck at this point, but I have serious reservations about killing a fellow member. Have we done this before?"

"No, Feng. To my knowledge, no member of the corps has been killed by another member."

"Shut up, Feng. Do as your told. This is what we signed up for," said Dong.

"Dong is right, Feng. You took an oath to the corps to obey. I will forget about this incident quickly, but do not push the issue. You have your assignment. Am I clear?" asked Zhang with a stern look on his face.

"Yes, Guozhi. But I don't like it. I signed up to disrupt the damn communists, not kill fellow associates. Nevertheless, I will do it."

"Good. Glad we have an understanding, Feng," said Zhang.

"What are my orders?" asked Dong.

"You will travel with him and ensure the mission is accomplished. Feng has the lead. You provide whatever logistical support he needs."

"Okay, Guozhi. When are we to leave?" asked Dong.

"Immediately. I'm going to take a few days of vacation. I will rejoin you in Urumqi when Wu is dead. Liu wants a meeting after that which will coincide with our visit to Korla to check on preparations for next month's missile launch."

Feng and Dong soon departed the conference room. Before returning to his home in the city, Zhang needed to place a brief call.

"The operation is proceeding as planned. I'm hopeful we'll have good news soon."

"Excellent, Zhang. Keep me posted," said the man on the other end.

Wakhan Corridor, 6 miles southeast of Baza'i Gonbad, Afghanistan, June 14, 2:45 PM

Michael Brennan remained the third man in line in the caravan of yaks and donkeys deliberately moving east to the Chinese border. Now drenched with dust from several days of trekking through the Wakhan Corridor, he couldn't wait to enjoy the creature comforts of China. He was willing to pay a thousand dollars for a hot shower at this point. Nonetheless, he pressed on with only five hours of sleep per day, along with his guides. Wasim and his men were somewhat impressed with Michael's stamina. Most men would have faltered within thirty-six hours due to the group's intense pace through the unforgiving mountain terrain.

"Michael, we are going to rest here for two hours. Then, we'll continue moving east toward the entrance of the Wakhjir Pass. We may run into Chinese patrols soon," said Wasim.

"Why would they be this far west of the border, Wasim?"

"They began random patrols a couple of years ago. Beijing initiated them after tensions rose in Xinjiang. They are worried about Muslim agitators."

"Agitators? You mean terrorists like Al Qaeda or Islamic State?"

"That's what Beijing calls them, Michael."

"Have you and your men run into them before?"

"We have. We encountered them during a shipment we were moving a few months ago. We have all our required signatures on the paperwork and extra cash in case we run into them. All is good, Michael. Nothing to worry about."

"Isn't that what you told me as we approached Sarhadd?" asked Michael with a grin on his face.

"Fair point, Michael. Let's warm some rations and rest the animals."

The five men enjoyed a quiet meal at an elevation of approximately sixteen thousand feet. The winds and temperature were mild, and the weather was holding. The solitude and quietness of the region appealed to Michael. He could spend an enormous amount of time here, he thought to himself.

"So, Michael. You have a woman back home?" asked Jamal.

"No. I did until a few months ago."

"You did? What happened to her?"

"Let's just say she got tired of my frequent travels, Jamal."

"I've never understood western women," said Asif.

"What do you know of western women? What's not to understand?" asked Michael.

"They are too independent. At least that's what I've read about them."

"What's wrong with that, Asif. Some western men, including myself, find that to be an attractive quality."

"Everything. They want to work, have children, and share home responsibilities. A strong woman belongs in the fields and at home," said Jamal.

"Maybe in these lands, Jamal. But where I come from, an independent woman is to be admired."

"Michael, if we encounter the Chinese, you will do and say nothing. Leave the talking to us," said Wasim.

"This is your operation, Wasim. I'm just along for the ride," said Michael.

"They will ignore us. I know the border commander well. He's been on our payroll for years."

The group cleaned up after themselves and soon began traversing the rocky terrain. China was less than six miles away.

Toutenhe, Xinjiang Province, China, June 15, 4:48 PM

Brian Wu remained alone inside his apartment. His children were back with their grandparents in a suburb of Urumqi. He told them he was leaving for a long business trip to Hong Kong and would be back in a few months.

His focus for much of the day had been on leaving Toutenhe and establishing a new residence near Dehong, China, an autonomous prefecture located in the western Yunnan province. A childhood friend was now stationed there with the Chinese Army and could probably assist him with the move. Then he heard a knock on the door.

"Mr. Wu. I am Inspector Yang Lin with the Urumqi police department. May I come in?"

"Of course, Inspector Yang. Please come in."

"I wanted to stop by and share some news of your wife's death. I am sorry for your loss."

"Thank you. What have you learned?"

"The killer appears to have been from Fukang. Have you heard of it?" asked Lin.

"Yes, it's located northeast east of Urumqi."

"May I show you a picture of him?"

"Why?" asked Wu.

"We are asking all the victims' families in case the killer was targeting a specific person."

"I thought it was a terrorist attack?"

"That's still the prevailing hypothesis. However, I'm part of a team looking at alternate explanations," said Lin.

"Okay, you can show me the picture."

"This is the man we believe killed your wife. Have you seen him before?"

"Never. Is this a prison photo?" asked Wu.

"Yes. I have several more if that would help."

"I don't think so, but let's try to be sure."

Lin showed a few more photos of the man and one caught Brian's attention. He was horrified yet kept his composure in front of the inspector.

"Does that say assassination corps on his arm?"

"Yes, it does. Does it mean anything to you?" said Lin.

"No. It's odd. Is that a prison tattoo?"

"I don't know where it was made. I received the pictures from the warden at Fukang City Detention Center after we learned of his identity."

"So, you have no idea who this man is, and you've never seen him before?"

"No, I am sorry."

"Thank you, Mr. Wu. I am going to find out why this happened. I give you my word," said Lin.

"Thank you."

Brian escorted Lin to the door and slowly closed it behind her. His anger had nearly reached a boiling point just a few moments ago. He quickly reached for his cell phone and dialed Liu Zhun.

"Zhun, this is Heng. My wife was killed by a member of the assassination corps."

"I am sorry, Heng. She was in the wrong place at the wrong time. I was going to tell you soon."

"How could this happen?" asked Wu angrily.

"Part of our operations to disrupt Beijing include ethnic unrest in several provinces."

"Why was I not told about this?"

"Each member of the corps has their orders, Heng, and we all have our roles to play. I did not discuss the operation with you last week because I didn't want to worry you. My sources said she did not visit the city often."

"Your sources were wrong, Zhun. And now my children

have no mother."

"I am truly sorry, Heng. Are you in Toutenhe?"

"I am home."

"Can I stop by this evening? I will personally explain what went wrong."

"I expect you here within two hours, Zhun."

"You have my word, Heng. I am leaving the office now."

Click

Brian Wu paced back and forth in his living room. He wondered what his next move would be. Should he leave now and simply vanish for a while? Or should he confront Zhun and seek vengeance for Yan? His answer would come soon enough.

Wakhjir Mountain Pass, Afghanistan, June 15, 5:35 PM

The group of five men, including Michael Brennan, now approached the entrance of the Wakhjir Pass. Having traversed parts of the Hindu Kush mountains for nearly five straight days, they were in striking range of crossing the border into China. The narrow valley surrounding the men was covered with snow-tipped mountains and the terrain was more forgiving than Michael expected. Within an hour or two, the men would arrive at the border crossing, move through a barbed wire fence, and continue to the Chinese outpost at Keketuluke. There, they would present their paperwork and tribute to the outpost commander and continue along a road until they reached the Karakoram Highway.

"Wasim, is that a group of men up ahead?" asked Michael.

Wasim reached into his pocket and pulled out a pair of high powered binoculars.

"It sure is, Michael. I see three Chinese military soldiers. Jamal, get a payment ready."

"Three hundred or shall we give them six hundred?" asked Jamal.

"I'm in a generous mood. Give them six hundred when we approach," said Wasim.

Approximately twenty minutes went by as Michael's group inched close enough to stop and state their intentions.

"Hello, sir. I am Jamal. We are traveling to see Major Li Wei. I have a tribute for him. We come from Sarhadd with a certain product. We have a tribute for you as well."

"Is the Major expecting you this evening?" asked one of the soldiers.

"He never expects us. He expects tribute which I will give him. We come through the valley several times per year," said Jamal.

"The Major is away on business. He will not return for several days."

"Then we will pay his deputy for safe passage."

"Maybe, but what payment do you have for us?" asked the soldier.

"I have six hundred US dollars. That's two hundred for each of you."

The soldier instructed Jamal to remain where he stood and moved five meters back toward the two soldiers who continued pointing their weapons at the group. The three Chinese soldiers then proceeded to have a brief discussion on the matter.

"What product are you bringing in?" asked the soldier.

"Major Li is aware of our product. It's none of your concern," said Jamal.

Asif chimed in.

"Why are you so curious? We are from Sarhadd and have all our paperwork. Do you want a tribute or not? You know what product we have, or we would not have offered you cash. What is going on here? Are you new to this outpost?"

The soldier raised his weapon, a QBZ-95 assault rifle, capable of firing thirty rounds from its detachable box magazine.

"No, sir. I am not new. But we've decided the tribute is not enough."

"Not enough? My associate just offered you six hundred US dollars. That's more than generous. I wonder what Major Li will say when we report this?" asked Asif.

"Well, Major Li is not here, is he?"

"I guess not. How much do you want?" asked Jamal.

"We each want one thousand US dollars. I am sure you

can afford it," said the soldier.

Michael stood approximately twenty-five meters from the group of Chinese soldiers. He had no idea what was being discussed but felt uneasy. Wasim appeared equally as anxious.

"We may be able to pay that much. Can we go back to our group and discuss the matter?" asked Asif.

"Take your time. We are here all night," said the soldier.

"Wasim, they want one thousand dollars each," said Jamal.

"A thousand per man? That's ten times as much as we've given in the past."

"Wasim, if we pay this amount now, what will they want the next time?" asked Asif.

"It is outrageous. But what other choice do we have?" asked Wasim.

"Let's negotiate a lower price and see what they say," said Jamal.

"Give it a try. Michael, you have your weapon close to you?"

"Right here, Wasim."

Jamal and Asif returned to the Chinese soldiers. Michael and Wasim looked on as Sabour remained in the rear of the group. Michael had come to appreciate his quiet demeanor since meeting him in Sarhadd. The man kept to himself and rarely engaged in small talk.

A few minutes later Asif and Jamal returned.

"They still want three thousand dollars, Wasim. They won't budge."

"Damn Chinese. Greedy bastards. Either way, we probably need to pay."

"I say we kill them and bury their bodies later," said Asif as he turned to Jamal.

"Tempting. But that could complicate future deliveries," said Jamal.

"What's complicated? We kill them now. If we're lucky, the Chinese will think the soldiers defected," said Asif.

"They might buy one or two, but three? I doubt that, Asif," said Wasim.

"If we don't kill these greedy bastards, they'll just want more the next time," said Asif.

"I'm with Asif on this one, Wasim. If we pay this much now, our prices will rise. This will complicate our business with the Chinese buyers," said Jamal.

"Michael, what do you think?" asked Wasim.

"I don't care about these Chinese soldiers or your problems in the future. I just want to get across that damn border. Decide what you want to do, but CIA has paid you good money to get me into China. And that's what we expect," said Michael.

"Okay, Asif. It's your call," said Wasim.

Asif turned to Jamal.

"I'll take out the two men behind the man you spoke to. You kill the greedy one."

Both men turned and walked toward the group of Chinese soldiers with smiles on their faces. All three soldiers held their weapons pointed down to the ground, clearly relaxed and convinced they were dealing with low-level opium traders. In the past, opium traffickers had followed Chinese rules implicitly and never acted violently. Until now.

Jamal approached the lead soldier and quickly pulled out a pistol from the sling he had under his Patu, a traditional Afghan shawl. A single shot to the soldier's forehead killed him instantly. Asif did the same but used a modified AK-47 rifle and finished off the two others.

"Sabour, come here," yelled Jamal.

"I know. You want me to clean up the mess, right?" asked Sabour.

"Yes, find a place for these greedy Chinese. Wait for us in Borak. We should be back there in a couple of days," said Jamal.

Michael turned to Wasim.

"Now that we've solved the problem, how will your men dispose of the bodies?"

"There are some remote caves near here, Michael. No one will find them," said Wasim.

"How long do we have until the soldiers are reported missing?" asked Michael.

"At least a day, if not longer. The patrols normally run for twenty-four hours. They are not efficient here and it could be longer. Either way, our contact will be on the road near the outpost later this evening. He will take you to the Karakoram Highway and then my work is finished."

Michael and the four men began moving eastward toward the Chinese border while Sabour remained behind and collected the bodies. If all went as planned, Michael would soon be safely on the Karakoram Highway to meet his British contact.

Toutunhe, China, June 15, 6:05 PM

Brian Wu remained in his apartment. Liu Zhun was arriving shortly, and Brian would have his vengeance. The lights inside his apartment were dim as he sat on a plush black sofa adorned with red cushions. On the coffee table was a beautiful crystal clock and small bamboo plant. Both were situated next to his Norinco NP-42 9mm pistol. The gun was given to him by his father, a former soldier in the People's Liberation Army.

"Heng, I have been delayed. I should be there at 7:15 PM."

"Okay Zhun. I guess fifteen minutes won't matter."

"I've asked Feng and Dong to join us. It was Feng's operation and he will explain what went wrong," said Zhun.

"I don't care what Feng has to say. He's Guozhi's pawn. I asked for you."

"I know, Heng. But I thought he could explain the tragic circumstances himself. As you know, I sometimes don't get bogged down with operational details. I would rather you hear it directly from him."

"Feng may have planned the operation, but it's you who I want to speak with."

"Okay, Heng. I understand. I will come alone."

"Be certain you are alone, Zhun."

Click.

Brian reached for his weapon and anticipated what would happen next.

"Do it," said Zhun.

Feng hung up the cell phone and quickly approached Brian's front door. Dong followed behind him as the men had their weapons drawn. Silencers were already placed on their pistols to keep away unwanted attention from the apartment building's tenants. As the two men arrived at the front door, Feng fired two shots at the exterior door knob and slammed his right foot against the door.

Feng rushed into Brian's apartment and was quickly shot three times. His body slumped toward the floor. Dong noticed Brian sitting on the left side of the sofa and managed to fire a single shot, but it was too late. Brian placed two rounds into the man's chest.

Brian noticed Dong was dead, however, he was unsure of Feng's fate. As he rose from the sofa, he saw Feng's left leg move. His view was partially obstructed from the kitchen counter where Feng fell. Brian slowly moved toward the injured assassin.

"Feng, what do you know of my wife's death?" asked Brian.

"Nothing, Heng. Guozhi ordered me to kill you. I don't know what happened to Yan. I swear it."

"Zhun tells me you planned the attack. Who was the man you used for the job?"

"I have been with Guozhi since our last meeting. After the missile test in Korla, we left for Beijing. I was there until a couple of days ago."

"So, Zhun is lying? I assume he ordered you here?"

"He did, Heng. Finish me. I can't stand this pain much longer."

"I see, Feng. You are bleeding profusely from your stomach. Why would I want you to have a quick death? My wife suffered, why shouldn't you?"

Feng said nothing and stared into Wu's eyes.

"You have nothing else to say, Feng?" asked Brian.

"You're a worthless swine. Your exit from Hong Kong was sloppy and put our organization at risk. All our plans and years of preparation might be wasted."

"You and Guozhi have only been with us for two years. I've been with the corps since it resurfaced. You took my children's mother away from them. And now you will die."

Brian placed a single shot into Feng's head. Zhun's assassins had failed. Brian wondered if the organization would fail like it did so many decades ago. But he didn't care. His first assassination with the corps would be against its charismatic leader, Liu Zhun.

Brian grabbed his backpack and quickly left the apartment. Upon reaching his car, he pulled out his cell and called Zhun.

"I am coming for you, Zhun. It won't be now. But I will come. Then I will find you and then I will kill you."

"I am sorry things did not work out, Heng. I had other plans for you. One of us will die soon. I wonder who it will be. Goodbye, my young friend."

Chinese Embassy, Pyongyang, North Korea,
June 15, 7:30 PM

Sun Boling joined his fellow officers inside the grand hall of the Chinese embassy. The crowd was large and included mostly well-dressed diplomats and their spouses, a few Chinese military personnel and members of the Workers' Party of Korea, including its deputy, Pak Yong-nam. Accompanying Pak was a large contingent of North Korean military officers and rising stars within the Young Pioneer Corps, a wing of the WPK.

"So, Boling. How do you like your new assignment?" asked one of the Chinese officers.

"I already miss Beijing. This is a wretched country."

"You get used to it, Boling. In time, you may appreciate the creature comforts here. We are treated like royalty. The North Koreans kiss our ass," said a nearby officer.

"I just want to get back to the fleet," said Boling.

After a few minutes of small talk, the men made their way to the reception line to greet Pak Yong-nam and his special guests. Sun Boling rendered his respects and quickly returned to the nearby group of military officers who were enjoying traditional Chinese hors d'oeuvres consisting of Cantonese style pork and shrimp dumplings, tea leaf eggs and crab Rangoon.

"Boling, have you heard that we may be meeting their great leader soon?"

"Great leader? No. I thought he kept to himself?" asked Boling sarcastically.

"We thought the same. Apparently, he has invited us to observe a missile test."

"Why would he do that?"

"To demonstrate a major leap in his missile program.

Did you hear about the recent test off the coast of Hawaii?"

"Yes, I read about that while I was on leave, just before I reported," said Boling.

"We believe his fuel technology still lacks the power to successfully place a miniaturized nuclear warhead on one of his long-range missiles. I guess he wants to prove us wrong."

"What will he use to simulate the warhead?"

"Good question, I guess we'll find out soon."

"Why would he do that?" asked Boling.

"He wants us to take him seriously and the Americans still do not believe he can fire a warhead onto their shores. Without proven technology, he can't negotiate for more food."

"I understand wanting to convince the Americans. But why try to convince us?"

"Leverage, Boling. He still believes we will support any move he makes on the peninsula."

"Unwise. He should know by now we have greater ambitions," said one of the officers.

"Agree. We already have military forces in Africa. Soon, our naval forces will operate in the Atlantic and in South America," said Boling.

As the men chuckled and scanned the crowd, Boling's cell phone buzzed. A message from the mainland came in.

Urgent. Please call right away.

Boling politely excused himself from the group and briskly walked to his office on the third floor. He then opened the top drawer of his desk and removed the subscriber identification module card and swapped it with the chip inside his government issued cell phone. A phone call to his commander was required.

"Hello, Zhun. Why the urgency?" asked Boling.

"Hello, Boling. We have had a minor setback here. Heng

is no longer with us."

"Heng? What has happened?"

"One of our operations in Urumqi went bad. Yan is dead and Heng has become a liability."

"How did Yan die?"

"In an attack. She wasn't supposed to be there. One of our members made a grave error. Heng is after me now. I am going to kill him and wanted you to know."

"Thank you, Zhun. How will this disrupt our operations going forward?" asked Boling.

"It will not. Guozhi will proceed with the second launch next month. How are things going at your new assignment?"

"Better than we anticipated. I should have some very good news for you soon."

"Keep me informed, Boling. There are other operations being planned and Beijing will soon be in disarray."

"I will. Should I reach out to Heng?"

"No. It's best he does not know where you are or the specifics of your operation. We can't risk another setback. He has nowhere to go."

"Alright, Zhun. Let me get back to work. I'll call when I have a good update."

Click.

Boling exchanged his SIM card and soon returned to the reception below. The problem with the Americans over the incident in Hong Kong may soon be over, he thought to himself.

Dafdar Village, Tashkurgan Tajik Autonomous County, Xinjiang, China, June 16, 3:55 PM

Michael Brennan and Wasim arrived at Dafdar, a Wakhi village just east of the Karakoram Highway. Their long journey through the Wakhan Corridor, Wakhjir Pass, and across the Chinese border was finally over. For the most part, the operation was executed swiftly and as its planners in Langley had envisioned. Michael was now on his own and would soon be joined by his British counterpart. Asif and Jamal had already said their goodbyes and were off in the nearby hills meeting with their local buyers.

"Okay, Michael. When will your contacts arrive?" asked Wasim.

"At six o'clock, Wasim."

"I am sorry for the problem we had in Sarhadd. I hope your superiors in Langley will overlook the incident," said Wasim.

"What incident is that, Wasim?" asked Michael with a slight grin on his face.

"Thank you, Michael."

"You did an excellent job, Wasim. Unexpected things happen in our line of work. It's just the nature of what we do."

"I appreciate that, Michael. For what it's worth, I am going to find Baqir's cousin. The Taliban won't get away with kidnapping him. I can't allow the Taliban to disrupt my operations back home. There is still much business to be made there."

"I understand, Wasim. Do what you must. Survival is a strong instinct."

The two men continued sitting inside one of the stone shelters used by local Wakhi tribesmen. Within minutes, Michael leaned back and began a short nap. He was tired, filthy, and anxious to move to the next phase of his operation. Safely inside China, and his contract with CIA nearly complete, Wasim would do the same.

At precisely 5:35 PM, Michael's alarm began buzzing from his wristwatch. His nap wasn't nearly long enough, he thought to himself. A quick kick to Wasim's left boot woke the Afghan contractor quickly. Then Michael's cell phone rang.

"Michael, it's Doug. Have you arrived safely in Dafdar?"

"Well, how the hell are you, Doug? I'm fine, thanks for asking."

"Ha. Do I really have to ask, Michael?"

"Nope. Things are good here, Doug. I should be meeting the British in about twenty minutes. I will feel better once I get my papers and a hot shower."

"I'm sure you will. I think we have some good leads for you to look at. I'll have someone send you the specifics when you get settled and log in."

"Sounds good, Doug. Have the requirements changed since I left?"

"No. I just need you to verify if the anti-satellite missile test was a deliberate miss or if they meant to hit us."

"Okay, Doug. With some luck and a bit of coercion, maybe I'll be back in Indonesia soon. I have a lot of work to do."

"I understand, Michael. Just get us the intel asap. This will get the President and the NSC off our asses."

"And it will get me the hell out of here. I've never felt more unprepared for an operation, Doug. I'm wondering why the British don't handle this themselves. They have better assets here."

"You know how Washington and London feel about joint operations, Michael. It makes the politicians feel better. Just get the job done quickly and we'll have you back in Jakarta soon."

"Have you finished an exit strategy?" asked Michael.

"It's going to depend on how the operation unfolds. If things go smoothly, I might just have the British fly you out. If not, I'm working on options with Shane in Beijing."

"Shane is a good man. A bit idealistic for me, but I'm sure he'll come through."

"Good luck, Michael. Let's get this done quickly. With a bit of good fortune, you'll be out of there in a couple of months."

Click.

Then it came. As Michael gazed across the plateau, he could see a black pickup truck moving closer and in his direction. This had to be the British, he thought to himself.

"Michael, I presume?" asked the passenger as he pulled up to Michael's position.

"Yes, I am. You must be John?"

"Correct. Hop in mate and let's get moving. We have a full night's travel ahead of us."

The two professional spies were soon on their way and operation Red Sky was now in motion. The operation had changed somewhat since Michael's last briefing in Kabul. He and John were to work directly together to determine Beijing's intent behind the missile launch.

Dabancheng District, City of Urumqi, Xinjiang, China, June 16, 9:00 PM

Liu Zhun sat down. Flanked by two members of the assassination corps, he reached for the phone and spoke softly.

"Guozhi, your men have failed. Wu Heng got away. He's coming after me now."

"Feng and Dong are seasoned operatives. How could they have failed?"

"Does it matter? I expect him to find me here soon. I told him about my farm many years ago. I suspect he'll take his time and strike when he's ready."

"Do you have enough men?" asked Guozhi.

"Plenty. I heard from our man in Pyongyang. He may have good news for us soon."

"That is good. When are you going to provide me some specifics? I don't like being left out of the loop on such an important operation. Maybe I can use my resources to assist?"

"No, Guozhi. You know I don't discuss such matters. You have your role in the organization. I value your contribution to the corps, but we should be fine. If something changes, I will let you know."

"Okay, Zhun. I understand. The situation with Wu Heng needs to be resolved quickly. He knows about the missile test next month. He could become a liability if Beijing's counter-intelligence organization determines who he really is."

"He doesn't know the specifics, Guozhi. All he knows is that we are planning to hit the American satellite next month. He won't be a problem and I'm confident he won't talk. He wants revenge for Yan and that should keep him quiet."

"I hope you are right, Zhun."

"I am, Guozhi. Trust me."

General Zhang Guozhi spent the next several minutes giving Liu an update regarding the second missile launch. A significant bribe for one of the engineers would ensure the missile's trajectory would "accidentally" hit the American spy satellite. Regardless of Beijing's official position, America's response would be immediate. At least that is what the men hoped.

"Will your man in Pyongyang complete his mission shortly after the missile launch?" asked Guozhi.

"That's the plan. Of course, it's all contingent on his access. If I think he has a very tight window of opportunity, then I will order him to strike immediately. Do you think Beijing would delay the launch if he is successful?" asked Liu.

"It's possible, but I think testing will continue despite whatever issues they face along the North Korean border," answered Guozhi confidently.

"We can only hope my friend. If we are not successful, we will have other opportunities," said Liu.

"Maybe, but I fear a massive crackdown if we lose the initiative," said Guozhi.

"Let's rid ourselves of these negative thoughts. Things are going to work out for the corps. I will eliminate Wu Heng as soon as possible. In the meantime, I'll transfer the funds to your engineer, so he is satisfied. However, I don't think he'll have time to enjoy it."

Liu chuckled a bit as if he was amused. Guozhi remained focused.

"Excellent. Let me know when Wu's situation is resolved," said Guozhi.

"Of course, Guozhi. I will call you soon."

Liu Zhun turned to one of his men and instructed him to call several of the corps' associates. Their presence and protection were required immediately as Wu Heng would soon arrive at the remote farmhouse. Liu Zhun put his trap in motion.

Blue Paradise Lounge, Urumqi, Xinjiang Province, China, Jun 18, 7:35 AM

Michael Brennan finally awoke from a long evening's rest. The hot shower from the night before, coupled with a hearty local meal, reinvigorated him. Shaven and dressed like a western businessman, Michael was eager to start Operation Red Sky, the joint intelligence operation between CIA and SIS inside China. The cozy apartment on the third floor he woke up to would be his home for the foreseeable future. Though modern with all the creature comforts he needed, he missed Virginia. Back in Montclair, summer had begun, and tourists began flocking to Washington, D.C.

While waiting for his coffee to brew, Michael fired up his laptop and made the secure connection with Langley using one of its communications satellites in low earth orbit. The message he was looking for was waiting in his inbox. It included several individuals Langley thought were working on or near the Korla military complex. They would be his first targets the agency would recommend during his spotting phase, the first step in recruiting human assets. Langley suggested floating the names with his SIS counterpart and that they would provide an update when necessary.

Langley also included several high-resolution overhead images of the Korla military complex. The imagery, provided by a top secret NRO satellite, had a national imagery interpretability scale of seven, which could identify fenced areas, cars, and street lamps. Michael already knew his chances of getting onto the complex were slim, and probably not necessary. His strategy would be to identify local restaurants, bars, and brothels where some of the facilities' employees were likely to be found before or after their shifts. It would be in those locations he could strike up conversations and begin the process of learning what he could about the missile launch.

A few minutes later, he heard a knock on the door. Accompanying John Dearlove was Mei, the brothel's owner and long-time SIS source in Xinjiang.

"Good morning, Michael. Ready to get started?" asked Dearlove.

"I am. Langley just sent me some intel on Korla."

"Good. Let me look at it."

"I assume she is cleared?" asked Michael as he turned to Mei.

"Probably not, Michael. But she has been with us for decades. She will be part of this operation."

"Okay, John. No issues on my end," said Michael.

Dearlove looked at the screen. It didn't take him long to offer an opinion.

"This is garbage. The imagery is nice to look at, but we have no use for it. And these four individuals, well, most are no longer working there or wouldn't have the information we need. Your friends in Langley have nothing we can use right now."

Michael appreciated John's candor, despite his arrogance. But he knew John's assessment was probably right. Langley's intel in China was spotty at best.

"Agree, John. We'll need to drive through Korla and see where the employees like to entertain themselves. Unless, of course, SIS has something I don't know about."

"Mei and one of her associates will drive you to Korla this morning. Did you have time to review your paperwork last night?" asked Dearlove.

"Yes."

"Any questions, Michael?"

"Nope. Let's get started."

"Great. I have matters to attend to here in Urumqi. Let's meet back here in a few days after your first recon. Sound good?"

"Absolutely, John. Thanks."

Michael turned to Mei.

"Do you have something secure I can put my laptop in?"

"Of course, we can use my safe downstairs. Let us get going," said Mei.

A few miles into their drive south toward Korla, Michael turned to Mei.

"Is John always that pleasant in the morning?" asked Michael.

"Only when he has something else on his mind."

"Care to elaborate?"

"No. He tells me what I need to know. He is a serious man."

"That's good, Mei. Then there shouldn't be any surprises."

Dabancheng District, City of Urumqi, Xinjiang Province, China, June 18, 9:16 AM

"Sir, it's Lin. Wu Heng is driving into the Dabancheng District."

"I wonder what he is doing in Dabancheng? He doesn't have family there. Oh well, keep an eye on him. Something about the man doesn't feel right."

"Understand, sir. I agree."

"Any idea what the hell he is doing there?"

"No idea, sir. I've been following him for fifty minutes. I will provide an update later this afternoon," said Lin.

Inspector Yang Lin continued following Wu through the streets of Dabancheng. The grief-stricken man she met just days earlier, was clearly in a hurry to get to wherever his destination would be. Yang wondered if her target was aware she was following him.

Wu Heng turned east toward the outskirts of town and began driving on a dirt road at one of the entrances to the Dabancheng Wind Farm, one of the largest in the world. Powered by nearly three hundred turbines, most blades were half the size of a football field. Winds up to forty miles per hour could be felt ripping through the air originating from the beautiful Tian Shan range and Tarim Basim.

Yang only had seconds to decide if she should follow Wu. At that point, he would surely know he was being followed. Nevertheless, she had her orders and turned onto the trail, used mostly by maintenance crews to keep the facility operating at maximum efficiency.

Yang maintained a distance of one hundred and fifty meters as Wu slowly navigated through the wind farm. At the end of the trail, Wu stopped at one of the remote buildings and quickly exited his vehicle. He turned back toward

Yang's car and stood there.

A few moments later, Yang reached for her pistol and approached Wu.

"Inspector Yang. Why are you following me?" asked Wu.

"My boss asked me to keep an eye on you. What are you doing here?"

"My cousin works on the farm. He said I could come here to be alone."

"Why not remain at home, Wu?"

"The city is crowded and noisy. I need to be in a quiet place and reflect. There is no need to point that weapon at me."

Yang lowered her weapon, sympathetic to the man's recent loss.

"We have counselors in the city who could help you," said Yang.

"Ha. No, Inspector Yang, they cannot. My children no longer have their mother."

"What is inside the building?" asked Yang.

"Want to see?"

"Okay, Wu. But you go in first. A woman can't be too careful."

Wu Heng reached into his pocket and pulled out a key. As Yang entered, Wu immediately slammed the door and knocked the policewoman to the ground. He quickly sprung to the floor and snatched Yang's weapon from her hand.

"Stand up, Inspector Yang," said Wu as he pointed the weapon at her.

"What is this, Wu. I am a police officer. Give me my weapon, now," shouted Yang.

"No, Inspector Yang. Now sit down."

Yang had no choice and self-preservation kicked in.

"I have done nothing to you, Wu Heng. I am simply following orders."

"What are your orders, Inspector Yang?"

"To follow you. My commander wants to know more about you. You apparently exhibited special training at the hospital where you foiled the terror attack."

"Really? I simply tackled a would-be assassin and your commander thinks highly of me?"

"Yes. There is no record of you serving in the armed forces."

"Maybe I just got lucky?"

"You now have the gun, Wu Heng. I doubt you got lucky."

"What have you learned from following me?"

"Nothing, really."

"What made you follow me here?"

"I already told you that. I was following orders."

"Do you always follow your orders?" asked Wu.

"Always."

"I used to blindly follow orders as well."

"From who?" asked Yang.

"The assassination corps. Have you heard of us?"

"Never."

"The group began in Hong Kong over a hundred years ago. It's been resurrected."

"I can help you, Wu Heng. Let me bring you to one of our counselors and I'll forget this incident ever happened."

"Ha. I doubt that, Inspector Yang. If I let you go, I'll be in prison. I cannot let that happen. Do you have children, Inspector Yang?"

"A boy, he is seven years old."

"Is his father a good man?"

"He is. Enough of this nonsense, Wu. What happens to

me, now?"

"You die, Inspector Yang."

Wu Heng fired a single shot into Yang's forehead. At least he was merciful.

Brian Wu sat and stared at the woman's lifeless body. He was genuinely remorseful since the woman was a mother to a young boy. He wondered how her family would feel when news of her death would be reported.

It didn't matter, however, as Brian Wu's fierce vendetta against Liu Zhun was coming to a speedy conclusion. Nothing would prevent his confrontation with the leader of the assassination corps despite whatever collateral damage would occur. Brian Wu had finally become the ruthless assassin Liu Zhun hoped he would be.

Korla, Mongol Autonomous Prefecture, China, June 18, 4:55 PM

Michael and Mei arrived in Korla and soon checked into their hotel. The Garden was a five-star luxury hotel, situated along the Kongque River. The location was ideal and provided the group an excellent venue to begin their reconnaissance of downtown Korla. Ping would join them later after a brief visit with his cousin at a nearby apartment complex.

Korla was a bustling city of over five hundred thousand people, rich with water and lush farmlands. Well known for its production of aromatic pears, Korla sat near the oil fields found in the Taklamakan Desert. A booming economy fueled by a rise in energy jobs helped explain the city's thriving population.

Korla was also home to the People's Liberation Army Unit 63618, the agency responsible for China's ballistic missile defense. Its scientists, engineers, computer software analysts, and other personnel could be found roaming the streets in search of tasty food and entertainment. The city was a target rich environment for human intelligence collection and Michael was ready to begin identifying individuals who had access to information, also known as the *spotting phase*.

"I'm going to take a shower and freshen up. Let's meet in the lobby at six o'clock."

"Okay, Mei. I'll be at the bar. There's something I want to try," said Michael.

"Please ensure you have your papers in case you are questioned. Korla doesn't have many westerners. The police are unlikely to stop us but be prepared."

"I'm just a freelance photographer for BBC, Mei. I got it."

"And your reason for being here?" asked Mei with a smile.

"I'm doing a story on the city's growth due to increased oil exploration over the past few years. I'm fine, Mei. I studied the file last night."

Michael entered his room, secured his luggage and quickly turned his attention to the hotel's bar where a small sampling of local drink was in order. He had been waiting anxiously for twenty-four hours to try one of China's most famous beers, the Sinkiang Black Beer. The ale, similar in color to a dark American lager, was manufactured in northwestern China. Michael found the drink to be flavorsome with a slight taste of brown sugar and an excellent complement to his lamb dinner.

Mei arrived at the bar about an hour later. She wore a beautiful red dress with white heels and ankle ties.

"Wow. Where are we going, Mei?" asked Michael.

"You mean, where am I going, Michael?"

"Okay, where are you going?"

"Ping will take me to one of the nightclubs here in the city. My research suggests there are senior personnel from the missile complex who visit there. Many are military officers. You and Ping will visit another location. It's a bar in the western part of town."

"I assume we have other locations to scout as well?" asked Michael.

"Of course, Michael. John and I have several places in mind. We'll spend a few hours at each location and determine where to put our efforts in the coming days. Now, our only objective is to confirm locations where employees of the complex like to hang out."

"Sounds perfectly reasonable to me, Mei."

The two quickly exited the hotel and found Ping. The

trio would spend several hours at multiple locations throughout the evening. Michael found the exercise necessary despite little success. At approximately 12:40 AM, their luck had changed.

"Mei just texted. She's having a drink with someone who claims they work in flight control," said Ping.

"So soon? Damn, Ping, we just got lucky," said Michael.

"It doesn't surprise me that she already found someone who may be useful. She is very persuasive, Michael. Be careful," chuckled Ping.

"I know the type, Ping. It takes more than looks to capture my attention. How long have you worked with her?"

"She recruited me a few years ago in Urumqi. I usually drive her associates to places like this where they watch."

"Watch who?" asked Michael.

"Whoever the targets are, Michael. They include Chinese police, People's Liberation Army units, western businessmen and others."

"Have you done much surveillance yourself, Ping?"

"A little. Mei is still training me. I guess she is trying to teach me patience."

Michael felt insulted as it was clear that he was working with an amateur. Tonight's surveillance objectives were minimal, and Ping's ability to identify Chinese military personnel by rank was really all that was required. However, John's insistence to remain in Urumqi bothered Michael despite the operation just getting off the ground.

"How long have you opposed your government, Ping? I assume you're no fan of the Communist Party or you wouldn't be working with Mei."

"As long as I can remember. I actually met Mei at a protest in Urumqi."

"What were the people protesting?"

"The Uyghurs were upset over the lack of jobs awarded them by the government. They claimed they were being racially targeted and secluded from competitive government contracts. It remained mostly peaceful until a group of anarchists arrived. Then it got a bit violent. That's where I met Mei."

"Who were the anarchists?" asked Michael.

"I have no idea. I just heard some people in the crowd talking about them."

The two men continued their pleasantries for another thirty minutes. Mei texted a second time and insisted that she be picked up right away. Ping and Michael arrived approximately fifteen minutes later.

"I'm meeting the man again tomorrow night. He's my best lead."

"Good news, Mei. What else do you know about the man?" asked Michael.

"That his wife and two sons are in Beijing. He moved here without them and flies to Beijing once a month."

"Better news. That means he's lonely and just needs someone to talk to. Do you think he's the talking type, Mei?"

"It may take a few weeks, but I can probably get him to open up about his work soon. I'm going to ask John to confirm his identity. If it checks outs, I'll run with it."

The group arrived at the Garden Hotel and Michael and Ping would enjoy one more round of drinks together while Mei returned to her room.

"He is an American spy. He's working with John to determine if the missile launch was intended to hit the American reconnaissance satellite."

"We expected this contingency, Mei. Keep the American occupied for a few more days. Then kill him," said the voice on the other end of the line.

"That will bring me unwanted attention. How will I ex-plain it to John?"

"Leave that to me, Mei. I'll send some men to Urumqi when you return."

Toutunhe, Xinjiang Province, China, June 18, 8:49 PM

John Dearlove returned to Toutenhe. He had spent the last few days exploiting SIS contacts to determine if recent intelligence on Brian Wu was accurate. Wang Yong promised he would assist and the search for Brian Wu began to narrow. A photo of Brian had been circulated throughout the city to Wang's associates, including legitimate businesses operating within Wang's commercial empire. Wang's associates reported Brian Wu's whereabouts in the city but could not confirm an address. The missing information John was waiting for had finally arrived.

"John, It's Yong. We have the address for Brian Wu and will text it to you shortly. However, my informant at the police department says his name is Wu Heng. His identification has been confirmed. Does the name mean anything to you?"

"No, Yong. He did not have such an alias. Are you sure of the address?"

"I am. My sources are reliable, John. I have fulfilled my end of the bargain. Will you be needing anything else?"

"For now, nothing, Yong. Thank you."

Dearlove quickly drove to the apartment complex and arrived twenty minutes later. The secure building required a contactless smart card for access. John would have to wait for someone to exit and slip into the building. The opportunity came after John spotted a young couple approaching the front door.

John easily entered the building. The couple was too focused on their smartphones to notice him. He made his way to the elevator and quietly arrived at the front door. John noticed the door looked brand new and nothing like the other older doors he passed. Nevertheless, he reached into his pocket and pulled out a credit-card lock pick set he had used hundreds of times over his career.

John noticed the smell right away. There was a strong odor emanating from one of the rooms. The smell of death was in the air, he thought to himself. He raised his weapon and walked toward the hallway. A few steps later, two bodies lying in the bathtub became visible.

Dearlove examined the men and searched their bodies for identification. There were no wallets, phones or other items found in their clothes. Dearlove then decided to search for tattoos to understand what might have transpired in Brian's apartment. He found the markings of the assassination corps, like what he and Chi found on the dead bodies near Taiyuan. John surmised that Brian was being hunted by the assassination corps. But why, he thought to himself. And then he recalled Yuan's death from the recent terror attack in Urumqi. It started making sense.

"Yong, it's John. I'm afraid I have another request."

"Now what, John? I don't remember being one of your British spies."

"Have you heard of the assassination corps?"

"I've read about them. They existed long ago but are now a footnote in history. Why?"

"I'm in Wu Heng's apartment. There are two bodies here with the inscription. I saw two others in Taiyuan with the same markings and words. I wonder if someone has resurrected the group?" asked Dearlove.

"Ha. Don't be silly, John. If they existed, I would know about it."

"It seems you don't. I'm going to send you their pictures. Can you circulate their faces throughout your organization and help me identify them?"

"Why not, John. I'm happy to help an old friend."

Click.

John hung up and immediately called the Hong Kong operations center.

"Elizabeth, it's John Dearlove. I'm sending some pictures your way. Please have them analyzed in our database. I doubt we'll find a match but give it a go."

"Yes, sir. How long will you be staying on the mainland?"

"Until I accomplish my mission, Elizabeth. Please contact me when you have the results."

Click.

Dearlove placed one more call.

"Mei, it's John. How is the reconnaissance in Korla going?"

"Good, John. I believe we have a target for your American friend."

"Will you be seeing them tonight?"

"Of course."

"Good. Enjoy the evening and tell him you will be back next week. Let him wait a bit."

"I had planned to. But we have a couple of more days to go."

"No, you've made more progress than I expected. It will take some time to gather the information we need on the missile launch. I have other matters to attend to. Bring Michael back tomorrow afternoon."

"Alright, John. Can you tell me what other matters you have? I think it's best we remain in Korla as planned. Michael and Ping could help identify more targets and give us options."

"I understand, Mei. This is no longer negotiable. Get back here tomorrow."

Click.

John Dearlove exited the apartment complex and returned to his car. He needed to update Alex Sawers right away.

"Alex, it's John."

"Hello, old chap. How is the operation going with the American?"

"Good. He is in Korla with one of my assets. They've identified a target for exploitation. But there is something else."

"Have you found Brian?"

"I'm getting closer. He may have been involved with a group called the assassination corps."

"Never heard of them, John. Should we be concerned?" asked Sawers.

"I'm not sure yet. But I'd like some Intel on them. They existed from 1910 until 1912 and then vanished. There is little evidence of them found in the history books."

"John, I appreciate the update, but we promised the Americans our full support on this missile launch. The Prime Minister has called me twice."

"The Intel will come, Alex. Please be patient."

"Okay, John. I'll talk to analysis right away and see what we can dig up."

"Thank you, Alex. Don't worry about the operation. You and the Americans will get your answers soon."

Dearlove began driving to his hotel and wondered if Brian's affiliation with the assassination corps was voluntary. After all, his treachery in Hong Kong began before Yan's sudden death. There was something missing, he thought to himself. The uncertainty plagued him for the remainder of the evening.

Urumqi, Xinjiang Province, June 19, 8:50 PM

"Michael, I'd like to speak to you about a sensitive topic. May I come in?"

"Of course, John, grab a seat. I'm getting an update from Langley. Can you give me a minute?"

A short while later, Michael closed his laptop and the two men began talking.

"Langley is happy about the target we found in Korla. If we're lucky, the operation could be over in a few weeks."

"We can only hope, Michael. Mei is very good at what she does. I have another matter to discuss. Have you heard of a group called the assassination corps?"

"Can't say that I have, John. Who the hell are they?"

"They formed in 1910 with the goal of ending the Qing dynasty. The Xinhai Revolution occurred soon after and they disbanded. I've had the pleasure of making their acquaintance recently, four to be exact, and think one of my former assets has joined the group."

"John, my mission is to find out what China's intentions were with the missile launch, nothing else. I'm not interested in chasing a bunch of clowns who call themselves assassination corps."

"I don't blame you. If I were in your position, I would say the same thing. But there's something going on and I'm convinced my former operative is behind it."

"Why should I care, John? It sounds like an SIS mess to me. Why should CIA help you clean it up?"

"I'm not asking for CIA. I'm asking for you, Michael. We could work on this together and remain focused on the operational requirements. I believe we can achieve both."

"Not interested, John. The only thing I give a damn about is the Intel. The quicker we can determine what happened during the launch, the quicker we can get back to our business. I have another operation in Indonesia that requires my attention."

"What if this assassination corps business and the missile launch are linked?"

"How the hell do you figure that, John?"

"My operative went rogue right around the time of the launch. He funded an operation to assassinate five of my assets in Hong Kong. He did not have access to the resources to support the operation. And now he's been spotted here in Urumqi. It's a bit too coincidental for me, Michael."

"I think you're reaching, John. How is he connected to the missile launch?"

"That's what I'm trying to figure out. I've got nothing right now. Look, Michael, we have a solid target in Korla. Mei will return in a few days to get the man talking. My guess is she'll have the information within a few weeks. I'm quite certain that both of our governments expected this to last longer. In the meantime, I want to be surrounded by people I can trust."

"What about Mei or some of your other assets?" asked Michael.

"I'm keeping her out of this for now. I want her focused on the Korla issue."

Michael sat back in his chair and clearly appeared annoyed. He knew John was serious and understood his need to determine what happened to his former asset. Michael had experienced the same pitfalls over previous operations. He entertained the proposition out of professional courtesy.

"Who is your former asset?" asked Michael.

"Brian Wu. I found out recently he goes by the name of Wu Heng."

"Did you say Wu Heng?" asked Michael as he reached

for his cell phone.

"Correct," said John.

"Is this the man you are looking for, John?" asked Michael as he displayed Wu's face on his smartphone.

"That's him. How the hell did you get his picture, Michael?" asked John in astonishment.

"This is your guy? You must be fucking kidding me. I recently picked up an asset in Indonesia, a Chinese naval officer. He was filmed having sex with Wu Heng in Hong Kong. Indonesian intelligence alerted us."

John sat back in his seat and couldn't believe what he was hearing. He began to chuckle.

"This is bloody stunning. What are the odds?"

"I've seen similar situations, John. Indonesian intelligence says they weren't close so I'm sure my asset can't help us," said Michael.

"You're probably right, Michael. Care to help me find this guy?"

"What the hell, John. We have a few days to kill until Mei returns to Korla."

The two men continued talking for another fifteen minutes. John shared the location of his safe house and some additional assets in the area. Michael was impressed with John's logistical infrastructure and access to much needed resources.

"Thank you, Michael. I'll be back in the morning and we'll get started."

"You got it, John. Good night."

Michael opened his laptop and decided to send a quick message to his operations center.

I need all the Intel we have on a group called the assassination corps. Reference all open source documents and include dark web searches going back ten years. I do not need historical data before 2008. Request everything you can find within twenty-four hours. MB

Wu Heng and the assassination corps just became the target for two of the world's deadliest spies.

Dabancheng District, City of Urumqi, Xinjiang
Province, China, June 19, 9:35 PM

Brian Wu arrived at a patch of trees, just one kilometer from Liu Zhun's farmhouse in the Dabacheng District. The skies were cloudy and little illumination from the moon was visible. The air was cool and crisp, as a breeze blew across the lush fields. The remote farm offered Brian the opportunity to approach Zhun's suspected location from a safe distance. He reached into the trunk and pulled out a rifle, the Chinese QBZ-03, complete with a night scope.

The QBZ-03, also known as the Type 03, was a gas-operated selective fire rifle capable of firing six hundred and fifty rounds per minute. It included a thirty-round box magazine and weighed approximately three and a half kilograms. The QBZ-03 was a deadly weapon, despite a poor reputation among international arms dealers. Brian expected the rifle to perform its task for the evening.

Brian carefully searched the farmhouse and adjacent lands as he peered through the night scope. He noticed six men conducting roving patrols while two remained on the front porch. Liu Zhun had more men than he expected. He wondered if the assassination corps was bigger than he thought. It didn't matter at this point.

The former SIS operative remained in his position, just behind a clump of trees, and waited. The vantage point offered him an excellent location to continue observing the farmhouse and studying Liu's men and their patterns. He didn't see Liu as blinds covered the windows and prevented his observation of the interior. It didn't matter. Brian was certain that Liu was hiding inside.

There were four SUVs at the front of the farmhouse. Brian estimated the size of Liu's protection force to be around twenty men. Too many, he thought to himself. Brian was confident he could kill at least five of Liu's men from his location, but the rest would be a problem. Brian Wu sat back and thought about his next move.

Brian decided to remain in place and continue his observation of the farmhouse. Liu Zhun would eventually have to come out, he thought to himself. The assassin would wait for his opportunity to strike. John Dearlove, his former spymaster, taught him well.

Wu learned the art of patience soon after John recruited him. Dearlove once directed him to observe a yacht at a marina in Hong Kong for five days. Brian's task was to report anything that moved on the boat during the night time hours. His patience wore off on the fourth day where he took a short nap immediately after sunset. Unbeknownst to Brian, Dearlove filmed the entire incident and on day five revealed the mistake. As Brian lay napping, an older man went topside and walked by his position on the dock. Dearlove made the young operative pay for his 'sin' and conducted a similar event lasting fifteen days. On that occasion, nothing moved as Brian remained alert the entire time. Brian learned that boredom often consumed a spy's time and became their best friend. It was simply the nature of the business.

A few hours later, Wu scanned the property. The same men he observed earlier were walking alongside the farmhouse, while two men remained on the front porch. There was no sign of Liu and Wu Heng would wait until the following morning to decide his next move.

Blue Paradise Lounge, Urumqi, Xinjiang Province, China, June 20, 1:20 AM

Michael Brennan remained awake. He had difficulty sleeping as he wondered if John's request would be too much of a distraction. After all, his mission would come first, and the assassination corps didn't really concern him. He empathized with John's position and understood how painful Wu's actions were. The man double-crossed his spymaster and John was determined to make him pay a price. He considered John's proposal a fair request and had done the same a few times in his career. Pay it forward, he thought to himself. How credible was an organization calling itself the assassination corps anyway?

Michael stared at the ceiling. The room was nearly pitch black as an old fan barely circulated the air throughout the room. Then a faint sound emanated from the kitchen. Michael Brennan was no longer alone. He reached for his Glock 19 pistol and sprang from the bed.

A second distant sound came from the hallway. The weight of a stranger's body was pushing onto the hardwood floor. Michael could barely hear it but he knew someone was coming. He waited patiently along the wall adjacent to the door and prepared to strike.

The doorknob began to turn. A few seconds later, Michael quickly grasped the stranger's right hand. The unexpected move surprised the intruder who reacted by firing several rounds into the walls. The individual never had a chance.

Michael began furiously punching the would-be assassin as blood began oozing from the person's broken nose. A few moments later, the individual fell to the floor and was unconscious. Michael noticed the long hair right away. The assassin was a woman wearing a traditional Chinese dress. He carefully moved through the hallway and checked the remainder of the apartment, a studio style apartment with a combined kitchen and living area. The small room was secure. Michael returned to the hallway and turned on a dim light. Mei lay barefooted on the floor. He shook his head and called John Dearlove.

"John, it's Michael. You need to get your ass to my apartment right away."

"What's going on, Michael?" asked John groggily.

"I'm not sure, but Mei just tried to kill me. Your God damn asset snuck into my apartment with a weapon. Get moving, John," said Michael coldly.

John arrived at the Blue Paradise Lounge within forty-five minutes and worked his way to the top floor. Michael sat at the kitchen table pointing his weapon at Mei. Dry blood covered her left nostril. Michael then turned his weapon toward John.

"John, please have a seat."

"Point that damn weapon somewhere else, Michael."

"Not until I can figure out what the hell is going on here. Sit down, John."

"There must be a bloody good explanation for this," said John as he walked toward the table and sat down.

Mei stared at Michael and remained still.

"What happened tonight, Mei?" asked Dearlove.

Silence. Mei remained defiant.

"Mei, what the hell is going on? Why are you here?" asked Dearlove a second time.

"I doubt she's in the mood to speak, John," said Michael.

"We need to get her to one of my safe houses. There are too many people at this location during the day. Get up,

Mei," barked John.

"John, we're not going anywhere until I'm satisfied I know what the hell is going on. She is your asset. This is your mess."

"Michael, I don't have time for this bloody nonsense. I understand how you feel. Come with me and we'll figure this out together. If you're going to shoot, then shoot. If not, move your ass."

Michael respected John's attitude and demeanor. Dear-love was clearly disappointed in Mei, and Michael wondered what he planned to do with her. Nevertheless, Michael remained alert as he stood up and followed the SIS operative to his car. John drove while Mei remained in the front passenger seat. Michael sat in the rear with his left hand firmly holding the Glock. He figured John had no idea of what was going on but remained cautious. For the moment, Michael Brennan would trust no one.

Dabancheng District, City of Urumqi, Xinjiang Province, China, June 20, 10:06 AM

Wu Cheng remained alert. He had not slept the previous night as he continued observing Liu Zhun's farmhouse. The air was unusually chilly, but not cold enough to impact Wu's reconnaissance efforts. There was very little activity at the farmhouse except for Liu's roving patrols. They appeared disciplined, attentive, and prepared. He did not recognize them but that was Liu's genius. He only shared information with people who needed to know. He was not unlike British intelligence who compartmentalized data in hopes of maintaining secrecy. This was Liu's power as the commander of the assassination corps. A few members did know of each other, but this only occurred recently as Liu's plans began to unfold. Wu Heng accepted the practice long ago but never really liked the uncertainty. He wondered if the organization was much larger than Liu had indicated.

As he searched through his scope again, he noticed an SUV approaching from the west. It didn't appear to be moving quickly, and there was only a single passenger inside. A few moments later, Wu identified the driver as Guozhi. Guozhi was not in uniform and clearly hadn't replaced his lost associates from Toutunhe. Wu wondered why the hell Guozhi was there in the first place and remained perched alongside the tree.

A few moments later, Guozhi drove up to the group of vehicles in front of the farmhouse. As the vehicle came to a stop, Liu Zhun exited the front door. Guozhi glanced towards Wu's location as he exited the vehicle and turned to Liu. Wu wished he could hear the men speak but sat patiently as the situation unfolded.

Liu entered the farmhouse as quickly as he exited.

Guozhi followed him and shut the door. The roving patrols continued their duties while activities around the farmhouse continued as they had for the last twenty-four hours. Wu remained patient and ready to strike if the opportunity presented itself.

"Thank you for coming, Guozhi. How are things?" said Liu.

"It was no trouble. I'll be heading to Korla this afternoon to check on the preparations for the second test. The operation appears to be running smoothly. The loss of Dong and Feng are still disappointing. It will complicate my plans with the engineer at the facility, but I'll manage. I've already wired him a deposit for the job."

"Good. I am sorry we lost Feng and Dong. That was my responsibility and I apologize. Their loss will not be in vain. They will be avenged."

"I appreciate the invitation, Zhun, but why have you asked for a meeting? My staff is beginning to ask questions."

"It's about our operation in Pyongyang. Our asset has informed me that he will not be near the target until later next month. Can you reschedule the second test for July 27th?"

"I thought your man was close and would soon have access to him?"

"I'm afraid my information was inaccurate. These things happen, Guozhi. You know that."

Guozhi sat back and appeared slightly annoyed. Nevertheless, he understood how important the missile launch was in the grand scheme of things. The destruction of America's newest surveillance satellite was an integral part of Liu's plans. The assassination corps had to successfully complete simultaneous missions in hopes of turning Beijing upside down.

"I can reschedule the launch, Zhun. But Beijing will not

be happy. Can you assure me your man will deliver?"

"You know I cannot guarantee success. But I'm confident he will take out the target. He is prepared to die and understands that he likely will. We are fortunate to be in this situation, Guozhi."

"I agree, Zhun. Is there anything else?"

"Yes. There is another matter I'd like to discuss."

"Go ahead," said Guozhi.

"As you know, there are five senior members of the Communist Party we are targeting for assassination to coincide with the missile launch and the operation in Pyongyang. I want to add President Xi to the list."

"Have you lost your mind, Zhun? His security is impenetrable. We couldn't get close enough."

"No. But you can, Guozhi," said Liu coldly.

"Me? And how do you propose that?"

"That's not my problem. You know him, don't you?" asked Liu.

"Yes, but I do not meet with him alone."

"Guozhi, you are a rising star in the party. There must be some way."

Guozhi thought the idea was preposterous. The nearly dozen operations the assassination corps had planned would bring significant pressure on Beijing. The loss of President Xi might prevent the group from achieving its strategic goals.

"This is a bad idea, my friend. If Xi were killed, the party would simply replace him. Our operations are intended to put pressure on the regime and show the people how inept it is. Xi will be blamed for his inability to provide order. We need him alive, Zhun, not dead."

Liu was displeased. However, Guozhi's assessment made some sense. He would try again later.

"Okay, Guozhi. I understand. But can we discuss this

again soon? I'm confident he will want to speak with you after the American spy satellite is destroyed. You must give me a chance to convince you. Fair enough?" asked Liu as he smiled.

"Fair enough, Zhun. I need to get to Korla. I have a flight to catch in an hour. I will update you in a few days with preparations for the second launch."

"Thank you, Guozhi. And thank you for your frankness. I appreciate it."

Guozhi exited the farmhouse and returned to his vehicle. He quickly sped away and Wu Heng wondered what the men discussed. The former British SIS operative didn't care and continued waiting for his opportunity to kill the commander of the assassination corps.

Midong District, City of Urumqi, Xinjiang Province, China, June 20, 10:55 AM

John Dearlove and Michael Brennan remained tucked away north of Urumqi, in the Midong District. They had moved Mei quietly in the night into a remote safe house owned by one of John's assets in the region. Mei was unaware of the secure facility and John was certain none of her associates would come there looking for her. John's resources in the Xinjiang Province were vast and most of his assets were unaware of each other's existence. A professional spy rarely shares such information, unless pressing circumstances require it.

Mei's brothel house served John well over the years, but mostly as a hotbed of intelligence gathering. The isolated home located near the Lucaogou Railway Station had rarely been used by John or SIS operatives, but its proximity to the railroad offered easy entry and departure from the city. Its owner, a Uygher gentleman in his late eighties, profited handsomely from the arrangement.

Michael eventually settled down from Mei's attack earlier in the morning and smoothed things over with John. The two men had spent the last few hours interrogating Mei. She never spoke and both men were getting frustrated. Neither man was willing to use enhanced interrogation techniques, for now. Then Michael's phone rang.

"Michael, it's Doug. What the hell is this business about an assassination corps? Why did you make the request and how does it tie into the missile launch?"

"Our British colleague has encountered several of them since his arrival on the mainland. It may be nothing, but there's a chance the group could somehow be involved."

"Are you fricking kidding me, Mike? This was a missile

launch directed by their armed forces. You know a civilian group wouldn't have access to a Chinese military facility."

"No, Doug. I know it sounds farfetched and I'm not sure I believe it at this point, but this is a joint operation and I'm going to help. We asked them for assistance on this operation and I'm going to help the man. I don't see an issue."

"Do his people know what the hell you two are spending your time on?"

"I don't know, and I don't care. Would you like me to ask him, Doug?" asked Michael sarcastically.

"Where are you now?" asked Doug clearly annoyed with Michael's tone.

"North of Urumqi."

"How are things proceeding in Korla?"

"Not good. One of our assets turned on me last night. We are now in the process of questioning her. We are going to resume reconnaissance in a few days."

Doug sighed and changed his tone.

"What happened, Michael?"

"The damn woman tried to kill me, Doug."

"What did the British say?"

"He's pissed off and probably more embarrassed than anything else. These things happen, Doug."

"Do you think you will be back in Korla soon?"

"Yes. I won't be fucking around on this for long."

"Okay. You'll be getting a file in a couple of hours. There doesn't appear to be much on the group, but we found some open source Intel. It's not much but it may be beneficial to the British."

"Thanks, Doug. I'll be in touch soon. Keep the bureaucrats off my ass. This operation is likely to take months."

"You are probably right, but you know how impatient the White House can be."

"I get it, Doug. Out here."

Michael returned to the room where John sat directly in front of Mei.

"So, are the suits in D.C. concerned?" asked Dearlove.

"Of course. They think this is a wild goose chase," said Michael.

"What do you think, Michael?"

"I don't. If you want to continue wasting time trying to get her to talk, be my guest. I'll sit back and watch the show. You've got two days, John, and then I have to insist we get back to Korla."

"I'll get her to talk."

John stood up and moved toward an old wooden cabinet in the corner of the room. He opened one of the doors and removed a black polypropylene syringe case. The tiny case could have housed a fountain pen.

"Sodium thiopental?" asked Michael.

"Indeed."

Rajin Naval base, Rason, North Korea, June 20, 1:30 PM

Sun Boling finally arrived at the ice-free port city of Rason. Rason, home to the Rajin naval base, was also situated along the border with China and Russia. Both countries had leasing arrangements with the city and it was used extensively by China as a gateway for access into the strategic waters of the Sea of Japan. Rajin also served as a training facility for many of its commissioned officers and commanders within the Korean People's Navy. Today, Boling would meet with senior North Korean officials and naval officers to discuss the YJ-18B, an anti-ship cruise missile also known as the "eagle strike eighteen."

Western intelligence analysts believed the missile had an operational range of five hundred kilometers and could travel Mach three in its terminal, or final phase of flight. Boling would spend much of his time discussing the acquisition capabilities of the missile, despite Beijing's insistence that any missiles sold would not have access to its satellite network. This would severely limit Pyongyang's operational capabilities, but North Korea was eager to acquire and test a variant of the missile in the future.

As Boling finished his presentation, his personal cell phone buzzed. Liu's text message was short but insistent.

Please call right away. It's urgent. I must speak with you at once.

Boling excused himself from the remaining group and ordered his driver to prepare for the return trip to Pyongyang. He found a bathroom on the top floor of the facility and carefully checked his surroundings. The timing of Liu's message couldn't have been worse but he would obey his commander's directive. The bathroom appeared empty and

Boling faced the window furthest from the bathroom's opening as he dialed Liu's number.

"Hello, Liu. What is it? I'm in Rajin. Please make it quick," implored Boling.

"You must not strike too early. We have many operations planned for next month, specifically the 28th. Will you have access around that timeframe?"

"I told you earlier, I cannot be certain when their great leader will appear at the facility. I've only heard it will be in a few weeks."

"If you strike too early, then our plans are in serious jeopardy."

"Why? Our operations will put a strain on Beijing. Does it matter if they are closely coordinated?"

"Of course, Boling. One or two events are not going to cause enough pressure in Beijing. It will take all our efforts around the same time. Our efforts will only be realized if they occur within days of each other. I know you are in a difficult situation, but I am confident you will find a way. It must be around the 28th, give or take a few days."

"I will kill him, Liu. You can be certain of that."

Click.

Boling noticed the reflection of a man standing behind him and slowly turned to his left. He wondered what the stranger might have heard. It didn't matter. As Boling shifted his body, he quickly reached for the blade in his uniform pocket. The small knife, only four inches in length, remained hidden as he faced the North Korean counter-intelligence agent.

The man stood at nearly six-foot-tall, much taller than the average North Korean male. He was a member of the North Korean Ministry of State Security, the domestic spy which reported directly to President Kim and ran North

Korea's prison camps. Its primary focus was to ensure the survival of the regime and Kim's direct family. The career intelligence officer never had a chance.

"Who are you speaking with?" asked the man confidently.

Boling immediately threw the knife into the man's throat. Blood began oozing profusely onto his neatly pressed uniform as he fell to the floor a few moments later. Boling lunged toward the man and grabbed his left arm. He knew he was in trouble and had to get away as quickly as possible.

Boling had little time to move the man into a nearby stall. He kept the man's upper torso elevated as he began dragging the lifeless body across the floor. He would have to worry about the bloodied floor later. Boling quickly propped the man onto the commode into a sitting position with his head leaned back. He wondered how much time he had left until someone else walked into the bathroom. Sun Boling was in a vulnerable position. Nevertheless, he closed the stall door and focused on cleaning the fresh blood now firmly visible on the floor. Luckily, it wasn't as much as he feared.

A few minutes later, Boling cleaned the blood drops from the floor and disposed of the paper towels into the stall next to the dead North Korean operative. For the moment, the unexpected confrontation appeared to have been resolved.

Boling exited the bathroom, walked down the hall and made his way down the staircase leading to the building's entrance. He was pleasantly surprised to find it nearly empty as most of the North Korean delegation had already departed. Boling wondered if the body would remain concealed for the remainder of the afternoon. If so, his death would have to wait for another day.

White House Situation Room, Washington, D.C., June 20, 2:35 PM

President Trump arrived at the White House situation room. The past two weeks were taking a toll on the first term President. Since Pyongyang's test of its intercontinental ballistic missile earlier in the month, media outlets around the world were in a dizzied frenzy over the growing tensions between North Korea and the United States. President Trump's use of Twitter did not abate the fears of millions of people around the world. His plain spoken and direct communication skills were being heard in Pyongyang. No one knew if it was working.

"Nice to see you again, Oliver. I assume you have more good news for me?"

"Good to see you, Mr. President. I wish I had better news."

"You and me, both, Oliver. So, what do we know about North Korea's latest test?"

"Sir, North Korea's test confirms our assessments that President Kim can fire an ICBM onto American soil. As you know, the intelligence community's view was that North Korea would likely develop a working ICBM capable of reaching the United States sometime in 2018. The telemetry data we've analyzed confirm they've made the appropriate strides in their fuel technology. Since we spoke last about the issue, I believe they are six months from having the capability to protect a miniaturized nuclear warhead capable of re-entry and reaching our shores."

"Why six months? Why can't they reach us now?"

"There was extensive damage to the missile shroud of the vehicle. It doesn't appear they have perfected their re-entry capability. I don't think a warhead, nuclear or otherwise, could withstand the intense heat of re-entry into earth's atmosphere."

"How confident are you of your assessment, Oliver?"

"Very confident, sir. The telemetry data doesn't lie. The shroud was badly damaged."

"What if you are wrong, Oliver?"

"It won't be the first time, Mr. President. If I'm wrong, we can still shoot them down with our missile defense. We have enough interceptors for at least twenty vehicles," said Oliver.

The President appreciated his humility and wished more analysts in the IC felt the same way. Their arrogance frustrated him at times, but he appreciated their expertise and judgment. Oliver was a straight shooter. He was concise and clear, another attribute the President valued.

President Trump turned to his National Security Advisor.

"Herb, what do you think?"

"All we have is the data, Mr. President. If we use anything else in our assessment, we'd just be guessing. I trust Oliver's assessment, but it may not be universal within the IC."

"Could we knock out twenty missiles?" asked the President.

"We could, sir. But not many after that. We only have sixty interceptors deployed in Alaska and California at this time. In addition, Mr. President, we have THAAD batteries in South Korea and Guam. If they launched everything they had, some missiles might get through."

"How many missiles do they have capable of hitting the United States?"

"We don't know for sure, Mr. President. The estimates range from thirty to sixty vehicles."

"I told the American people I would keep them safe. What options do we have for a preemptive strike?" asked the President as he turned to his national security advisor.

"Several, sir. But there would be no good outcomes. Regardless of its success, there would be massive casualties in Seoul and to our armed forces stationed nearby."

"What are the estimates?" asked the President.

"Ten to thirty thousand, Mr. President. And if they fire their full complement of ICBMs, it could be in the millions here at home."

"How many more interceptors could DOD build over the next six months?"

"At least two dozen if we diverted funds from other programs."

"I want to see a plan for five dozen more. Let me know what you propose diverting and the impact to those programs. Can you have something for me in a few days, Herb?"

"Yes, Mr. President. I'll have some options for you."

The President turned to Oliver.

"I hope you are right, Mr. Tanner. We need six months."

"The data is accurate, Mr. President. We have a little more time."

"Sir, if I may. I think we need to tone down the rhetoric a bit. The Chinese are getting nervous and some are worried Kim will make a strategic miscalculation. He is still young and isolated. If we allow him a diplomatic victory in the short run, we'll have the interceptors in six months to ensure he can't hit us. It's a small price to pay for our security and some normalcy will return to the Korean peninsula. Once the interceptors are deployed, we'll have the strategic advantage," stated the national security advisor.

The President leaned back in his chair. He understood the optics of backing down and the impact it might have on his political base and some members of Congress. He was a strong-willed President but understood how continued saber rattling could confuse Kim and his advisors. President Trump became conciliatory.

"Okay, Herb. I'll tone it down a bit and direct the staff to refrain from further threats. That includes me. We'll do it your way for the foreseeable future."

"Thank you, Mr. President. I'll get the options on your desk in a few days."

A few moments later, the President returned to the oval office. Oliver was one of the last individuals to leave the situation room.

"Oliver, I need a minute," said the national security advisor.

"Yes, sir?"

"I have a friend on the J2 staff. She is convinced the North Koreans need another year to perfect their re-entry capability. I've known her for a long time and never known her to be wrong about these technical matters. The President trusts you, as do I. But I want you to look over the data some more. I think you'll find she may be right."

"My numbers are accurate, sir. Are you suggesting that I change my assessment?"

"Run the numbers again, Oliver. We need to give the President some assurance he has time until we exhaust diplomatic options. In six months, we'll have the interceptors. But I'm afraid he'll put Kim in a corner."

"Sir, with all due respect, that's not my problem. My job is to give you and the President my very best assessment. I don't care if it runs contrary to your policy options. The North Koreans will have a re-entry vehicle within six months. Are you suggesting I change the assessment?"

"That's exactly what I want you to do."

"I will not do it. I won't be pressured to change my analysis."

"Run the numbers again and speak with J2 or I'll contact the Director and get another analyst over here."

Oliver Tanner was a senior intelligence analyst with the Defense Intelligence Agency. He had served DIA for over twenty years and had a proven track record regarding his analytical production. He was admired throughout the IC and even had allies in Congress. This wasn't the first time the career intelligence officer had been pressured. It was uncommon for policy makers to exert direct pressure on the intelligence community, but it did occur from time to time.

"You're not threatening me, are you, sir?"

"Oliver, there are things going on behind the scenes that you are not aware of. I'm trying to prevent a God damn war with North Korea. The President is a good man, but we need to give diplomacy more time. Six months won't do it. We need him to believe the re-entry vehicle will not be ready until next summer. Can I count on you?"

"No, sir, you cannot. Why don't you have your analyst at J2 do the next briefing?"

"The President has come to trust you. Your reputation is superb, and he wants to get the Intel from you."

"I will not change my assessment, sir. I will, however, highlight the dissension from J2. That's all you're going to get."

"Fair enough, Oliver. In the meantime, think about what I said. Kim will not launch first, but will if cornered. A snake strikes when cornered, Oliver. We need to give diplomacy some time. The risks are too great if we don't."

"Again, that's not my concern, sir. What you and other policy makers do with my assessment is on you. My job is to present the data and my analysis objectively. If I did other-

wise, intelligence analysis would become an impractical endeavor. I'm an analyst. Let me analyze. Focus on policy, sir."

Oliver quickly turned to the exit and walked out of the
situation room. The National security advisor was impressed
with his bravado. He wasn't normally accustomed to that
from intelligence analysts. Herb McMullen smiled and
walked to his office determined to give the President more
time.

Midong District, City of Urumqi, Xinjiang Province, China, June 20, 5:00 PM

John Dearlove and Michael Brennan returned to the kitchen table in the remote SIS safe house. Their efforts to get Mei talking had failed all afternoon. John had already placed the syringe filled with sodium thiopental, also known as "truth serum," in front of Mei to intimidate her. The ploy proved ineffective though rumors of its lethality remained fresh in her mind.

The drug had been officially banned from most intelligence agencies around the world, including law enforcement. However, intravenous barbiturates were used in India during the interrogation of a suspect linked to the Lashkar-e-Taliba terrorist group in 2008. Unverified sources suggested the "truth serum" worked.

"Are you thinking of using the drug, John?"

"I think it's time, Michael. Mei will not bloody talk. I'm convinced this is our only option."

"I've heard the drug doesn't work in most cases. What makes you think yours will?"

"Our scientists have studied this for years. The problem they encountered was the inability to accurately isolate neural circuits that govern emotions like fear, depression, and others. A few years ago, they figured out how to manipulate those circuits that govern one's ability to speak the truth."

"What's the downside?" asked Michael.

"The dosage required to manipulate the neural circuits are often lethal. If I give her too much she will die. If I don't give her enough we won't find out why she attacked you or figure out what the hell is going on."

"Do I get a vote in this, John?"

"You do," said Dearlove.

"Do it. We can't screw around with this assassination corps business much longer. D.C. is on my ass regarding the missile test. If you want to chase ghosts, do it on your own time."

Dearlove sat back and thought for a moment. He knew Michael was right and London had similar concerns. It was now or never.

"Okay, Michael. I will administer the entire dose. We'll have to cross our fingers and hope for the best. Mei is a small woman and I doubt she'll survive."

"I'm sure you have sentenced many individuals to their deaths, John. We both have. Let's get to it."

John returned to the room where Mei sat. He placed the syringe on the table directly in front of her.

"Mei, why did you attack Michael?"

Nothing. Mei stared into John's dark eyes in continued defiance of her former employer.

"Mei, I will not ask again. If you do not answer I will administer a drug that will make you talk. However, it's likely to kill you. Is that what you want?" asked John coldly.

Still nothing. Mei continued her bold stare into John's eyes.

"I warned you, Mei," said John as he stood up and walked in her direction.

John Dearlove injected a full dosage of the sodium thiopental in her left arm. A few moments later, the first sign of the drug's impact became apparent. John waited a bit longer until Mei began chuckling. Mei also felt light-headed and drowsy. One of the drug's side effects included symptoms of drunkenness and disorientation.

"Hi, Mei. How are you feeling?"

"Happy, John. What am I doing here?" asked Mei as she continued giggling.

"Michael and I were worried about you. Do you remember, Michael?"

"Yes. How is our American friend?"

"He is doing well."

"Good to hear, John," said Mei as her speech began to slur slightly.

"Why did you try to shoot Michael last night?"

"Zhun asked me to do it. I guess I failed, huh?"

"Who is Zhun? Is he one of your friends?"

John didn't have much time and had to be direct.

"Ha. I guess you could call him that," said Mei as her speech became more rapid.

John knew the dosage was extreme and he worried her heart rate would begin to accelerate.

"I want to meet Zhun. Where can I find him?"

"You can't."

"Why is that, Mei?"

"He finds you," said Mei as she began laughing loudly.

Mei's body began to shake a bit and she became erratic. John's fear was coming to fruition. Mei was experiencing cardiac arrest.

"Where can I find Zhun?" asked John.

"Near..." said Mei as she took her last breath and hunched forward in her chair.

Unbeknownst to John, Michael was standing in the room's entrance.

"I assume the freak show is over?" asked Michael.

"It is, Michael."

"Did it work?"

"Not really. The only name I got was Zhun. There are hundreds of thousands of men in the area with that name. I'm afraid we didn't get much."

"Did you say Zhun?"

"I did indeed."

"We're in luck, my friend. Let me show something," said Michael as he smiled.

The two men returned to the kitchen table. Michael's laptop was open as a secure connection with Langley was ongoing.

"I just received these files from Langley. Read the first document," said Michael.

John skimmed the document and noticed the paper's author. It was Liu Zhun and the article was entitled *The rise and fall of the Assassination Corps, 1910-1912*.

"Now look at this document, John."

The second article, written in 2004, was entitled, *Whatever happened to the Assassination Corps?* Liu Zhun was also its author.

"This has to be your man, John."

"Where did you find this?"

"I found nothing. CIA located the articles on a dark website. The paper was uploaded from an IP address in Brussels."

"How the hell did he get it there?"

"I don't care, John. I know they used open sources. That's really all I know. You can worry about that later. We have a name. Now we just need an address. I assume you have assets that can assist with that information?"

"I bloody well do, Michael. This is helpful. Thank you."

"What do you want to do with Mei?"

"I'll send a team to dispose of her body. They should be here within an hour."

"I'm sorry about Mei, John. I know it hurts when our assets turn on us. It's the nature of the business."

"True. But the real nature of our business changes us, Michael. We eventually become what we go after."

Michael Brennan could not have agreed more.

Korla Missile Test Complex, Korla, Xinjiang Province, China, June 20, 5:15 PM

General Zhang Guozhi remained in the executive conference room after a series of meetings focused on Korla's second test of the Dong-Neng-3 exoatmospheric vehicle. His team of technical wizards and programmers had already successfully launched the anti-satellite missile to within a razor close margin of the American spy satellite. The second test was designed to prove the missile's ability to greatly alter its trajectory in midflight. Beijing ordered the second test to come nowhere near western satellites as it simply wanted to prove its immense capabilities to a watchful United States intelligence community.

The plan seemed logical as Beijing concluded any military conflict with the United States would likely occur in outer space. Most western analysts agreed despite the possibility of a conflict in the South China Sea or along the Korean peninsula.

Guozhi turned to his new driver, a young soldier hired by his Chief of Staff, while in Beijing.

"Min, I'd like you to get the address for Wang Jin, our lead software engineer. I want to speak with him alone. Perhaps over dinner, if you can arrange it."

"Yes, sir. Shall I wait for you outside?" asked Min, as she understood the commander's directive.

"Yes, thank you. I'll be there shortly. Tell my aide to return to the hotel. I'll join him later for dinner."

Guozhi finally had the conference room to himself. Korla's base commander and his staff had already returned to their offices while the scientists, engineers and civilian staff began their trips home.

Guozhi dialed the phone and spoke deliberately.

"I am in Korla. The second test is on schedule. I will be meeting with Wang Jin within the hour. I expect no issues."

"That is excellent news, General Zhang. Do you think he will accept the money?" asked the man on the other end.

"Oh, yes. I am sure of it."

"Why are you so certain?"

"He's a pompous ass and underpaid for what he does. I've known Jin for several years now. He's too smart for his own good. He'll accept it."

"What if he doesn't?"

"Leave that to me. He's a pawn in our efforts. Let's not worry about that now."

"When will you return to Urumqi?"

"Tomorrow afternoon. I am going to make another play for the information."

"You think we'll get the information we seek?"

"Probably not, but I must try," said Guozhi.

"Okay, General Zhang. I hope to hear from you in a few days."

Click.

Guozhi returned to his vehicle a short while later. The drive to Wang Jin's residence would only be thirty-five minutes. Min had already reached Wang and indicated he was honored to receive the general at his apartment. Guozhi expected nothing less.

The last few days had plagued Guozhi. He grappled with how he would approach Wang and get him to agree to alter the guidance system that would ensure a direct hit at the American spy satellite. He wondered if he should present himself as a member of the assassination corps, worried the brilliant and introverted engineer might get scared off. Guozhi also considered creating a story that Beijing wanted the missile to deviate from its course and strike the satellite. However, Beijing would only include a few individuals to ensure its success. Guozhi thought the approach might work and Wang would consider it plausible. It might also stroke Wang's ego to be entrusted with the information while the money would buy his silence and allegiance to Beijing. Guozhi knew it would be a tricky proposition, either way.

Guozhi had decided earlier in the day to go with the assassination corps angle. There were simply too many variables to consider and he eventually believed that involving Beijing in the story would scare the engineer, rather than motivate him.

"General Zhang. It is an honor to have you in my home. Please come in, sir," said Wang.

"Thank you for seeing me, Jin. You have a lovely home. I assume my driver informed you that we would eat dinner?" asked Guozhi.

"Yes, sir. I have already started to cook. Will your driver be joining us?"

"No. I have important matters to discuss. May I sit down?"

"Of course, General Zhang."

"I am a member of an organization in Beijing that believes our government is too appeasing to the United States. I am a loyal man to the country and to the party, but some members of my organization fear the Americans do not respect us. We fear their arrogance is what keeps them deploying warships off our coastlines. They do not respect our rights in the South China Sea and continue challenging our strategic interests in the Pacific region. We believe they are doing this because they perceive our military capabilities are weak," said Guozhi.

"I'm not sure what this has to do with me, General Zhang. I'm just an engineer."

"How do you feel about American warships patrolling near our borders?"

"I don't care. I trust my government will protect me," said Jin.

"We can, Jin. However, our interests are being hindered. If America knew our true capabilities, many of us in Beijing believe they would give us greater flexibility to achieve strategic goals. Does this sound unreasonable to you?"

"I know nothing of these military matters. I am a software engineer."

"An underpaid engineer?" asked Guozhi.

"That is true. I am confused. Where are you going with this, sir?"

"I want you to alter the missile's flight path during the second test. I want you to guide the missile into the American spy satellite."

"The same satellite we just flew by?"

"The same one, Jin."

"Wouldn't that start a war with the Americans?"

"No. We believe the news will be kept out of the public media," said Guozhi.

"What will you tell Beijing? They will trace it all back to me."

"I will accept full responsibility for the error. I am close with many members of the party and President Xi. They will attempt to make amends with the Americans, but our true capabilities will be known. I want you to program the missile's trajectory five hours before we fire. Once the satellite is hit, manipulate the program the best you can to make it look like an accident. I will leave that to you. You are the only one I know who can make this happen. You are one of the finest engineers in the country. This is the right thing to do, Jin. I need you."

Guozhi was clearly appealing to his ego as he sat back and remained stunned by what he heard. He let him process the information like any good engineer would.

"We will pay you an incredible amount of money, Li. You will never have to worry about money again. If you want, I'll make sure your work here continues after the investigation."

"How much money are we talking about, General Zhang?"

"Enough. You could even leave the country if you wanted. My organization will ensure your paperwork is approved for anywhere you want to go."

"Anywhere?" asked Wang.

"Wherever you want to go, Jin. We love our country but sometimes we are too patient. If the Americans are convinced we can destroy their high earth orbit satellites, our government can achieve far greater success. Can I count on you?"

"You can, sir. And I want to go to Paris. I want the paperwork before the launch day. When will you transfer monies to my account?"

Guozhi was impressed.

"There will not be a transfer. You will have the first installment in cash next week. The second installment will be delivered two days after the launch. We cannot risk the Ministry of State Security checking your bank accounts or other digital transactions. They will become suspicious."

"I didn't think about that," said Jin.

"Good. Let us eat. Tell me about Paris."

Guozhi chuckled inside. The engineer would make a lousy spy.

Liu Zhun will be pleased, he thought to himself. Wang Jin would feel differently after the launch.

Dabancheng District, City of Urumqi, Xinjiang Province, China, June 21, 9:10 AM

Brian Wu remained hidden in the brush approximately one kilometer from Liu Zhun's farmhouse. Now on his second day, he wondered when the moment to strike would occur. He also wanted a fresh shower and a prepared meal. Wu was human after all and stunk after prolonged exposure to the heat. It would have to wait. Liu was in his crosshairs if he could just find an opening. It would come soon enough, he thought to himself.

"You think he has any idea we know?" laughed the man sitting with Liu.

Liu's property had several infrared and live video cameras placed throughout the property. The tiny cameras were expensive and considered next-generation technology. Liu spared no expense in preparing the property for such an occasion.

"No. But we need to give him an incentive. I want you to take most of the men back to Urumqi. I'll remain here with Kun and Shuang. I want Wu to feel confident and make a move. I cannot remain here much longer. We'll set a trap. I'm sure Wu will fall for it."

"Why?"

"His British training will kick in. He will see just one vehicle outside and convince himself he has the element of surprise. Do not worry, Shi. I will be fine."

"When do you want us to leave?"

"Now would be fine. I will quickly escort you and the men outside. I want him to see me. I will also take my time walking inside."

"What if he decides to shoot?" asked Shi.

"He won't. This is personal for him. He wants to look

me in the eyes."

"What if you are wrong, Zhun?"

"Then I will die, my friend. And you will assume leadership."

"Do you think he knows his wife's death was accidental?"

"It no longer matters, my friend. He must be killed."

Shi and Liu exited the farmhouse while Kun and Shuang remained in the living room. Shi barked orders for the men to prepare for departure. One by one, members of the assassination corps began piling into their vehicles. Liu casually walked to the front door as the convoy quickly sped off.

Liu Zhun had prepared his trap.

Brian Wu continued peering through his scope. It was now time to attack, he thought to himself. He quickly sent a text message before jumping into his vehicle and drove toward the farmhouse. The message would serve as an insurance policy in case he failed. Brian figured Liu's bodyguards would number two or three men. A few minutes later, Brian arrived in front of the farmhouse with his weapon drawn. He saw no signs of activity and it was eerily quiet. Nevertheless, he cautiously approached the entrance as his heart rate became slightly elevated. He was, after all, unsure of just how many of Liu's men were inside.

Wu slowly turned the doorknob. It was unlocked. Not a good sign, he thought to himself. He decided to enter anyway.

Brian kicked in the front door and stormed into the farmhouse. Kun and Shuang were sitting on a beige couch staring into their smartphones. Liu told the men to relax until nightfall as Wu would likely wait until then to strike. The two men were new members of the assassination corps and former Triad narcotics dealers. They never had a chance.

Their sacrifice would ensure Liu's survival exactly as he had planned.

Brian fired a single shot into Kun's chest as Shuang reached for his weapon. Brian turned his sights toward Shuang and fired three shots into his chest. The former SIS operative quickly scanned the room and saw no further threats. He then noticed Kun was still alive and promptly put him out of his misery with a single shot to the head. Where the hell was Liu? he thought to himself.

Wu slowly peered around the corner and noticed the vacant kitchen. The table had several cups of soy milk and steamed baozi stuffed with beef and vegetables. The pungent smell permeated throughout the air as he searched for signs of Liu Zhun.

Nothing.

Brian carefully walked down the narrow hallway as he firmly held his weapon. He could see the openings of two bedrooms alongside the hallway. Ahead, the hallway opened into what appeared to be another multi-purpose room with an entrance leading to a back porch.

"Heng. Stop moving and drop your weapon," said Liu.

Brian Wu froze. How did the commander of the assassination corps get behind him? he thought to himself.

"Well done, Zhun. How did you manage that?" asked Brian as he dropped his gun to the floor.

"Keep walking forward, Heng. Do you see the door to your right? I knew you would come as soon as Shi and the others left. I waited for you to strike and now here we are," said Liu coldly.

"Okay, Zhun. Now what?"

"Turn around and sit down, Heng."

Brian Wu was about to die. And he knew it.

"Why did you order the attack in Urumqi?" asked Brian.

"It was a small part in our strategic plan here in the region. Shi has several more attacks planned around the time of the launch. Yan's death was unforeseen. I am truly sorry she died, Heng."

"I doubt that. I might have lived with it, Zhun. But why did you send Feng and Dong to kill me? You owe me that much."

Liu Zhun scoffed. Nevertheless, his recruit deserved the answer.

"You became a liability, Heng. It's as simple as that. How long did you think it would be before British intelligence found out about Yan? Her death, as unfortunate as it was, would lead them straight to us. I could not jeopardize our plans. He is already here and looking for you. You knew the risks when you joined. There are things more important than our lives or those we love. This is who we are."

"I could have taken care of John Dearlove. That would have been easy if you had given me the chance."

"That is possible, Heng. But we will never know."

Liu Zhun fired his weapon. The single round entered Brian's forehead and he slumped to the ground. Blood began oozing from the abrasion ring of the surrounding skin. Brian was unconscious but slowly breathing. Liu noticed some blood oozing behind Wu's head. The velocity of the bullet had caused an exit wound through the occipital bone.

Liu Zhun stood coldly over Brian's motionless body. He wondered if he should fire again or let Wu Heng bleed to death. The ruthless commander of the assassination corps decided on the latter.

Chinese Embassy, Pyongyang, North Korea, June 21, 9:22 AM

Sun Boling sat at his desk inside the Chinese embassy. He had spent the last thirty minutes responding to a group of North Korean officers who still had questions regarding the acquisition and guidance capabilities of the YJ-18B missile. He had expected inquiries despite carefully informing the group there would be restrictions. China shared very little sensitive technological data with North Korea despite growing fears in the western intelligence communities.

Then Boling's phone rang. It was his administrative assistant.

"Sir, I have a call from a gentleman named Lieutenant Kim Jang. He works for the Ministry of State Security. He says its urgent."

Boling expected the call, but not this quickly.

"Patch him through, Tang," said Boling.

"Captain Sun. I am Lieutenant Kim Jang from the Ministry of State Security. I have some questions I would like to ask you."

"Of course, Lieutenant Kim. How may I assist you this morning?"

"One of our officers was found dead this morning at Rajin Naval base. He appears to have died shortly after your presentation. May I stop by your office this morning to discuss the matter?"

"I am sorry to hear that, Lieutenant Kim. What happened?"

"We do not know. We believe he was killed."

"Killed? How?"

"He was likely struck with a sharp instrument. Probably a knife of some sort."

"I would be happy to assist, but I'm not sure what I could do for you, Lieutenant Kim."

"It's a formality, Captain Sun. I need to speak with all the participants at the meeting. I won't be taking much of your time."

"Feel free to come right away, Lieutenant Kim. I have a light schedule today. I'll make the arrangements at the front gate."

"Thank you, Captain Sun. I will be there at ten o'clock."

Click.

A sense of anxiety overcame Sun Boling. He recalled the events at Rajin the day before and believed he had slipped away from the naval base without being detected. Or so he hoped.

Lieutenant Kim Jang arrived at the front gate of the Chinese embassy precisely at ten o'clock. The North Koreans were always punctual, at least from what Boling had noticed in his short tenure as a staff officer in the embassy. Jang received his badge and Boling's assistant escorted the counter-intelligence officer to Sun's office.

"Hello, Lieutenant Kim," said Boling.

"Thank you for meeting me, Captain Sun. I will not take much of your time."

"I am happy to help, Lieutenant Kim. So, who was the man you said was killed?"

"This is his picture. Do you remember him from the presentation you made?"

"No. I do not recall seeing the man."

"Are you sure," asked Jang.

"I am certain. There were many individuals at my presentation."

Jang sat back in the old wooden chair facing Boling's desk. He sighed ever so slightly and reached into his briefcase. The middle-aged officer pulled out a small video camera and placed it on Boling's desk. Sun knew what was coming next.

"Is that you going to the bathroom after your presentation, Captain Sun?"

"Yes, it is me."

The tape continued to play as Jang stared into the eyes of Sun Boling.

"Do you see the man entering the bathroom, Captain Sun?"

"Yes. Is he the one who was killed?"

"It is, Captain Sun. If you let the tape continue playing, you will see yourself exit a few minutes later. The victim never left the bathroom."

Sun Boling began to perspire a bit. Jang knew he was nervous and recognized the Chinese officer's anxiety. He reached for the video camera and hit the stop button.

"I know it was you, Captain Sun. I have made a copy and placed it in a secure location. I am seeking asylum. I want to leave North Korea immediately."

"Who else knows about this, Jang?" asked Boling as military courtesy was no longer necessary.

"No one. The man worked for me and was instructed to follow you until you exited the facility. I took personal control of the video a few hours later after it was apparent what happened."

"How can I guarantee you asylum? You know it's nearly impossible, Jang."

"I understand, Captain Sun. I am patient and will wait for the opportunity. You will find a way. If not, then the tape will be sent to your commanding officer. How long do you think it will be before my government has the approval to arrest you?"

"This tape proves nothing, Jang."

"To some extent, that is true, sir. But we both know how the Chinese government will react to this. There will always be tension among our nations, Captain Sun, but it's clear what happened. Your government will come to the same conclusion."

"Why do you want to leave, Jang. You seem to have a good life here. You are well paid, well fed, and among the elites in North Korea's society. Why give this life up?"

"I have my reasons, Captain Sun. However, a family member of mine was recently taken to the Kaechon internment camp for an outlandish accusation. I now have several members of my family in prison. We often imprison our citizens because of guilt by association. How much longer before I am sent to meet my demise, Captain Sun?" asked Jang.

Boling was aware of the infamous Kaechon internment camp, also known as Camp 14. Situated along the Taedong River, the one-hundred and fifty-five-kilometer squared area housed approximately fifteen thousand prisoners living in horrific conditions. The forced labor camp was known as a house of horrors where its residents went to die. These "unredeemable" human beings spent their remaining lives farming and working in dreadful factories for no wages. A smell of death persisted in the prison and its ruthless treatment of political prisoners was known across the international community. Boling had little doubt that Yang was speaking the truth.

"It will take some time, Yang. This will not be an easy endeavor for me. How quickly do you want to leave?"

"Now, Captain Sun."

"That is not possible, Jang. Give me a few weeks. Will that work for you?"

"I'm not sure I will have that much time. I will need to

provide an update on the investigation soon. How about one week?"

"Done. How can I reach you?" asked Boling.

"You can't. I will follow up with you in a few days. Please provide me a good contact number."

Yang left a few minutes later and insisted that Boling escort him out of the building. Boling had little choice and would need to quickly determine a reason for the visit as his colleagues would likely ask questions.

Sun Boling's life just got a bit more complicated. Liu Zhun would be kept in the dark.

SIS safe house, Midong District, City of Urumqi, Xinjiang Province, China, June 21, 9:17 AM

John Dearlove and Michael Brennan sat at the kitchen table contemplating their next move. Then John's cell phone buzzed. He reached into his pocket and noticed the text message was from an unknown sender. The message was short and unexpected.

In case I fail. Find Liu Zhun and Zhang Guozhi. They must be stopped. I am sorry for your troubles, John. BW

"My god. It's from Brian. He has contacted me, Michael," said John.

"Huh, are you sure? Why the hell would he do that?" asked Michael.

"It's him. Look."

"That's your man, John. Who is this Zhang character?" asked Michael.

"No idea. But we are going to find out shortly. Can you get Langley to zero in on him? I'm going to call GCHQ and find out what I can about this number."

"On it, John," said Michael.

Dearlove immediately placed a call to his friend, Robert at GCHQ. Michael reached for his laptop and quickly made a secure connection with Langley.

"Robert. It's urgent. I've caught a break this morning. I just received a call from 86153289665. I want to know where the signal is coming from. Now please, Robert."

"It will take some time, John."

"Right away, John. Your technical wizards should find it quickly."

Robert knew it would be difficult, but he expected nothing less from the career MI6 operative. John Dearlove was no different from any other intelligence officer not intimately familiar with signals intelligence gathering techniques. Though powerful with global reach, GCHQ was not the omniscient agency many portrayed it to be. Its reputation was earned, but its capabilities were often exaggerated. Nonetheless, Robert would make it a priority and support his good friend's request.

"I'll do my best, John. Will you need anything else?" asked Robert.

"Not for now, Robert. And thank you."

Click.

The two men continued waiting at the safe house for another three hours. Neither man could proceed with the operation or determine more about the assassination corps until actionable intelligence was provided to them. The professional spies were used to situations like this and often passed the time getting to know one another.

"Are you married, John?" asked Michael.

"I was once. She died from cancer years ago."

"I'm sorry to hear that. It must have been devastating. Do you have children?"

"Two sons. They are attending Cambridge. How about you?"

"Not married. I came close once but the job requires more commitment than a marriage. I should have retired years ago. As you know, we often become like what we search for."

"What happened?" asked Dearlove.

"She got tired of being alone, John."

"Our profession takes a toll on us, huh Michael?"

"That it does, John. I only hope that I look back many years from now and find solace in what I did."

Michael's cell buzzed.

"Michael. Do you have any idea who Zhang Guozhi is?

How did you get his name?" asked Doug sitting in his comfortable chair in Langley.

"That's why I sent the request, Doug. I don't. Our British colleague asked me to get what Intel I could."

"General Zhang Guozhi is the Director for the General Armaments Department of the People's Liberation Army."

"Is that supposed to mean something to me, Doug. You know I've not worked an operation here."

"China's ballistic missile program falls under his leadership, Michael."

"Outstanding. That's the first good news I've heard yet. Let me put you on speaker, Doug."

"How did you guys get locked onto Guozhi?" asked Doug.

"I received a text earlier this morning from a former operative in Hong Kong. He's tied up in this assassination corps business. He said both men needed to be stopped. We know about Liu Zhun from what your staff provided us. I'm not certain why Zhang's name came up, but I have my suspicions," said Dearlove.

Michael chimed in.

"John, Zhang must be involved with the assassination corps. John's asset would have no other reason to implicate him. He will have the information we need regarding the missile launch. Unless you disagree, I'm going after him."

"Would it matter what I think, Michael?"

"Not one bit. Let me do my job, Doug. It's what I do best."

"You continue to be a pain in my ass, Michael. No, I don't disagree. But he's a high-ranking PLA officer and he's going to be hard to get at. We think he's in line for a major party position in the future. He'll be a dead man soon enough if we can prove his involvement. I wouldn't be surprised if

Chinese intelligence is watching him closely, regardless. But we need the Intel on the launch. That is your first priority, Michael. John, I'll leave it to you to talk with Alex."

"I have my target, Doug. Let me and John worry about that. If we can get at Zhang, we can kill two birds with one stone. There's a clear connection between Zhang and the assassination corps. I can feel it."

"Concur, Michael. Keep me in the loop. We may have caught a break on this but I'm frankly not optimistic about Zhang. Maybe you can get to one of his military aides. Look for a target folder from operations this afternoon. We'll get you guys whatever we have on the man. Good luck, gentlemen."

Click.

John Dearlove's cell buzzed a short while later.

"More good news, Michael. I have a location for Brian's cell. It's not far from here."

"Great. I'm already tired of sitting here on my ass. We've got good Intel. Let's get to work."

General Zhang Guozhi just became one of the most sought-after targets in China. Michael and John would be in his shadows soon enough. But first, both men would need to visit a farmhouse in the Dabacheng district.

Defense Intelligence Agency, Joint Base Anacostia-Boling, Washington, D.C., 21 June 10:21 AM

Oliver Tanner remained at his desk. It was covered with piles of sensitive technical data from multiple agencies within the United States Intelligence Community. Most of the items included telemetry data from collection systems including L-band radars, overhead assets, and ground-based X-band radars. One such radar, the AN/TPY-2, could acquire, track, classify and estimate the trajectory of a ballistic missile. It was also deployable by air, land, and sea giving the Department of Defense flexibility to position the system anywhere around the globe. The AN/TPY-2 was also integrated with the Terminal High Altitude Area Defense system.

Oliver's phone rang.

"Olie, it's Margaret. The Director is ready to see you now."

"Thanks, Margaret. I'll be right there."

Oliver had waited patiently since he returned from the White House the day before and stormed into the office of the Director's executive assistant. He wasn't sure if the tactic worked but he was, after all, one of the most respected intelligence analysts in Washington, D.C. Oliver was a confident man but had the well-earned reputation of being easy to collaborate with and was anything but arrogant.

"Olie, how the hell are you?" asked Director Richardson.

Lieutenant General Stephen Richardson, the first African American Director at the Defense Intelligence Agency since its inception in 1961, had a sterling reputation. He was bright, compassionate, decisive and well respected within the intelligence community. A career Marine officer, he began as a tank commander where his talents eventually led him to Marine intelligence. Oliver considered him a father figure.

"Thanks for seeing me, sir. I'd like some advice on something."

"You mean the incident with Herb?" asked Richardson.

"Ha. I guess he already made the call. I expected that. The damn maniac wants me to change my assessment, sir. I can't square it."

"What can't you square, Olie?"

"I'm sure my analysis is correct. I've got the best technical data money can buy and I know North Korea is only six months away from having the capability to hit us."

"So, Olie, what's the problem?" asked the three-star general as he sat back in his chair.

"He's putting pressure on me to change the assessment. That's the problem, sir."

"I've always spoken the truth, Olie. I've always been a straight shooter when it comes to my assessments. I understand his motivation to give the President of the United States more time to exert diplomatic and economic pressure on the regime. It's well intentioned and some could argue its noble. Regardless, if the data says six months, then it's six months. There's nothing to square, Olie. Our job is to give POTUS our best assessment. Ultimately, policymakers decide what they want to believe. You know how this works. I'm sure Herb will find someone who disagrees. Be prepared for that at your next briefing. I have your back."

"So, I will give POTUS the next brief?" asked Oliver.

"Absolutely. I've already told him to pound sand. I can't promise what happens after that, Olie, but the President trusts your judgment. I trust your judgment. You know this material better than anyone in the IC. Stand by your conclusion," said Richardson.

"Thank you, sir. I will."

"I expect nothing else, Olie. Now get the hell out of here and get to work," said Richardson as he smiled.

Oliver felt reassured. The "old man" was a brilliant officer and true intelligence professional. All intelligence assessments, no matter how unnerving or contrary to policy they might be, had to be made in an unbiased way. Oliver had always known this, but Richardson's reminder was all the analyst needed.

If Herb McMullen wanted war, he got it, Oliver thought to himself.

Dabancheng District, City of Urumqi, Xinjiang Province, China, June 21, 5:07 PM

Michael Brennan and John Dearlove were just minutes away from reaching the location of Brian's cell phone. Robert's team at GCHQ had come through and provided John with the geolocation data they needed. The GPS enabled chip used satellite information to calculate its location. John never understood how GCHQ could intercept such information, but he had a good imagination.

The trip from Midong to Dabancheng took them approximately two hours. Traffic was lighter than usual, and it gave the men more time to get to know one another. John was surprised to learn that Michael's love for football was not the New York Giants, but rather, Manchester United. John didn't mind Michael's support of one of the most respected and hated clubs in the English Premier League. Dearlove preferred his beloved Chelsea FC, playing in London to its most ardent fans.

"It's taking us to that trail over there," said Michael as he pointed in a northeastern direction.

"Near that farmhouse up ahead?" asked Dearlove.

"Yes, but we're going to pass it," said Michael.

"Why the devil are we going into the brush?"

"We'll find out soon enough, John."

Dearlove pulled onto the trail as dust began rising into the warm air. Moments later, Michael told John to stop alongside a clump of trees.

"We're here," said Michael.

"Great, GCHQ led us on a wild goose chase. Are you sure this is it?" asked John.

"I am, my friend. Let's look around."

Michael exited the passenger side and began searching

for the cell phone. John did the same on the other side of the trail. Michael noticed the clump of trees had a good vantage point of the farmhouse. There was an open field and flat ground leading to it. The vegetation provided an ideal spot to conduct surveillance of the farmhouse. This was the general area for finding Wu's device, Michael thought to himself. It actually made sense with the remote farmhouse being the only structure within sight.

"I'll bet your man was here, John. The phone is here unless we've got bad Intel," said Michael.

"You're right, Michael. The trees provide good observation. Brian was here. I just know it."

A few minutes later, Michael found the phone neatly placed on the tree's stump. It was standing upright and clearly meant to be found.

"Okay, here we go," said Michael.

"The damn thing is out of battery. Let's get to that farmhouse," barked John.

The two professional spies returned to their vehicle and began driving toward the remote farmstead. Nothing moved, and it appeared abandoned despite the outward signs it was well maintained. John's mind raced contemplating the unfolding development. Why the hell did Brian contact him now? he asked himself. And why did Brian leave the phone?

"You think Liu and Guozhi were here, John?"

"That I do, Michael. We'll know soon enough."

John soon pressed on the brakes and the vehicle came to a stop. Both men drew their weapons and cautiously exited the vehicle.

"Let me go around the back, John. You enter from here," said Michael.

Michael slowly made his way alongside the structure. His hands maintained a firm grip on the weapon with his thumbs pointed forward. He quickly peered around the corner and noticed the back porch. The door appeared open.

As Michael continued moving toward the door, he noticed the feet of a man lying on the floor. Dry blood became evident. The man must surely be dead, he thought to himself. Michael recognized John's asset seconds later.

Brian Wu was near death and barely moving. A few moments later, John came through the door and stood behind Michael. He motioned for Michael to continue moving and check for signs of activity as he knelt in front of Brian.

"Why did you do it, Brian?"

Brian laid motionless. The only sign of life was his chest moving up and down gasping for air.

Nothing.

"Why the hell did you turn on me? Can you hear me? Can you understand what I'm saying?"

Nothing. And then Brian uttered a few words that were barely audible.

"He killed my wife, John," said Brian softly. His head never moved.

"Liu Zhun?" asked John as Michael returned.

"It's just us, John," said Michael.

"Yes," said Brian softly.

"What about Zhang Guozhi?"

Brian attempted to speak one last time.

"Just kill me and end this pain, John. I am…"

"You're what, Brian? Sorry? Not good enough."

Nothing.

"What about Zhang Guozhi?" shouted Dearlove.

"He's done, John. Put him out of his misery," said Michael as he placed his hand on Dearlove's right shoulder.

John Dearlove stood up. He knew Brian would expire quickly. Compassion was never one of Dearlove's stronger qualities. He fired anyway. The single shot to Wu's head killed him instantly. Brian Wu's membership in the assassination corps was over.

"We've got to get his cell turned back on soon, John. Maybe we'll get lucky and get some Intel."

"I doubt it, Michael. He used this cell phone for one purpose."

"Insurance?" asked Michael.

"Yes. But we'll check to be sure."

The two men made their way through the farmhouse and toward the front entrance. Though unlikely, John and Michael had hoped to find some Intel on the group. The rooms appeared to have been recently used, as evident by the unkept beds and condition of the kitchen. Nothing stood out for exploitation. There were no laptops, PDAs, or even old-fashioned paper. Then Michael noticed the car.

"John, look outside," said Michael.

"Ah, we have friends coming. Let's welcome them."

There were three men inside the approaching vehicle. They looked relaxed but the intensity in their eyes meant they had a job to do.

"Shi, there is a vehicle at Liu's property. Did you call others?" asked the man sitting in the passenger seat.

"No. Approach with caution, Gao. Dispose of them quickly, along with Wu."

"Okay, see you later tonight."

Gao and his men exited the vehicle and drew their weapons. Two men flanked the perimeter walls and began walking toward the rear of the farmhouse. Gao remained standing near the front entrance as Michael and John remained hidden inside.

A few minutes later, one of the men noticed Wu's body on the floor. He and his partner carefully entered the room but saw nothing else.

Then suddenly, Dearlove peered around the corner and shot both men. Their bodies quickly fell to the ground. Gao heard the shots and immediately rushed through the front door. He never had a chance as Michael popped his head from the kitchen and quickly fired two shots into Gao's chest. Gao's lifeless body hit the floor.

"We're clear, John. Let's see if we can find out who these bastards are."

John approached the two men and searched their pockets. Neither had identification on them. He then rolled up their sleeves and found the markings he was looking for. Members of the assassination corps had clearly come to dispose of Brian's body, he thought to himself.

"Michael, both men were members of the assassination corps."

"This guy has no identification, only a cell," said Michael.

"Roll up his sleeves. I'll bet this one is a member as well."

"What now, John?" asked Michael.

"Grab his cell, Michael. There's got to be something on one of these damn phones we can use."

"We'll get some Intel from this, John. What do you want to do with Brian?"

"Leave him. I'll eventually find out where his children are staying. They deserve to know what happened to their father. I owe the traitor that much."

Michael and John exited the farmhouse and began their trip back to the Midong district. GCHQ would provide actionable intelligence soon enough.

CITIC Bank Mansion, Urumqi, Xinjiang Province, China, June 21, 9:02 PM

Liu Zhun and his deputy, Li Shi, were sitting along the executive conference room table on the fifty-ninth floor of the China CITIC Bank Mansion in Urumqi. The location had been the de facto headquarters for the assassination corps since 2016. Liu Zhun, the son of one of the most successful bankers in Xinjiang, had inherited the family business after the death of his father. This vast wealth included real estate holdings, stocks, bonds, and foreign treasuries. This allowed Liu to rapidly build up the assassination corps and prepare for its crusade to topple the Chinese government. Ten members of the assassination corps were present.

"Ladies and gentlemen, our operations are on schedule. We have encountered a setback in Hong Kong. As many of you are aware, Wu Heng's operation in Hong Kong has failed. His former boss there uncovered the operation and has isolated the targets. My sources indicate he is here in Urumqi. However, he is on a wild goose chase. His knowledge of our organization has died with Heng. We are now in the final preparations to begin the collapse of the Xi government," said Liu Zhun.

"How do we know Wu did not share information with the British?" asked one of the women sitting directly in front of Liu.

"I can assure you, Iris, our plans have not been compromised."

"How can you be sure, Zhun?" asked Iris.

"I am certain. I killed him myself earlier today."

"I will ask again, Zhun. How can we be certain our plans are not in jeopardy?"

Liu Zhun quickly grew tired of her insubordination. He

rotated his head to other members of the group and finally locked onto the eyes of the man sitting next to Iris.

"How is the operation in Shanghai proceeding?" asked Liu.

"We are on schedule. The Vice Chairman will be killed by a member of his staff."

"That is good news, Han. Any chance his schedule changes? Who have you selected?"

"The Vice Chairman rarely makes a schedule change. His driver, Zhun. He has been paid well," said Han.

"General Zhang. How is the second test coming along?" asked Liu.

"The engineer has received the first half of his payment. He will alter the guidance system just before launch. I will override any concerns the flight director may have regarding the software changes. It is likely he will not even notice it until shortly before impact."

Liu received a short update from each of his members. Simultaneous operations occurring throughout China were planned and apparently ready for execution.

"Why have you been so vague with our operation in Pyongyang, Zhun?" asked Iris.

"I'm growing tired of your insolence, Iris. The operation in Pyongyang is one of our most critical. I am personally overseeing it. It is proceeding as planned."

"Who is the assassin?" asked Iris.

Zhang Guozhi chimed in.

"I think Iris asks a good question, Zhun. We have all shared our plans with you. But you keep us in the dark with respect to Pyongyang," said Guozhi.

"Shi," said Zhun as he turned to his deputy.

Shi drew his Husa knife, also known as an Achang knife, and threw it directly toward Iris' throat. Iris slumped forward in the chair as several members looked on with astonishment. Guozhi stared at Shi and expected the same. His defiance impressed Shi as the two men never really cared for another.

"The operation in Pyongyang is proceeding, Guozhi. I will not entertain any further questions. Am I clear?" asked Liu.

"Quite clear, Liu," said Guozhi as he sat back in his chair and stared at Shi.

The Achang knife derived its nickname due to its origin with the Achang ethnic group in Longchuan County in southwestern China. Their reputation for brilliantly made knives, including sheaths made of leather and silver, were widely reported for nearly six hundred years. Shi and many members of the assassination corps used the knife during the conduct of their operations.

"We must remain focused on our operations. The hour is approaching. I have asked General Zhang to plan for the assassination of President Xi. Where are we Guozhi?" asked Liu.

"I have made no progress, Liu. But rest assured, after our missile strikes the American satellite, I am certain President Xi will want a personal update. I will use that opportunity to dispose of him."

"How will you escape, Guozhi?" asked one of the members.

"I will not. It's my honor to make the ultimate sacrifice for our historic operation. I am prepared to die."

"Your sacrifice will be recorded for eternity, Guozhi. History will look upon us favorably for what we are about to do," proclaimed Liu.

Liu Zhun made a few remarks to close out the meeting. This would be the last gathering of key leaders within the assassination corps until their operations were executed. They and any remaining survivors were instructed to make their way to Bugat in western Mongolia, located approximately sixty miles from the Chinese border. Liu Zhun would await them and prepare for subsequent operations.

General Zhang Guozhi wondered if Liu's plan was a bit ambitious. Nevertheless, he was determined to do his part. Would history judge him the way Liu suggested it would? he asked himself. Only if the events unfolded as the commander of the assassination corps had envisioned. He then recalled a well-known Chinese proverb; *deep doubts, deep wisdom; small doubts, little wisdom.*

Chinese Embassy, Pyongyang, North Korea,
June 22, 8:25 AM

Sun Boling sat quietly at his desk. It had been two days since he spoke to Lieutenant Kim Jang from North Korean intelligence. The man would want some details soon, Boling thought to himself. He was determined to provide them and get back to his primary task as directed by Liu Zhun. Jang's request could not have come at a worse time. He would have to support Jang's request for safe passage to China or face a firing squad. There was little to think about.

The only assets he had at his disposal were embassy vehicles and they were strictly monitored by North Korean counter-intelligence upon departing embassy property. He would have to come up with a damn good reason to use them in the first place. The Ambassador had use of a business jet on loan from Beijing, but Boling would never be granted such access. In addition, the border with China was tightly monitored. He heard of gaps along the fences separating the two countries but unsure how many random patrols occurred along the border. North Korea was a country built to prevent its citizens from leaving and his limited access to Chinese transportation left him with few options. Sun Boling was in a bind and he knew it.

He thought Jang's request was preposterous. How could the North Korean counter-intelligence agent expect a Chinese naval officer to help him escape? he thought to himself. The farfetched request unnerved Boling, but he was caught red-handed in Rajin. Sun Boling concocted the only plan he thought was possible. He had to kill Lieutenant Kim Jang. There were simply no other viable options. His possible meeting with the great leader would come in just a few weeks so he had little time to spare. Jang's deadline of a week was quickly approaching. He reached for his phone.

"Jang, it's Boling. Can we meet tomorrow evening at 8:30 PM?"

"Of course, Boling. Where did you have in mind?"

"Outside of my apartment. I am sure you know where it is. You will pick me up and we will travel to the China-North Korea River Bridge."

"I will not have the required documents. How will I be able to cross it?" asked Jang.

"Leave that to me, Jang. The three-hour trip will take us to Dandong. From there, you will be debriefed by my intelligence services and ultimately released. You will have a fresh start."

"That is very risky for me, Boling. How can you be so sure I'll get through my country's security on the North Korean side?"

"Your job is to get us safely to the Bridge. I will take care of the rest, Jang. We need to trust each other."

"Okay, Boling. But do not forget I have the video from Rajin."

"I know, Jang. There is no need to remind me. But you will bring it with you."

"If I don't?" asked Jang.

"Then you can arrest me at my apartment and end this tomorrow. This is non-negotiable, Jang. We need each other but I need assurances the video stays with us until we reach Dandong."

"That is reasonable, Boling. I will bring it with me."

"Excellent, I will see you tomorrow evening, Jang."

Click.

Neither man blindly trusted the other, but their fates would be inextricably tied together. Boling then studied the map on his cell phone. His computer had access to the internet but he knew Chinese intelligence was monitoring his activities from inside the embassy. Google Earth provided all the imagery he needed to visualize the location where he would kill Jang. The small city of Anju, along the Chong-chon River, would be the last thing Lieutenant Kim Jang would ever see.

SIS safe house, Midong district, Urumqi, Xinjiang Province, June 22, 9:21 AM

"Good morning, John. It's Robert."

"I hope you have good news, my friend. Has GCHQ performed another one of its magic tricks?"

"We have, John. The cell number you provided us has been found. We picked up its signal near the town of Hami. We even identified the owner. It's registered to an individual named Li Shi. I'll send the coordinates to your cell phone shortly."

"What else do we know about the man, Robert?"

"Nothing. You think we have an army of analysts working on this, John?"

"I do, Robert. I must get to the bottom of this. I'm also working with the Americans. Shi is affiliated with a group called the assassination corps. One of its members is a high-ranking PLA officer with intimate knowledge of a recent missile test. If we find Shi, we find our target."

"John, I'm drowning in requirements from the Prime Minister's office. I cannot continue tasking precious resources on this."

"I understand, Robert. Will it help if I get Alex to contact your Director?"

"If you wish to, John. But I can't promise he'll approve it."

"Oh, I think he will, Robert. But thank you for this information. I'll let you know what more I may need."

"Be safe, John."

Click.

"We have a name, Michael. He's been identified as Li Shi. He's near Hami, a city about six hundred kilometers from here."

"What are we waiting for, John. Let's get to it," said Michael.

The two men packed several items for the trip including high powered rifles, three shotguns, several hundred rounds of ammunition, and even a handful of HK-100 mini-drones. Both men prepared for the long journey and did not expect to return to Urumqi anytime soon. The remote SIS safe house had served its purpose and given the professional operatives a chance to finally prepare for their confrontation with the assassination corps. GCHQ's intelligence was actionable; however, both men wondered how long Shi would remain in Hami.

Hami, known as Kumul by Uyghurs living in Xinjiang, was a large city of approximately five hundred thousand residents. The city was best known for its Hami melons and its origins dated back to the First Millennium BCE. Founded by a people known as the "lesser Yuezhi," a great wall once encircled the city with iron gates on the eastern and western sections of the metropolis.

"Do you have any assets near Hami?" asked Michael.

"I do not, Michael. But I've contacted a friend who will meet us there."

"I hope he's a better friend than, Brian," said Michael jokingly.

John appreciated Michael's humor. He knew the American was kidding as being double-crossed in the espionage business was not uncommon. But it always stung. Michael had shared his story of betrayal by an asset in Jamaica he once worked with a few years ago. The long-time CIA contractor had conspired with the Islamic State terror group and nearly got Michael killed.

"Do you think we can get some imagery of the location, Michael?"

"I'll try, John. I'm sure NRO has some birds in the sky. It will depend on how quickly CIA can get the request approved. How long before we get there?"

"Nine hours."

"That's a tight window," said Michael as he tilted his head toward the clear blue skies.

Michael knew there were dozens of low earth orbit satellites above. The problem was that these satellites orbited the earth every ninety minutes. Depending on their arrival in Hami, and the inevitable bureaucratic approval process, imagery might not be available. Other factors included camera angle, availability, and weather, depending on the model being tasked. Michael was not optimistic and shared his lack of enthusiasm with John. He called Langley.

"Doug, it's Michael. We got a lead. The individual we're now looking for is Li Shi."

"Why this guy, Michael? What does he have to do with General Zhang Guozhi?"

"John and I were ambushed yesterday. We picked up a cell phone from one of the men and got his number. GCHQ did the rest. We think finding Shi will lead to Guozhi."

"I agree. But what if you can't find Li?"

"Then we'll adjust fire, Doug. John's resources in this region have become an endangered species. We have few options right now."

"Do you guys have anyone working the Korla missile complex right now?"

"Yes, one of John's assets is back there now looking for possible sources."

"Okay, Michael. It's your call. But let's not get bogged down with this. Your priority remains the missile test."

"Do you think you can get us imagery of Li's location in Hami?"

"When do you need it, Michael?" asked Doug.

"Within six hours."

"Are you frickin kidding me, Michael? That will not happen. I can't get a request through NRO that quickly at this time of day."

"Just try, Doug. We don't want to go in there blind."

Then a thought occurred to Doug.

"Have you heard of the X-37b aircraft, Michael?"

"I read something about it once. Why?"

"There's one flying now, Michael. Send me the coordinates of what you need to be photographed. No promises, bud, but I'll see what I can do."

Click.

The X-37b orbital test vehicle had once spent over seven hundred days in space. The mini space shuttle was lifted into orbit aboard an Atlas V rocket. Its length was less than ten meters, while its wingspan measured less than five meters. The tiny Air Force unmanned aircraft had incredible collection capabilities and pundits from around the world debated its true mission in space. Doug Weatherbee and others at CIA knew its tremendous capabilities and the ability to quickly maneuver in space made it an ideal overhead asset. Doug would have to convince an old friend at the Pentagon to help him.

"Langley is going to try, John. But I doubt they'll come through."

"Not enough time, Michael. We'll have to approach Li's location with extreme caution."

"How long has that vehicle been behind us, John?"

"Thirty minutes or so."

"Who do you think they are?" asked Michael.

"They could be Chinese counter-intelligence. If they wanted to stop us, they would have done so by now."

The black Mercedes SUV had joined them on Highway 312 soon after their departure from Midong. Its occupants remained approximately one hundred meters behind John and Michael and made no overt effort to remain hidden.

"I'm going to get off the highway in Turpan. We'll see if they follow," said John.

Both men stared out the window and wondered how their encounter with Li Shi would end. John pondered how his sons' studies were proceeding back home. Cambridge was, after all, one of world's renowned academic institutions and the opportunities they would find upon graduation would be immense. Michael was anxious to return to Indonesia and hoped the intent behind China's missile launch would soon be revealed. He could feel John's frustration with how events had unfolded and was determined to help his new friend in whatever capacity he could. Michael had been there before, he thought to himself.

Sinanju region, Anju city, near the Chongchon River, North Korea, June 23, 9:25 PM

Sun Boling and Kim Jang were making steady progress toward the China-North Korea Friendship Bridge, connecting the two countries along the Yalu River. There were few automobiles on the road and only the occasional bus, moving workers from central Pyongyang to the city of Anju. The bridge had been known as the Yalu River Bridge until it derived its current name in 1990. It had been constructed by the Japanese Imperial Army during World War II and was a vivid reminder to the North Korean people of Japanese aggression and occupation. The North Korean regime used the bridge as propaganda to remind its people of the atrocities committed by Japan which contributed to the tensions shared by both nations to the present day.

"What are your plans once my government releases you?" asked Boling.

"I want to own a business," said Jang.

"What kind of business?"

"I want to buy and sell CDs, DVDs, and records," said Jang as he smiled.

Boling sensed the professional counter-intelligence officer was letting his guard down. He was feeling comfortable and thought his life in North Korea was coming to an end. The optimism beaming from his eyes was almost infectious, Boling thought to himself. Boling did not have the heart to tell him these products were considered ancient history by much of the world. In North Korea, they were luxuries collected mostly by the elite ruling class. There was an underground black market for smuggled goods and only the wealthiest North Koreans could buy them.

"What kind of music do you like, Jang?"

"American Rock-n-Roll, Boling. Is there anything else?"

"What will your government do to your family once they realize you are gone?"

"They are already dead, Boling. They live a lie and are plagued with propaganda from birth to death. Many in my family are old now. There are only a few of us at my age. I will miss them dearly but there is no life for me here. They had their opportunities but did not have the courage to try."

"How can you be sure the life you choose in China will be better?"

"Anywhere in the world is better than here, Boling. You should know that by now."

Boling made a sharp turn left and slowly accelerated as he guided the car north. He knew from the map that the bridge in Anju was quickly approaching. He thought he was within two thousand meters of the bridge that would carry the men across the Chongchon River. To the east, there was a large clump of trees as Boling expected from his map reconnaissance earlier in the day. Up ahead was an open field surrounded by state-owned farms. There were no buildings or structures and they would remain on the remote road for several more kilometers.

"What is that over there, Jang?" asked Boling.

Jang turned his head to the east and saw nothing. It didn't matter.

Sun Boling used the opportunity to quickly remove the knife hidden under his left leg. He used the ice-pick grip, also known as the reverse grip, and struck the sharp dagger into Jang's chest. Then again. Then again. All in all, Boling struck Jang six times in under ten seconds. The man never had a chance.

Boling drove toward the bridge and found a trail just

thirty meters from the riverbank. He slammed on the brakes and quickly exited the vehicle. Boling opened the passenger door and pulled Jang onto the dirt road as he continued struggling to breathe. He then took his knife and cut Jang's throat as blood began oozing down his chest and onto his shirt. Jang would be dead in moments, Boling thought to himself.

He dragged Jang's body to the riverbank and looked for a suitable place to bury the body. He was lucky as the soil was soft and loose, rather than dry and compact. Boling quickly returned to his vehicle and released the trunk where he removed a folding shovel. The boron carbon steel blade on an aluminum shaft would do the trick. The small shovel even had a serrated edge in case he needed to cut through any roots or vegetation.

It would take Boling nearly fifty-five minutes to dig a ditch deep enough to conceal Jang's body. The cool breeze emanating from the west made the task a bit more bearable. Then his cell rang.

"Boling, how are things this evening?" asked Liu Zhun.

"I am well, Zhun. Is there a problem?"

"No. You may proceed with the operation when the opportunity presents itself, Boling. I have left Urumqi and our operations will begin to unfold in the coming weeks. I want you to exercise your initiative. Do not wait for my order from this point on. It's your decision when to strike."

"I understand, Zhun. But it will not be for several weeks."

"It does not matter. When their great leader is killed, chaos will ensue along the border. Of course, it would be best if done with our other operations, but I know access is problematic. Do what you can, Boling. It was an honor working with you and history will judge you kindly for what you will do."

"Thank you, Zhun. The honor was mine to have."

Click.

Sun Boling turned his attention to finishing the laborious task of burying Jang into the North Korean dirt. As with the rest of his family, Kim Jang would never leave North Korea.

White House Situation Room, Washington, D.C., June 22, 9:30 AM

"Good morning, everyone. What the hell are the North Koreans up to this time?" asked the President.

"Sir, North Korea has fired a single medium-range ballistic missile toward Micronesia. The missile, known as a Hwasong-12, splashed into the Pacific approximately eighty kilometers north of Bechyal."

"Don't we have some sort of defense agreement with Micronesia?" asked President Trump.

"We have a responsibility to protect the country under the Compact of Free Association agreement," said Herb McMullen.

"That looks damn close to Guam, Oliver."

"It is, Mr. President. I believe they were sending us another signal," said Oliver.

"What might that be, Oliver?" asked the President, though he had a good idea why.

"They were reminding us they have the capability to hit Guam with their medium-range missiles."

"We already know, Oliver," said the President.

"Yes, sir. It's just a friendly reminder."

"Herb, why do these guys keep firing missiles every other week?"

"As you know, Mr. President, the goal of the regime is to build an ICBM capable of hitting the United States. They learn from each test."

"What could they possibly learn from firing a missile near Micronesia?" asked the President.

"It's too early to tell, Mr. President. They may have been testing their new engines, guidance systems, or any one of the many things associated with their long-range missile program. Or it could have been a simple reminder. Remember what happened last year, Mr. President."

"I remember their threat. Believe me. I remember. Oliver, what do you think?"

"I won't see all the telemetry data for several days, Mr. President. At this point, they may simply be sending us a reminder. As you know, they do that from time to time."

"Would you characterize Kim as crazy, Oliver?" asked the President.

"Sir, he's only a technical analyst. We have others who could answer that question," said Herb.

Oliver did not appreciate the dismissive remark by the National Security Advisor. Neither did the President.

"Oliver, proceed," said the President.

"Mr. President, I do not believe he is crazy, insane, or unstable as many in this room have characterized him. He is calculating, and methodical. I believe he knows we are unlikely to attack first. I believe he made that calculation long ago. The test earlier this month could have come closer to Hawaii."

"Do you still believe he is six months away from having a re-entry vehicle?"

"Yes, Mr. President, six months," said Oliver as he turned toward Herb McMullen.

Herb McMullen became visibly irate and his piercing eyes said so. The President remained focused and never noticed.

"Sir, Oliver is one of the best we have. But we do have an analyst in J2 that believes its closer to a year."

"Well, Herb, which is it?"

"I believe Oliver's assessment is a bit ambitious, sir."

The President turned back toward Oliver.

"What do you say, Oliver?"

"I'm aware of the analyst at J2. Her technical assessment of the heat shields used in previous tests is wrong. I stand by my analysis, Mr. President."

"Oliver, if you're right, what should I do in six months?" asked President Trump.

"That is up to you, Mr. President. I'm not good at policy. I study missiles, Mr. President. Anything else, and I am probably winging it."

The President appreciated Oliver's candid remarks. He agreed with them, but he still wanted the man's opinion, nonetheless.

"Try again, Oliver. What do you recommend I do in six months?"

"Sir, I suggest turning your attention to the Chinese. They are the only ones who can exert pressure on the regime. We have tried and failed too many times. The North Koreans will not listen to us, Mr. President. Even you, sir."

The President knew Oliver was right and appreciated his candor. Though a confident man, President Trump was aware of America's limitations. He turned to Herb.

"Herb, I want the NSC to finish plans for retaliation in case shots are fired. In addition, I want a coordinated NSC plan to put pressure on the Chinese. I want the end state to be the conclusion of missile testing and a cessation of WMD production. Let's offer to stay out of the South China Sea except for our mission to ensure freedom of navigation. If they want to continue building up military facilities there, so be it."

"Sir, we have more time to negotiate. I don't think giving up the SCS is a good idea."

"Herb, it's not up for debate. I want the Chinese to solve the problem. Build up our interceptors and formulate a policy to get the Chinese on board. At some point, we have to make concessions to them."

"But sir…"

"Enough, Herb. I want a plan within ninety days. If you can do it without giving up the SCS, that's fine. But if not, they can have it. Our more significant problem is North Korea. Am I clear?"

"Clear, sir."

Herb McMullen sat back and appeared frustrated. The President knew it, and so did the rest of the participants. Oliver Tanner just ruined his plans to give the North Korea problem one year. Six months was probably not enough time, he thought to himself. Nevertheless, his commander in chief had spoken and a new diplomatic effort to appease the Chinese would be underway.

Turpan, eastern Xinjiang Province, China, June 22, 12:35 PM

Michael and John were about three hours into their drive. The two men were still being followed by a mysterious Mercedes SUV soon after their departure from the SIS safe house in Midong. The vehicle maintained a steady pace of about one hundred to two hundred meters behind John and Michael. The two professional operatives were now sure the vehicle belonged to China's Ministry of State Security. The behemoth counter-intelligence apparatus was well known for following western businessmen and government officials while visiting China.

"Hello, Chi. Meet me at Wang Yong's place at 1:00 PM," said John.

"I'm already outside, John. Take your time, my old friend."

"Who is Chi?" asked Michael sitting in the passenger seat.

"A long-time associate and asset here on the mainland. He picked me up in Beijing a couple of weeks ago. I've worked with him for a long time. He can be trusted, Michael."

"Good, we're going to need him."

John pulled off Highway G312 onto Gaochang Road and began driving south into the Gaochang district within the city of Turpan. The two men would eventually grab a quick bite to eat on their way to Hami. It would also give John an opportunity to coordinate for another favor from Wang Yong, Xinjiang's largest opium dealer.

Michael and John arrived at Wang's upscale apartment. The man known as a "blue lantern" to the Chinese Triads was waiting. The Mercedes SUV parked alongside the road behind John's car, approximately eighty meters away. As expected, the men sitting in the vehicle maintained an unassuming nature and made it clear they were going to keep a close watch on their western visitors. Chi remained in his car after a brief discussion with John.

"Hello, John. I see you have brought a friend," said Wang Yong.

"Yes, Yong. This is Michael."

"Another western spy. That's all I need. Please sit down," sighed Yong.

"Thank you, Yong. I need your assistance once again. There is a black Mercedes SUV parked alongside the apartment complex. I'm certain they are Chinese intelligence. I want you to get rid of them."

"Why would I want to get mixed up with them?" asked Yong.

"You probably don't, Yong, but I bet some of your Triad friends would."

"Maybe, John. What do I get for this support?"

"My gratitude, Yong. Nothing else."

"Why don't you lose them yourself?" asked Yong.

"We are on a tight timeline. We need to be elsewhere in a few hours. We do not need the attention, Yong."

"Does he speak?" asked Yong sarcastically as he looked at Michael.

Michael said nothing and simply stared into the man's eyes. Wang Yong immediately knew he was a serious man.

"Well, Yong. Will you help us or what?" asked John.

"I cannot promise the Triads will do anything, John. They operate in the shadows as do we. They will need to be motivated."

John Dearlove figured he would need to pay Yong, regardless of his earlier request. The man was correct as the

Triads were fully committed to anonymity as Yong was.

"How about I wire one hundred thousand US dollars to your account?"

"When will I see the money?"

John Dearlove reached for his cell phone and established a secure link with Vontobel Bank in Zurich, Switzerland. A few seconds later, the wire transfer to Yong's bank in Hong Kong was completed.

"How does now sound, Yong? Pay the Triads whatever you want," said John as he showed Yong his cell phone.

"Okay, John. What exactly do you want to do with the SUV?" asked Yong.

"I want it to stop following us. We will continue traveling west along Highway G312 for several hours. Whatever it takes, Yong."

John was vague as he intended to be. He didn't care how the job was done. The end state was clear, and Yong and his associates could use their imaginations.

"I cannot promise how the Triads will accomplish the task, John."

"I don't care, Yong. Just get it done. Michael and I are going to have lunch at the restaurant across the street. We'll leave in about thirty minutes."

"Alright, John. I may do this job myself. The vehicle will not be a problem."

"Thank you, Yong. I will be in touch if I need anything else."

"Nice talking with you, Michael," said Yong sarcastically.

Michael simply walked by Wang Yong and paid no attention to the opium dealer. Michael's dismissive nature and fierce eyes made Yong feel uneasy. But it didn't matter. Wang Yong was now one hundred thousand dollars richer and had a nearby associate in mind to finish the job.

John and Michael grabbed Chi, who remained waiting in his vehicle, on their way to the restaurant across the street. After a short lunch, the three men returned to their vehicles and prepared for the remaining journey to Hami. Hami was still about four hundred kilometers away and it would take the men approximately five hours of normal driving time.

John stepped on the accelerator and soon began driving toward Highway G312. Chi followed closely behind. Then suddenly the men heard a loud explosion. The black Mercedes SUV was in flames as they turned and looked behind them. Smoke drifted into the skies above as nearby pedestrians began screaming and scrambling away from the burning vehicle. For the moment, both men would have no distractions as they prepared for their fateful confrontation with Shi in Hami.

Yiwu County, Hami city, eastern Xinjiang Province, China, June 23, 9:20 AM

Liu Zhun and Shi, along with several other members of the assassination corps, were making final preparations for one of their operations in Beijing. They were in a remote building in the northern sector of the county, adjacent to the Qarlic Shan Mountain range. Despite its proximity to the Gobi Desert, Hami city was a fertile oasis, though its economy was mostly dependent on natural resources such as iron, gold, and copper. Liu's fortune included a controlling interest with a mining company focused on nickel extraction in the region. Hami was the perfect location for Liu to get final updates on his operations before crossing into Mongolia toward Bugat.

"Did you and Guozhi make peace yet?" asked Liu Zhun.

"Not really. But I have asked him to arrive this evening for dinner," said Shi.

"I need him focused on the missile launch. Smooth things over with the man."

"As you request, Zhun. But I cannot promise that we will be good friends."

"How was he able to adjust his schedule and arrive so quickly?" asked Liu.

"His organization needs resources. He has informed his staff he will be inspecting our mine for procurement. I am sure his staff will not become suspicious. He will depart from the airport with his driver."

"He wouldn't come if he thought it unwise, Shi. Anyway, in a few weeks, it will not matter. He will be dead, along with President Xi."

The men chuckled a bit as they had supreme confidence in Guozhi's abilities. Neither man really liked Guozhi because of his career in the PLA. He was, after all, a member of the government they wanted to see collapse. Nonetheless, years of loyalty to the organization had assuaged their fears. His destiny was tied to theirs, or so they thought.

"Will you be leaving after lunch?" asked Shi.

"Yes, I will be in Gubat this evening. I want you there within one week. There is nothing more we can do at this point except to ensure the transfer of funds to our operatives. I want you to oversee the remaining payments. How many men do you want to keep here?"

"I only need a handful. I'll send the rest with you this afternoon, Zhun."

Shi and Liu finished their meal and the commander of the assassination corps prepared for his journey across the Mongolian border. He figured the location was ideal and offered safety from any operational setbacks or missteps from his operatives. His plans always included contingencies and Shi would see to those details. The sheer number of operations across China offered the organization insurance as most would likely be executed as planned. A failure here or there would not prevent the collapse of the Chinese government. Liu's bold plans also included a social media campaign targeting China's youth and those most likely to support a new government free from Communism and corruption.

General Zhang Guozhi arrived in Hami a few hours later. He had spoken with Liu and wished him a good trip to Mongolia. Guozhi assured his driver she was not needed and suggested she go back into town and enjoy a few hours for herself. He would remain on-site for a while and call when ready to return to the airport.

Shi greeted Guozhi soon after his arrival at the mine.

"Guozhi, I am sorry for the incident the other night. Iris was becoming a problem and Liu grew tired of her questions. My job is to maintain order and discipline. I am sure you understand."

"I understand, Shi. Still, there was no reason to kill Iris. She was loyal. Her concerns were shared by many of us in the room. Why have you and Zhun kept the operation in Pyongyang so secretive?"

"It is our most sensitive operation, Guozhi."

"More sensitive than our missile launch?" asked Guozhi with a bit of sarcasm in his voice.

"Yes, of course. As you know, our plan relies heavily on massive refugees coming across the border from North Korea. This strain is key to exerting pressure on government leadership, or what's left of it. Our tactical objectives and assassinations cannot topple the government by themselves. The stress of refugees is what we believe will ultimately lead to the collapse."

"Yes, I know, Shi. I've heard that before. But many of us remain troubled. We want to know the details. We all share the risks equally if our plans fail."

"Zhun and I share your concern, Guozhi. We decided long ago that our operation in Pyongyang would be excluded from the rest of the organization. You and the others will just have to trust the plan."

"We do, Shi. Let's enjoy some dinner and try to put our past differences behind us," said Guozhi.

"I would like that very much."

The two men were joined by some of Shi's lieutenants. Tensions between the men abated somewhat, but Shi still sensed Guozhi's anxiety. There was an uneasy truce between them as history would soon judge their deadly campaign to topple the Chinese government.

Liu Mining Company, Hami, Xinjiang Province, China, June 23, 8:12 PM

Michael and John arrived at the outskirts of the Liu Mining Company. Doug Weatherbee and Langley had come through and provided the much-needed imagery of the facility where Shi was believed to be hiding.

The X-37b unmanned aircraft was able to execute an orbital inclination change much to the loathing of Air Force planners who reluctantly agreed to burn the fuel necessary for the maneuver. Nonetheless, the weather was ideal and crisp imagery of the complex allowed Michael and John to plan their insertion. Doug had asked for a NIIIRS level of seven, but got a nine, which would allow Michael to observe things like chain locks, rakes and shovels.

The two men and Chi would drive to the northeastern section of the mine. There were sand dunes approximately four hundred meters from the facility which they hoped would conceal their movement. The imagery did not show perimeter guards around the facility, but the men knew the "snapshot" from low earth orbit was just that; a snapshot in time. Both men agreed the facility would likely have roving patrols.

Michael and John parked their vehicle behind the sand dune nearest the facility. Chi would remain with the vehicle to secure it and their remaining equipment. The sun was quickly setting across the horizon and visibility became poor. However, the beautiful orange and red colors flaring upwards toward the skies were breathtaking.

John reached into the rear of the vehicle and unpacked a pair of Steiner military grade binoculars. The compact devices, modified by British SIS, were also laser range finders capable of acquiring targets nearly two thousand meters away.

They weighed in at less than fifty ounces and were perfect for operatives in low light conditions. He also reached for an L115A3 long range sniper rifle, capable of firing five rounds of 8.59 mm caliber ammunition. The all-weather sights ensured John would easily acquire and engage any targets from his vantage point atop the sand dune.

Michael would carefully make his way toward the fence along the northeast portion of the facility and use a pair of titanium bonded wire cutters to create a gap large enough for him and John to slip through. Michael then reached for a British military combat shotgun. The twelve-gauge weapon included a magazine capable of firing seven buckshot cartridges that would be perfect for any close combat situation he and John might find themselves in. Michael grabbed the second shotgun and slung it over his shoulders. He would hand it to John after they successfully breached the perimeter fence.

"Are you ready, Michael?" asked John.

"Absolutely. Let's find this son of a bitch. There's a treasure trove of Intel inside."

Michael stared through the binoculars. He did not see movement inside the facility. Then a man came into view walking north from the eastern side of the building.

"You see him, John?"

"I do, and now there's a second man along the western side."

"Got him," said Michael.

A few minutes went by and it appeared there were only two roving guards surrounding the building. It was time for Michael to carefully approach the northeast portion of the perimeter. John would cover his approach and kill the roving guards before sprinting to Michael's position.

Michael arrived at the fence and quickly began using his

wire cutters. Three minutes later, the gap was wide enough for him and John to slip through. He turned toward John and gave a thumbs up.

John took a deep breath and exhaled. Then another. He then squeezed the trigger of the L115A3 sniper rifle. The first man was hit in the head and quickly fell to the ground. John then turned his sights on the man alongside the western edge of the building. He fired a single round into the back of the man's head. Down he went. The British operative then placed the rifle on the apex of the sand dune and rushed toward Michael's position.

"Roving guards are dead, Michael," whispered John as he grabbed the extra shotgun.

"Good, that building can't hold more than five or six people, John."

"My guess is less than five," said John.

Michael led John across an undeveloped area toward an exterior outhouse. They were now within thirty meters of the building. According to the X-37b imagery, the building only had a front entrance and there were no windows. Two vehicles remained parked approximately fifteen meters adjacent to the southern end of the structure. Then a man exited through the front entrance on his way toward the outhouse.

Michael fired his shotgun as several pellets pierced into the man's chest. The loud sound of the shotgun gave their position away as they rushed toward the open door. Michael and John could hear men barking instructions inside.

Michael peered into the building's entrance. Two men were positioned behind a sofa and sprayed a volley of bullets in his direction.

"Two men with assault rifles behind the sofa on the right," yelled Michael.

John remained crouched alongside the exterior wall

and pushed the door open with his left hand. Michael leaned against the wall and found the left portion of the room was empty. There was no furniture or other items that could be used for cover or concealment.

"There's an office in the back. Looks like at least one man went inside," said John.

Michael turned his body to the right and fired two shots toward the sofa as John went storming through the front door.

John fired two rounds as both men remained pinned down behind the sofa. Michael quickly followed him inside.

Then suddenly both men attempted to stand up and fire their weapons. They never reached a standing position as Michael and John quickly finished them off with one shot each.

Shi and Guozhi remained in the back office. Shi peered around the corner and fired several shots toward John. One of the bullets hit John near the shoulder but he barely felt it. Adrenaline had kicked in and the injury would not be felt for some time.

Michael immediately turned toward the narrow hallway and fired two more rounds to keep the men inside pinned behind the wall.

"Who is there?" yelled Shi from inside the office.

Nothing.

Michael fired another round toward the door as John approached the hallway and positioned himself along the corner wall.

"I am looking for Shi," yelled John in Mandarin.

"What do you want with Shi?"

"I want to speak with him now," yelled John.

"You will die for this," yelled Shi as he attempted to peer around the corner and fire a few rounds.

"Maybe. Where is Shi?"

"I am Shi."

Michael and John heard a single shot coming from inside the office. Unbeknownst to both men, Guozhi had fired a single shot into the back of Shi's head.

"Where can I find Shi?"

Nothing.

Then suddenly, Michael and John heard the roars of a helicopter hovering outside the building. Michael turned toward the front entrance and noticed several soldiers approaching the building.

"What the fuck is this?" asked Michael.

"They must be PLA. We're in trouble, Michael," said John.

"God dammit. What the hell is the PLA doing here?"

Michael quickly moved to the front door and noticed at least twelve soldiers approaching the building with their weapons raised. However, they did not fire. He slammed the door shut as John remained focused on the office entrance.

"There are at least a dozen fucking soldiers outside, John."

"Shi, I want to speak with you, now. Let's end this. We're surrounded by the PLA."

"I am Zhang Guozhi. I am coming outside. Do not fire."

"Throw out your weapon and let me see your hands," yelled John.

Guozhi leaned forward and showed his hands but did not exit.

"Are you satisfied?" asked Guozhi.

"I am. Come out."

Zhang Guozhi exited the office and walked down the hallway toward John.

"Where is Shi?"

"Dead. Lying on the floor in the office. Would you like to look for yourself?"

"Not really. What the hell is going on here?" asked John.

"Good evening, gentlemen, I am General Zhang Guozhi, Director for the General Armaments Department of the People's Liberation Army and senior intelligence officer with the Ministry of State Security. You have complicated a very sensitive operation. Please lower your weapons."

Michael Brennan and John Dearlove looked at each other in bewilderment. They were in deep trouble and wondered what the hell would come next.

Barkul, Kumul Prefecture, Xinjiang Province, China, June 25, 8:00 AM

General Zhang Guozhi sat in the rear seat of his vehicle. His driver remained focused on the road ahead for the short trip to an isolated safe house controlled by the Ministry of State State Security. Guozhi reached for his cell phone and called Liu Zhun.

"Zhun, I have troubling news to report. Shi is dead along with several of our men."

"Where? At my mining facility?"

"Yes. It appears he was ambushed."

"How is this possible? Who could have known of our facility, Guozhi? And how on earth would you know this?"

"I was scheduled to meet him for dinner. We had some things to discuss. I found him and some of our men inside after my arrival. They were assassinated."

"Why did you not inform me immediately?" shouted Liu.

"Would it have mattered, Zhun?"

Liu Zhun took a deep breath. The commander of the assassination corps wondered if his plans were in jeopardy.

"Of course not, Guozhi. What do you think happened?"

"Shi had gambling debts. He may have owed more than we thought. The Red Diamonds gang may have had a part in this. I doubt this was the work of the government. I believe our plans are intact."

"How can you be sure, Guozhi?"

"I can't, but I intend to proceed with the operation. I suggest you do the same, my friend."

"Shi has been with me for a long time. I will want retribution."

"Let us focus on what we can, Zhun. You will have time

for that later," said Guozhi.

"Will you be heading back to Korla soon?" asked Liu.

"I will be there in a few days. I have a conference in Beijing."

"Shi will be avenged, Guozhi. I know you and he had differences, but he was one of us."

"I know you will have it, Zhun. I must go. I will call again soon."

Click.

Guozhi instructed his driver to speed up. He was anxious to get an update from his interrogators in northern Barkul. Barkul was located near the border and used extensively by the Ministry of State Security to meet Mongolian operatives reporting on their activities inside Mongolia. The region was famously called "the land of ten thousand camels" due to the substantial number of long-necked creatures reproduced there. Barkul was also the temporary home of Michael Brennan and John Dearlove.

"How are our guests doing?" asked Guozhi.

"Neither man is talking. We know of the British agent based on your report. We assume the American is CIA."

"Never assume anything, Hao. It's likely, but we cannot assume," said Guozhi as he made his way to the interrogation room housing Michael.

"Good morning. How may I address you?" asked Guozhi.

"Whatever you want," said Michael.

"I am Zhang Guozhi. What is your name?"

"What do you want it to be?"

"I do not care. I just want to know who I'm speaking with."

"Call me Michael."

"Michael, I've known about you and Mr. Dearlove for

several days now. You killed my men in Turpan. That was disappointing."

"What is it that you want?" asked Michael.

"What is your mission here? Why are you working with Mr. Dearlove?"

Michael chuckled a bit.

"I came to find you, General Zhang."

"You want to know about the missile launch, is that correct?"

"Of course. You know that. What are we doing here, Zhang?"

"I have a proposition for you, assuming you want to listen?"

"What might that be?"

"By now, I suspect you know the missile launch was never intended to hit your satellite. We were demonstrating our true power in space. It is no longer yours to command. I will allow you to inform your government of this after you accomplish something for me."

"Go on," said Michael a bit intrigued.

"The man you are looking for is now in Mongolia. He is not far from here. I would like to send you and one of my operatives across the border to question him."

"You're going to just let me leave? I would not advise doing that, Zhang. There's a good chance your operative will die, and you will never see me again."

"I expected an answer like that, Michael. Do you want to see John imprisoned or executed?"

"How do I know he's not dead already?"

"You will have to trust me, Michael. If you agree to my terms you will have an electronic chip device implanted into your neck. This will allow us to monitor your movement. It will also serve as insurance if you decide to flee."

"Doesn't sound like that would prevent me from doing anything, Zhang."

"That is possible. But the chip can be remotely detonated. The tiny explosion will sever your carotid artery. You would die in minutes."

Michael heard of such devices but was not aware they were used by intelligence services. Their signal could be intercepted and traced back to their point of origin. He wondered how the Chinese could mask their originating points, but it didn't matter.

"What kind of information do you want me to collect in Mongolia?" asked Michael.

"A man named Liu Zhun is the self-proclaimed leader of the assassination corps. By now, I am sure you know this. One of his operatives is now in Pyongyang and has been instructed to kill their great leader. I want to know who that man is."

"Sounds like his man would be doing the world a favor. Why do you want the information?"

"We cannot allow that, Michael. We do not care for him either, but his loss would bring millions of refugees into my country. And his death would risk our strategic buffer with South Korea and your country."

"So, you want him alive?"

"Yes. And I am certain your country agrees, despite what we hear in the news."

Michael wasn't so sure about Zhang's assessment, but he understood the strategic implications of the man's death and the uncertainty it would bring along the Korean peninsula.

"I want John to accompany me and your operative."

"That will not happen, Michael. John will remain here until you and my operative return."

"Forget it, Zhang. John goes or neither of us go."

Michael had already decided he would do it but wanted to see how flexible Guozhi might be.

"This is not negotiable, Michael. He will not leave this facility until you return."

"Then go fuck yourself, Guozhi. Find someone else."

Zhang Guozhi stood and turned toward the door. An individual had remained there with watchful eyes focused on Michael.

"Think about it, Michael. I do not have much time. I will return later."

Michael sat motionless and considered his options. They were far and few in between. His survival instincts kicked in and the opportunity to give Langley the Intel on the missile launch was too good to pass up. After all, this was his primary mission and it had to be accomplished at all costs. On the other hand, he did not trust Guozhi. Michael feared John was already dead and he would soon be joining him after his return from Mongolia. His mission would, therefore, serve Guozhi interests and leave Langley searching for answers.

Michael decided on his course of action a few minutes later. He would head to Mongolia and confront the commander of the assassination corps.

MI6 Headquarters, along the Thames River, London, England, June 25, 11:55 AM

Alex Sawers grew concerned. The man known as "C" had not heard from his top operative in China for two days. The Chief of British SIS had been receiving regular updates from John Dearlove but wondered why the career operative went silent. He decided to call Doug Weatherbee at CIA.

"Good morning, Doug. I am sorry to wake you. I have not heard from my operative in China. Has your man there checked in recently?"

"I've not heard from him for several days, but he does that from time to time. What are your concerns, Alex?"

"My man can be a thorn in my side, but he's my best. And he's my most reliable. His instructions were to update me daily. He has not done so for two days now. His last report indicated a reconnaissance into Hami."

"Let me see what I can do, Alex. I'll try to get back to you later today. How does that sound?"

"Excellent, thank you, my friend."

Click.

Alex Sawers summoned his administrative assistant, Teresa Holland.

"Teresa, I need a secure link with Lewis MacDonald in Stonehaven."

"Right away, sir."

Teresa patched the man through a few minutes later.

"Lewis, it's Alex. How are you, my old friend?"

"I am well, Alex. I assume this is not a social call?"

"No. I am missing an operative in China. I want you to prepare your team for recovery."

"Who is it, Alex?"

"John Dearlove."

Lewis MacDonald knew John well and even worked an operation with him in 2009. John had vouched for Lewis after the Macao incident but was unsuccessful in changing the minds of the bureaucrats in London.

"The location, Alex?" asked Lewis.

"We're not sure yet. He last reported traveling to Hami."

"That will be expensive, Alex."

"Indeed. The contract will pay three million US dollars."

"China is very dangerous. I will need four million, Alex. My expenses will be substantial."

"Done. But I am making no commitments. I have no idea where John is now. I just want you to prepare for the time being."

"My team will be ready to go within twenty-four hours."

"Excellent, I will be in touch soon."

Click.

Lewis MacDonald was a former SIS operative who was forced to retire early after an incident in Macao, China in 2011. While collecting intelligence on a prominent real estate businessman and casino owner, he lost his cool and killed several members of the man's security detail. Rumors in London were that he was simply being questioned by security personnel and "snapped." SIS investigators later determined the operative's decision was unwarranted and a bit too "high profile" for SIS to ignore. He barely escaped Macao and had served as a contractor ever since. Known as cold, calculating, and brutal, most officers in SIS simply referred to him as *Iceman*.

After his dismissal from SIS, MacDonald moved to Stonehaven. The small community was made up of mostly fisherman, and known by locals as Stoney, was situated along the coast in northeastern Scotland. MacDonald and his group of mercenaries lived in the small coastal town when in between contracts for SIS. The group of six individuals was composed of mostly ex-SIS officers and military personnel. MacDonald's group was the perfect choice for SIS when requiring "off book" operations without the scrutiny and oversight of Parliament. Used sparingly, the group had proven itself reliable over the years while earning significantly more money than serving the British government.

Alex Sawers reached for his phone and decided to try John Dearlove again. The phone rang and rang until it went to voicemail. Alex sat back and stared toward the Thames River. He wondered what had become of his best spy.

Chinese Embassy, Pyongyang, North Korea,
June 25, 1:38 PM

Sun Boling returned from lunch. He entered his office and dreaded the mundane paperwork ahead of him. Kim Jang's threat to expose Boling's actions in Rajin naval base was behind him and he could now turn his attention to killing the great leader, the President of North Korea.

Boling hoped the opportunity would present itself in a few weeks at a gathering of embassy personnel scheduled to meet senior North Korean naval officers near Rajin. A brief appearance by the great leader was expected. The reclusive President would discuss his vision and expectations for North Korea's expanding submarine program. There were two key pieces of information Boling was waiting for.

First, the list of participants from the Chinese delegation would be announced sometime in the afternoon. He had to be on the list or determine a way to be added. The second was the all-important seating chart. Boling had no control over the seating arrangements as those details would be approved by North Korean intelligence and President Kim's chief of staff.

About an hour later, the email hit his computer. Sun Boling was invited and would sit with the Commander of the Korean People's Navy, Fleet Admiral Li Jong-yu. Liu Zhun would be pleased, he thought to himself. He wished he could call his commander, but Liu's instructions were clear; Boling was now on his own and could execute when ready. There would be no further communications or guidance given.

Boling leaned back in his chair and figured he would be within twenty meters of the North Korean president. It was close, but he had hoped to be closer. Then he remembered seeing footage of public appearances by President Kim. He rarely surrounded himself with his top generals and advisors. This was by design and a form of insurance developed by a security detail who constantly worried about an assassination attempt on the great leader. Surrounding the delegation would be dozens of security officers supported by visual surveillance teams within the complex. The likelihood of success was low, but Boling was committed to making it work.

Sun Boling was a highly trained military officer with an opportunity, something very few people have ever had in North Korea. Western intelligence services would kill for the opportunity presented to the career naval officer. Boling now had the daunting task of planning the assassination. There would be security checks prior to and during the event. Boling figured it would be impossible to smuggle a weapon inside. He had to get creative, he thought to himself. But how?

Boling's excitement and prospect for a place in history had distracted him for nearly an hour. Then the deputy ambassador arrived.

"Commander Boling. Have you seen your email?"

"Yes, sir, I have. It appears I will join you and a few others in Rajin."

"Yes. There will be extensive security checks and interviews. We will begin in a few days."

"Who are the security checks with?"

"North Korean Ministry of State Security."

"They will not allow anyone to go near President Kim. These are not traditional background checks because of our status. Rather, they will be informal oral interviews."

"Will they question all of us?" asked Boling.

"No. They will only question our military staff."

"Where will the interviews be conducted?"

"Here in the embassy. The Chief of Staff will notify you

when the interview will be conducted."

The deputy ambassador soon departed Boling's office. Boling stared at the picture of President Xi hanging over the wall. He wondered how the President of China might react to the events that would soon unfold.

Boling finished his remaining duties for the afternoon and traveled to his apartment near the embassy. Planning the death of the great leader would consume his attention for the next few days. But how? he thought to himself.

Barkul, Kumul Prefecture, Xinjiang Province, China, June 25, 4:14 PM

Zhang Guozhi returned to John Dearlove's interrogation room. It would be their second meeting since John's captivity at Hami. John was tired but well cared for. He had not been subjected to enhanced interrogation techniques or physical punishment. Chinese interrogators had spent most of the evening with the man attempting to establish rapport.

Chinese interrogators were known to be harsh and brutal toward their prisoners. However, these were Chinese citizens, traitors or dissidents. Rarely did they brutally interrogate foreign spies like British SIS, American CIA or others. When these operatives were caught, they were either imprisoned or quickly executed.

"Mr. Dearlove, have you considered my proposal?" asked Guozhi.

"I have. You can go to hell, Guozhi. I will not reveal my network inside your country."

"Would you rather die or be imprisoned for the rest of your life?"

"I am prepared for both."

"Would you like to know how I found you?"

"Go on."

"Your friend, Chi. He has been working for our organization for two years. He reported your arrival in Beijing and we've been monitoring your activities ever since."

"Why did you not simply arrest me in Beijing?"

"We wanted to know what you were up to. We figured we could identify some elements of your network in Xinjiang. Chi helped in that regard. We always suspected Wang Jong but were not certain until recently. The loss of our officers in Turpan was unfortunate."

"Where is Chi now?" asked John.

"Far from here, Mr. Dearlove. I doubt you will ever see him again."

"What now, Guozhi. You know I will not betray my country."

"I am counting on it, Mr. Dearlove. You will have to pay for Turpan. However, if you tell us what we want to know we can spare your life."

"That will never happen. I would rather die."

"Then die you will, Mr. Dearlove."

Zhang Guozhi stood up and stared into John's eyes. He knew the career SIS operative would not willingly divulge information on his network in China. There was no reason to continue speaking to the man. He turned his attention toward Michael.

Guozhi arrived in Michael's room a few moments later.

"Michael, have you considered my proposal?"

"I have, Guozhi. I am willing to get your information. However, I want assurances that my friend will not be harmed."

"He will not be."

"When will I be able to notify Langley of the missile launch?"

"How about right now?" asked Guozhi.

Michael appeared a bit confused. He had not expected Guozhi to be so generous.

"Here, Michael. Use my cell phone. Be careful about what you share."

Michael called the Operations Center right away. An officer routed his call to Doug Weatherbee's cell phone.

"Doug, It's Michael. The missile launch was intended to send us a warning. The Chinese were not trying to take it out."

"How did you get the Intel, Michael?"

"Well, I'm sitting here with General Zhang as we speak."

"Huh? Where the hell are you and what is your exit strategy?"

"I am somewhere near Hami. John and I have been captured and the Chinese want me to collect Intel for them on the assassination corps."

Guozhi motioned for Michael to hand him the phone.

"This is General Zhang Guozhi. You have my assurances that Michael will be released once he finishes the job for us. No harm will come to him as long as he cooperates."

"What the hell is going on, Zhang?"

"Call this a spirit of cooperation between our countries. His mission will benefit both of us."

"You hold the cards, Zhang. It seems we have no choice. But why not use your own operatives? What do you need Michael for?"

"The assignment will be conducted in Mongolia. If the mission fails, one of our operatives gives us plausible deniability. Two makes things more complicated."

"My officer is not expendable, Zhang."

"I disagree, but he is a perfect choice. Liu will not divulge the information to us. He might to an American if he believes the assassination benefits your country. We believe if Liu is captured, he is more likely to cooperate with Michael to save himself."

Doug Weatherbee listened attentively. Michael's capture had given the Chinese a tremendous opportunity to bring in an outsider. But he wondered what information Michael was supposed to collect.

"What information are you looking for, Zhang?"

"Liu has an assassin in Pyongyang. We want to know who that is?"

"Why?" asked Doug.

"The operative has instructions to kill a high-value target inside North Korea."

"Who is the target?"

"That is none of your concern."

"I thought we were doing this to foster a spirit of cooperation, Zhang?" asked Doug sarcastically.

"Consider Michael's mission as goodwill. My country will return the favor."

"What support are you providing for Michael?"

"No more questions. I have your officer and he has agreed to assist us. You have my personal guarantee that he will be returned once the mission is over."

Click.

Guozhi made a few remarks to Michael before leaving the room. The procedure to implant the chip into Michael's neck would occur in the morning.

Doug Weatherbee sat motionless at his desk. His top operative had accomplished the mission but was now a prisoner of Chinese intelligence. The Director and members of the National Security Council would be pleased, but troubled by Michael's capture. Doug assumed Michael would die immediately after his mission and wondered if he could do anything about it. The President and others would do the same.

CIA Headquarters, Langley, Virginia, June 26, 7:30 AM

Doug Weatherbee arrived at Nikki Hastings' office, the Director of the Central Intelligence Agency. Accompanying Doug was Skip Mancuso, Directorate for Intelligence, the agency's Chief of Staff and the Deputy National Security advisor. The mood was tense as one of their own had been captured by Chinese intelligence. They knew his prospects for ever leaving China were dim. Most, if not all, believed Michael Brennan would soon be killed for espionage.

"Good morning, Doug. What more can you tell us?" asked Director Hastings.

"Not much, unfortunately. I spoke to General Zhang yesterday. He has Michael and wants him to collect Intel on the assassination corps. Their leader is a man named Liu Zhun. He is in Mongolia and has an operative working in Pyongyang. This operative, who we do not know, has instructions to kill a high-value target inside North Korea. That's all I've got now."

"What does DI have on this organization?" asked Hastings.

"It's a fringe group that existed in China from 1910 until 1912. Liu Zhun wrote a few papers on them many years ago. Frankly, we know nothing else," said Mancuso.

"We don't know a damn thing about them," added Doug.

"Doug, where are they holding Michael?" asked Hastings.

"We don't know that either. He said he was near Hami."

"What are the odds they release him, Doug?"

"The Chinese don't trade prisoners and I find it hard to believe they will let him go."

"Options?" asked Hastings to the group.

"I see very few. The man got us the Intel we needed. He

knows the risks," said Mancuso.

"Fuck you, Skip. That's a cheap shot coming from an analyst. Do you want to let him rot in a prison somewhere? We owe it to him to get him out, whatever it takes," snapped Doug.

"What do you suggest, Doug?" asked Hastings calmly.

"We wait. Let's see if the Chinese let him go. If not, then I recommend a trade. We caught one of their senior agents in Nevada a few years ago. Maybe the Chinese will want her back," said Doug.

"Doug is right. There's nothing we can do now. An extraction is impossible, and we don't even know where he is. What's to stop him from leaving Mongolia?" asked the Chief of Staff.

"I didn't get that far. If he can escape, he will. Zhang ended the call before I could get more information," said Doug.

"I can't imagine they will let him go to Mongolia if they didn't think he would return. What the hell would prevent him from escaping?" asked Hastings.

"Not sure. If he doesn't flee, there's got to be a damn good reason. My guess is that he has assurances the British agent will be let go," said Doug.

"Skip, what are some possible high-value targets in North Korea?" asked Hastings.

"If this assassination corps is real, and I'm not convinced they are as we have zero evidence, their targets are likely to be Chinese government officials. That's why they formed the group in 1910. It could be the Ambassador, it could be the embassy, or any one of several other targets," said Mancuso.

"Doug, what do you think?" asked Hastings.

"Skip is correct. It could be anything. We don't know

anything about the group or its objectives," said Doug grudgingly.

He hated to agree with Skip after his flippant remark earlier.

"Okay, so we wait, gentlemen. Skip, get some of your people on this. Send them to Doug and see if we can come up with a consensus. Let me know when you come up with a list of possible targets. Doug, I want you to sit tight on this. Our hands are tied. Let's wait and see what the Chinese do. Give the British a call and let them know where we are. I'll get an update to NSC on the missile launch. Skip, sit with me for a moment."

Doug and the Chief of Staff soon departed Hastings' office. They knew what was coming. Skip Mancuso was going to get an earful from the Director. His assessment of the situation was accurate, but his dismissal of Michael should have been addressed differently. Michael recognized the hazards of his chosen profession and performed his duties admirably. In the end, all that mattered was the information, but Michael was one of their own and he would not be dismissed. Skip Mancuso was about to learn that from the Director. Doug Weatherbee's turn would come later.

Doug returned to his office and immediately placed a call to SIS.

"Alex, it's Doug. Bad news, John and Michael have been captured."

"I suspected as much. John last reported he was leaving for Hami. That was many days ago."

"I spoke to Michael briefly and then General Zhang. Michael is helping Zhang get Intel on the assassination corps. He did not mention John."

"Where in the bloody hell are they now?"

"All we know is somewhere near Hami, Alex."

"What do you suppose happened to John?"

"No idea. I'm sorry, Alex. Michael reported he was a good man."

"He is a good man. What are you planning to do?"

"For now, I think its best we sit and wait. I'm sure Michael will contact me when he has the chance. My Director agrees."

"Doug, we have a finite window here to get our boys back. I cannot promise I won't order an extraction."

"Please don't, Alex. I want your man back as much as Michael, but we have no Intel and conducting an operation like that in China will likely fail. I'm sure you agree."

"You are probably right, Doug. But my government will want our man back as I presume yours does as well. I will contact you with any moves we make."

"Alex, please show restraint. I don't like this any more than you do and sitting on my ass is killing me. But the wise move is to wait until we know more."

"Agreed. I will contact you soon, Doug."

Click.

Doug sat back in his chair. He would have to wait. In the meantime, he would call his chief of station in Beijing and have him prepare an extraction team comprised of local contractors.

Barkul, Kumul Prefecture, Xinjiang Province, China, June 26, 8:05 AM

Zhang Guozhi entered Michael's interrogation room. The man looked well rested, he thought to himself. Accompanying Guozhi were two individuals. The first carried a black briefcase while the second simply stood behind Guozhi.

"Good morning, Michael. The gentleman you see in front of you will now implant the device. Just sit back and relax. It will only take a few moments."

The man carefully opened his briefcase and removed a steel plated syringe. The barrel appeared the same size as an ordinary syringe except it looked a bit wider, as did the hub and needle. The leading ring inside the syringe was connected to the actual chip, which was barely visible to the naked eye. The damn Chinese had perfected the ultimate motivator, Michael thought to himself.

The chip was firmly planted into Michael's neck just second later. He barely felt a thing except when the needle broke his skin. The man performing the act promptly left the room as Guozhi had instructed him.

"Michael, this is Echo. She will accompany you on your mission across the border. We will be monitoring her movements, along with yours. If she fails to report the device will be activated. If she is harmed, we will activate the device. If you make any attempts to flee we will activate the device."

"What exactly do you want, Zhang?" asked Michael.

"I want to know who Liu's man is in Pyongyang. That is all I require. Once you obtain this information, Echo will escort you back across the border."

"Where are we going?"

"In due time, Michael. Echo will lead you to Liu's location. I expect him to have no more than ten men with him.

Echo will serve as your tactical support."

"Do you care what happens to Liu?"

"Not at all, Michael. His organization will be dismantled the moment we know who the man in Pyongyang is."

"So, I have your permission to kill him?"

"Yes."

"What will happen when I return, Guozhi? I find it hard to believe you will just let me go."

"As I said yesterday, you will have to trust me."

"For the record, I don't."

"Do not be so cynical, Michael. This information benefits both our countries. I must tend to other matters. You and Echo will leave this afternoon. You will follow her instructions until you arrive at Liu's location. You will then have operational control."

"John had better be alive and in good health when I get back, Zhang."

"Or what?" snapped Guozhi.

Guozhi stood up and stared deeply into Michael's eyes for several seconds.

"Good luck, Michael. Keep Echo safe and I await your return."

The White House, Washington, D.C.,
June 26, 10:09 AM

Lieutenant General Herb McMullen remained at his desk. The President wanted an update on the North Korean missile launch earlier in the month. Recent missile tests over Japan had spooked some of the allies and the media wanted answers. He was determined to give the President another perspective that would differ from Oliver Tanner. His primary goal was to give the President and his senior foreign policy team one year to implement aggressive diplomatic and economic initiatives directed to curb President Kim's appetite for weapons of mass destruction. All efforts, as of now, were failing. Then his phone rang.

"Herb, it's Nikki. Do you have a few minutes?"

"Of course, I could use the distraction."

"Good news and bad news. One of my operatives has answered the President's requirement on the Chinese missile launch. As we hoped, the Chinese never intended to hit the damn thing. They were simply reminding us of their new capabilities. The Intel is good and we are confident of the assessment."

"Damn good news, Nikki. Nice job. What's the bad news?"

"The operative who provided the Intel has been captured. He actually spoke to us last night."

"I'm sorry to hear that, Nikki. What did he say?"

"He's been asked to collect Intel on an organization called the assassination corps. Don't worry about the specifics now, I'll send you a report this afternoon. What concerns us, is what the Chinese want."

"Which is?' asked Herb as he leaned forward in his chair.

"The Chinese are convinced this group has an operative working in Pyongyang with instructions to kill a high-value target."

"Go on," said Herb.

"They did not indicate who or what the high-value target was. My analysts think it could be the ambassador or other senior Chinese staff in the embassy."

"How did they arrive at that assessment?"

"This group actually existed from 1910 until 1912. They were targeting senior Chinese officials. So, the assumption is the resurgent group will do the same."

"Any idea on what their objectives are?"

"None. We have zero Intel on that now. They are ghosts."

"Why the hell would your operative be working with the Chinese?"

"We're wondering the same thing. They may be forcing him. He was, after all, working with the British on this. Their operative has been captured as well."

"Okay, Nikki. Thanks for the update. I'll inform the President right away. Thank god the Chinese were simply sending us a message on the launch. It would have gotten tense in here real fast. What are you planning to do about your operative?"

"Unfortunately, we have to wait. We don't where he is or where exactly he is going."

"Thank you, Nikki. Great work. I hope you get your operative back real quick. I'll be praying for him."

"Me too, Herb. Talk soon."

Click.

Herb McMullen was eager to inform the President and promptly made his way to the oval office. President Trump was at his desk and reviewing a draft speech he would deliver the following day to the National Rifle Association.

"Mr. President, do you have a few minutes?"

"Good timing, Herb. I need a damn break."

"The Chinese anti-satellite launch earlier this month was never intended to hit our bird. They wanted to let us know what they can do. Nikki says the Intel is reliable and she is confident of the assessment. But, it looks like we lost an operative."

"What happened?"

"We don't know. The officer is alive but currently imprisoned by the Chinese."

"What's going to happen to him?"

"No idea, sir. The Chinese have informed us that he will collect Intel for them against an organization called the assassination corps."

"Why the hell would he do that? And who the hell are they?"

"I'm sure he has no choice. I'm working on your second question, sir."

"Can we get him back?"

"I don't know, Mr. President."

"Get on it. We owe it to the man to try. Tell Nikki excellent work on this."

"Will do, Mr. President."

"One more thing, Herb. When we do the next North Korean missile brief, I want Olie back. I like him."

"Yes, sir."

Herb McMullen walked toward the White House Mess and grabbed a coffee. The small dining facility supported approximately fifty guests, but it was rarely full. Most staff employees ordered ahead and picked up their lunch from the take-out window. Beautiful paintings of Naval vessels adorned the wood paneled walls while fresh flowers were found at every table. Herb McMullen sat down and sipped on some black coffee. He acquired the taste as a young Marine infantry officer who served in Operation Desert Storm in Kuwait.

Herb sat back and wondered how he could get the President to listen to his officer from J2. Oliver Tanner was not going to budge on his previous assessment. According to Olie, North Korea would have the capability to hit the United States with an Intercontinental Ballistic Missile within six months. Herb and many other national security officials wanted another year before the President would be forced to consider any preemptive strike on the reclusive regime.

MI6 Headquarters, along the Thames River, London, England, June 26, 5:35 PM

Alex Sawers returned to his office. He looked forward to a hot cup of Earl Gray tea. He had just briefed the Prime Minister and Foreign Secretary on the Chinese missile launch. They were pleased, but saddened by the news of John's capture. Alex had anticipated the Prime Minister's cautious guidance. The Foreign Secretary advocated for an immediate extraction, if possible. Alex was to get the Americans onboard as soon as possible but SIS would have full operational control. Sawers reluctantly agreed since Intel on their whereabouts was nonexistent. It was time to notify Langley.

"Doug, I've just returned from a briefing with the Prime Minister and Foreign Secretary. They have ordered me to prepare for an extraction, if any Intel on our men is acquired."

"Alex, I thought we agreed to sit tight on this?"

"We did, and we are. I am going to deploy an extraction team near Hami. Nothing more."

"God dammit, Alex. If the Chinese get wind of this, our boys are dead. You know that."

"It's a risk we are prepared to take. We are not going to sit on this. The extraction team will be a small group of men with orders to sit tight. They will not conduct reconnaissance or make any overt attempts to find John or Michael."

"Not gonna work, Alex. Do they want a joint operation?"

"They wish it so, Doug. Whatever support you're willing to provide will be appreciated. We will do nothing unless we know for certain where they are and if we believe there is a reasonable chance for success."

"My Director is not going to be happy. And neither am

I, frankly. Why the opposition to waiting? We have zero Intel right now."

"Doug, I understand your concerns. We are simply deploying resources. They will do nothing unless we give approval. What if I convince the Foreign Secretary we will need your approval before any actions are taken?"

"It seems you already have your mind made up. I think it's risky. I want them back as much as you do, but we don't know a damn thing, Alex. We just talked about waiting. Michael will contact me when he has the chance. We have to wait until then," pleaded Doug.

"No promises, Doug. But, I will deploy the team this evening. They will be in Hami within two days."

"Okay, Alex. Let's see if we hear from Michael soon."

"I will speak to you soon, Doug."

Click.

Alex turned his attention to Lewis MacDonald and placed a call to the man's cell phone.

"Lewis. Is your team prepared to move?"

"They are. When will you send the instructions?"

"You will receive them when we are ready. For now, your team will move to Hami and sit tight. You are to do nothing, Lewis. Am I clear?"

"Sit tight? We can do that, Alex. But I need monies wired to pay initial expenses."

"I will wire one hundred thousand US dollars to your Bangkok account right away. I want to be clear, Lewis. There will be no overt movements. Go to Hami and remain at whatever location you have planned for. There mustn't be any mistakes."

"Understand, Alex. I will notify you once we are on-site."

"Good. Safe travels, Lewis."

Click.

Alex Sawers sat back and began sipping his tea. The smooth taste and solitude of the office allowed him to clear his head and think. John Dearlove, the most valued SIS operative of his generation, was missing and there was nothing Sawers could do about it. Waiting for information from Michael or other assets would take its toll on "C."

Burgastai Road, Bugat, Govi-Altai, Mongolia, June 26, 5:53 PM

Michael and Echo were traveling slowly along the bumpy trail on the outskirts of the Gobi B nature preserve near the Mongolian border. The Yongshi Warrior, China's latest jeep used by military forces, looked eerily like an American Humvee and included an all-metal fully enclosed body. The sandstone colored jeep rolled effortlessly over the soft sand littered with pebbles and small rocks.

"Where are we going, Echo?" asked Michael.

"We will be traveling to Bugat. It is a small town not far from here. Liu will be there," said Echo.

"How do we know he has not moved?"

"Guozhi is certain, so I am certain. He will be there, Michael."

"How long have you worked with Guozhi?" asked Michael.

"Never. He is a military man who serves our Ministry of State Security. I know very little of General Zhang. I just met him a few days ago. How long have you been with CIA?"

"Long enough, Echo."

"Why was your President so worried about our missile test?"

"I don't know, and I don't care. My mission was to find out why. I don't concern myself with such matters. I only care about the mission," said Michael.

Echo quickly realized Michael was not going to make small talk. She knew he was a serious man but tried anyways.

"We would not have been that reckless, Michael. Our country will soon be the most dominant economic power in the world. Our influence is growing, and we do not need to confront America. We will simply overtake you."

"Not my concern, Echo."

"Have you worked in China before?"

"Actually, no. Do you think I would tell you if I did?"

"Probably not, Michael. If we are going to work together, should we not get to know one another?" asked Echo.

"Echo, Guozhi has implanted a god damned chip into my neck. I have no logistical or intelligence support and I have no idea where I'm going. Why do I want to get to know you? We have a job to do. Let's do it."

Echo turned her attention to the gorge ahead. The Mongolian border was only three kilometers away. There would be a checkpoint a few kilometers after that manned by Mongolian border guards. Echo and Michael would enter the landlocked country posing as University professors from Hami studying the gray wolf of the Gobi B desert, its primary predator. Michael would be the primary photographer, an American professor at Oregon State University College of Forestry on a one-year faculty research grant.

Michael was impressed with the forged documents put together by Chinese intelligence. His American passport appeared genuine, along with his optical equipment. The Chinese had spared no expenses and he wondered how long it took them to gather the gear. Michael concluded the Chinese were probably as good at their tradecraft as was the CIA. It probably explained the enormous success the Chinese were having at collecting intelligence from American citizens inside the United States. For every documented failure, there were probably handfuls of successes. Chinese intelligence would be the beneficiary of an FBI intensely focused on homegrown violent extremism and not the tens of thousands of Chinese students and businessmen working and studying inside the United States.

Echo and Michael soon made their way toward the border. Up ahead, were at least two dozen black trucks used to export iron-ore into China. The trucks were returning to the Mongolian side as the narrow passage through the checkpoint was slow. Tourists were not typically allowed to cross here, however, border guards could easily be bribed. Echo hoped that her boss at MSS had already made the arrangements earlier in the morning.

"I see no civilian vehicles, Echo. This looks like a transportation gateway. Are tourists allowed to cross here?" asked Michael.

"No, but we have made arrangements. The border guards are known to accept bribes."

"Great, what if they don't?"

"They will, Michael. I have used this checkpoint before. Relax, we will be fine. If not, we will turn northwest and cross in Baitag Uliastai. We are in no danger."

"Oh, I'm totally relaxed."

About an hour later, Echo and Michael finally arrived at the checkpoint. There were two border guards awaiting them.

"This is not a checkpoint for tourists," said one of the border guards.

"We know, we are trying to save time and get to the Preserve this evening. Xi Wang has sent us and I believe he has spoken with someone here."

"Yes, I spoke to Xi. Do you have your payment?"

"Here you go. Xi thanks you for your troubles."

"It's no trouble, ma'am. I hope your research goes well," said the young man as he turned toward his comrade and smiled.

"Thank you, sir. I hope you enjoy your evening," said Echo.

Michael and Echo were now in Mongolia, also known as the land of the eternal blue sky. Echo continued along the Burgastai road for a few minutes and turned her jeep hard left onto the dirt trail leading north toward the Great Gobi B Protected Area. They would make their way to the remote region before midnight. Echo was scheduled to receive a secure file at midnight which would include satellite imagery of Liu's compound, and any intercepted communications coming from Liu himself.

One of the border guards who welcomed Echo and Michael just minutes before excused himself from his post. There were few trucks remaining at the checkpoint and he told his partner he would be back in a few minutes.

"Mr. Liu, you asked me to notify you of any unusual border crossings along the Burgastai road. There was a Chinese woman and an American professor who just crossed the border. They said they were going to the protected reserve to study wolves."

"Thank you, Davaa. You will be rewarded for this information. Which way did they go?"

"They turned north along the only trail leading into the preserve."

"Did they happen to mention how long they will remain there?"

"I do not know. I did not question them."

"Do you believe their paperwork was in order?"

"I do not know that either. My partner accepted a bribe from the Chinese woman. Tourists are not generally allowed to cross here."

"Thank you again, Davaa. Please notify me of any more unusual activity."

"I will. Thank you, Mr. Liu," said the sentry.

Click.

Liu Zhun had prepared himself well. A dozen Mongolian border guards along the Chinese frontier had been put on the payroll for months. It was easier than Liu thought despite his familiar knowledge of bitter tensions between the two countries dating back centuries. He wondered if the events along the border were truly as they appeared or if Chinese intelligence had somehow uncovered information about the plot or his whereabouts. For now, Liu Zhun remained comfortable, but his roving security detail would be increased just in case.

Munsu-dong Diplomatic Compound, Pyongyang, North Korea, June 26, 7:50 PM

Sun Boling finished dinner and continued his dialogue with a contingent of German diplomats inside the Munsu-dong diplomatic compound. There were several other countries represented inside the former East German complex, including Sweden and the United Kingdom.

Boling was relatively new to the Chinese mission in Pyongyang, but he had already grown tired of "dinner table" diplomacy. The constant dialogue between diplomatic representatives bored the career naval officer and his disdain for meaningless gossip and pleasantries were often on full display, much to the dismay of the Ambassador.

Boling had been a career submarine officer for the Chinese Navy. Commissioned as a young officer in 1999, he quickly rose through the ranks of the People's Liberation Army Navy, despite his Uyghur background. He was never an ardent supporter of the Communist party, but played along publicly to further enhance his career. He was an adventurer by heart and the lure of a naval career on the open seas attracted the young idealist.

It wasn't until 2011 that Boling began to seriously question his career choice. An altercation with his commanding officer in the South China Sea had nearly ruined his career. However, the incident left a black mark on his record and any hopes of achieving flag officer rank in the future were dashed. The constant deployment and time away from his family had also taken a toll on the officer whose constant requests for shore duty were denied. Boling's wife successfully petitioned for a divorce and Boling rarely saw his children. It was a chance encounter with Liu Zhun in Hong Kong that changed the man's political ideology and destiny.

Frequent email exchanges between the two men convinced Boling that China's Communist Party had to be dismantled from the inside. According to Liu, the Americans would never engage China militarily, and instead, focus on economic cooperation and interdependence. After years of being wooed, Liu agreed to join the Assassination Corps and help where he could. The unexpected assignment to the Chinese embassy in Pyongyang was more than Liu Zhun could have ever envisioned or hoped for. Sun's career was stalled, his wife and children had left him, and opportunities to institute changes in China did not exist. Boling's background and current assignment had to be exploited, Liu thought to himself.

"I hear you were chosen to be part of a small delegation that will meet President Kim soon," said one of the German diplomats.

"Yes. The invitation was quite unexpected," said Boling.

"You are fortunate. Very few individuals outside North Korea have met him."

"The same holds true for most North Koreans," said one of the other diplomats.

"I have heard the same. I assume I was chosen because of my work with his naval forces. I doubt he will want to speak with me," said Boling.

"I would be curious to find out what your observations are of him, Commander Boling. Would you be willing to share with us?"

"I don't see why not."

"Do you believe President Kim is a crazy man?" asked one of the Germans.

"No. He is a rational man. He does many provocative things, but I've seen nothing to suggest he is insane or unstable. What do you think?" asked Boling.

"Does it matter, Commander Boling? My country believes he is reckless and should put a stop to all the missile tests. It's our sincere desire to continue talks with his representatives, but they are very infrequent."

"I do not believe President Kim will commit suicide. He knows any aggressive actions will be condemned by my country and the United States. He and his family have much to lose. His tough talk is designed for his own people, not the rest of the world," stated Boling.

"Is your country prepared to conduct military operations if things spin out of control?"

"That is not for me to decide. However, I do believe my country will make the right decision when, and if, the time comes. It's the Americans I worry about," said Boling as he smiled a bit.

Several members of the German delegation chuckled as well.

"They can be a bit headstrong, Commander Boling," said one of the diplomats.

"That is correct, sir," stated Boling.

Sun Boling and the German delegation continued to speak for another ten minutes, mostly on trivial issues and world events. Boling promptly excused himself to use the bathroom.

"Gentlemen, thank you for a lovely evening. I am sure we will see each other again soon," said Boling as he departed.

Sun Boling soon exited the fortified compound. His driver, a young Chinese diplomat in her early twenties, quickly drove him home to retire for the evening. A short while later, Boling finally sat down on his couch. It was drab, and the red color had faded to an almost gold like color, clearly worn down by his predecessors over the years.

He began to formulate options for the assassination of President Kim. There would be no chance to smuggle in a firearm, he thought to himself. His best opportunity was to use the Husa knife, a favorite among the assassination corps membership. He had used it recently but the odds of coming close enough to greet the North Korean leader and use it was unlikely based on the schedule of events and his seating assignment. Boling concluded his best chance would be to throw the Husa knife and hope for a strike in the President's throat. If he could get within ten meters, not an unreasonable scenario, his chance for success was good, he thought to himself.

Boling would be near the young President in a few weeks. He wondered how history would judge his sacrifice and those of his fellow brothers and sisters in the assassination corps. Sun Boling soon drifted to sleep while thinking of his young children. He wondered where they were and what they were doing. More importantly, he wondered if they were thinking of him.

Great Gobi B Nature Reserve, Mongolia, June 26, 9:51 PM

Echo and Michael reached their destination for the evening. Tonight, they would rest inside the protected area of the Great Gobi B nature preserve. Echo would report to her superiors and await further guidance as Michael wondered when they would reach Liu's compound. The two had quickly erected a two-person tent and sat around a small fire while consuming Chinese military rations consisting of pork and mushroom Chow Mein. Michael was rather surprised at how tasty the meal was given it was a standard ration for Chinese soldiers. The meal didn't compare to an American Meal-Ready-to-Eat, but it came close enough.

"Echo, how much longer till we get to Liu?"

"We are very close now, Michael. We will stay here. If Liu remains at his current location, we will make our move tomorrow evening."

"What are we waiting for? If he's close, why can't we just get to him tonight?"

"My superiors in Beijing want to wait until tomorrow to verify Liu is still there. We have a satellite that will confirm his location."

"Good. How many men are protecting him?"

"We estimate around ten based on imagery and the number of vehicles at the location. You and I will arrive tomorrow evening and conduct a reconnaissance. There is a micro-drone in the vehicle."

"When will I be given operational control, Echo?"

"Once we arrive on-site. I have several types of weapons in the vehicle. They include sniper rifles, shotguns, and handguns. I will deploy the drone once we are near the facility."

"Okay, I'd like to see the weapons tonight and become familiar with them. Will that be a problem?"

"Not at all, Michael. May I speak to you about a sensitive subject?" asked Echo.

"Do I have a choice, Echo?" asked Michael as he smiled.

"There are many in China who favor closer ties with the United States. I am one of them and so are many of my colleagues within the Ministry of State Security. On the other hand, there are those who view your country as a threat and seek to confront America in the future. We are looking for…"

Then suddenly, shots were overheard coming from a nearby hill as several bullets struck the soft desert sand near the two operatives. Echo and Michael immediately rolled onto the ground and moved quickly behind their jeep. Michael spotted a vehicle in the distance traveling at a high rate of speed toward their position.

Echo quickly handed Michael a QSZ-92 semi-automatic pistol. It was already loaded with a twenty-round box magazine attached.

"I hope we have a hell of a lot more firepower than this, Echo," said Michael.

Echo opened the rear cab and quickly pulled down two rifle cases. The first case held a QBZ-97 assault rifle. The variant to the QBZ-95, the type 97, was a 5.56 mm rifle capable of firing almost eight hundred rounds per minute. Customers outside China included Cambodian special forces.

"Will this do?" asked Echo sarcastically as she handed Michael the rifle and three detachable thirty round box magazines.

"Much better, Echo. The shots were fired from the hill about two hundred meters away."

"I know, Michael. That's why I have this. Concentrate

on the approaching vehicle. I will take out the snipers on the hill."

Echo opened the second case and removed a QBU-88 sniper rifle used extensively by PLA infantry units and elite Chinese police forces. It included a tactical scope capable of day or night target acquisition and a folding bipod. Echo carefully positioned her body under the jeep and began scanning for movement. Michael moved alongside the jeep and waited patiently for the vehicle to get closer. It now appeared approximately three hundred meters away. Michael knew the maximum effective range of the QBZ-97 was approximately four hundred meters. Nevertheless, he waited and preferred to engage the vehicle at around one hundred meters.

Two more rounds hit the jeep as Echo was finally able to acquire the first shooter. She took a deep breath and carefully exhaled while gently squeezing the trigger. The first shooter would die quickly after the round entered his neck. Echo was certain that she saw movement along the eastern base of the hill and focused her attention there.

A few seconds later, the passenger in the approaching SUV leaned out the window and began spraying a volley of bullets toward Michael and Echo. Several rounds hit the front hood and pierced the window as Michael prepared to return fire. Michael and Echo found themselves in a firefight.

Michael remained concealed behind the vehicle and opened fire when the approaching SUV was approximately one hundred meters away. He squeezed off several rounds and aimed at the front tires. Several of the rounds hit their intended target and the vehicle began to slow. The driver appeared to lose control momentarily but slammed on the brakes to avoid a possible tip over due to the bumpy terrain. Michael continued to fire short bursts toward the vehicle and finally hit the driver as the SUV came to a stop. The passenger and one man in the back opened their doors and quickly ran behind the vehicle searching for cover. Michael stopped firing and took a few seconds to replace his magazine.

"Echo, have you taken out the snipers?" shouted Michael as several rounds once again hit the front of their vehicle.

"One target is down. There is a second shooter."

"I need the second shooter taken out, Echo. We are pinned down."

Echo did not respond as she focused on acquiring the second shooter. Then the opportunity struck. Echo was scanning the eastern edge of the hill where she finally spotted movement approximately twenty meters up from the base of the hill. The shooter was carefully moving his head up to scan Echo's position. Echo once again took a deep breath and slowly squeezed the trigger. The single shot entered the man's forehead and he fell instantly. Michael and Echo's threat from the nearby hill was eliminated.

"Michael, the targets on the hill have been eliminated. What is the situation?"

"There are two men behind the SUV. The driver is dead."

"Enough of this," shouted Echo.

Echo carefully moved toward the back of the jeep and stood up. She reached into the cab and pulled out another case. The case included a PF-89 next-generation light anti-tank weapon. The portable rocket launcher weighed at only twelve pounds and included an 80-mm high explosive warhead. Its maximum effective range was only two hundred meters, but the remaining threat was well inside that. Echo had used the lightweight weapon several times throughout her career and appreciated the negligible recoil the PF-89 had. A few moments later, Echo stood up and took aim at the SUV. The men behind the SUV never had a chance.

"You come prepared, Echo," said Michael.

"A woman always does. We need to relocate far away from here. Let's move north."

"I'd like to see if our friends on the hill have a vehicle located nearby," said Michael.

Echo agreed and began to clean up the site.

Michael walked briskly across the forgiving terrain and reached the hill in less than ten minutes. He kept his pistol firmly gripped in his hand as he walked around the eastern base of the hill. What he hoped for was now in plain sight just fifty meters away. An SUV used to transport the two snipers remained hidden behind the hill. Michael approached the driver door and noticed the keys were still inserted in the ignition. He would join Echo in just a few minutes.

Echo and Michael quickly transferred their equipment from their shot-up jeep to the newly acquired SUV. Echo would drive north as she indicated earlier and the two would have little trouble blending into the surrounding Mongolian landscape in the morning.

"How about we finish that conversation we started earlier, Echo?" asked Michael.

"In the morning, Michael. You will have to wait until then."

The two operatives spent the next hour traversing along the eastern edge of the Great Gobi preserve. Echo made a phone call and provided Beijing an update on the operation. The trail was bumpy, but the bright stars above provided them with some temporary solace and peace. Michael would stare into the night sky and wonder how John was faring. He did not have a choice helping the Chinese with their domestic problem. John was another matter entirely and he would do what he could to get the man back home to his sons. Guozhi had better be a man of his word, he thought to himself.

Qincheng Prison, Changping District, Beijing, China, June 27, 855 AM

John Dearlove arrived. He was escorted by three military soldiers from the PLA, and a member of the Ministry of State Security. He had been flown to Beijing the night before and remained at a State Security facility for one last round of questioning. His captors were unsuccessful in acquiring any information regarding his network of British spies inside the mainland. The continued interrogation was no longer necessary, and he would be imprisoned until a decision about his fate was reached. Dearlove's hopes of being released were dashed.

The career SIS operative was driven to the remote prison, first built in 1958 in the eastern foothills of Yanshan. The prison famously included inmates such as Yuan Geng, Bao Tong, and participants from the 1989 Tiananmen Square protests. Other inmates included former Communist leaders convicted of corruption and Tibetan nonconformists. Dearlove heard rumors that spies were housed here and guessed he would have many opportunities to get to know them.

"Stand here, and wait for my instructions," said the officer.

"What is your name?" asked a prison guard a few minutes later.

"John Dearlove," said the operative in Mandarin Chinese as his captor appeared impressed.

"You are a spy for the United Kingdom?" asked the guard.

"I come from England," snapped Dearlove.

"Do not bother. He has already been questioned," said the Ministry of State official.

Dearlove would soon be humiliated. He was forced to

strip down naked for a cavity search. It was unnecessary thought the security guard, but he had formal procedures to follow despite the man's former incarceration with the Ministry of State Security. A short while later he was given sheets, one pillow, a toothbrush, toothpaste and one bar of soap. A lifetime of service in MI6 had been rewarded with a prison uniform and basic toiletries inside a maximum-security prison on mainland China. John wondered momentarily if it was all worth it.

John soon found himself in a tiny cell measuring eight feet in length by five feet in width. The brown concrete walls were filled with paint chips and cracks. He was isolated, cut off from his chain of command, and completely unaware of his new surroundings. John Dearlove was in hell.

The British SIS officer sat in his new bed. He wondered how his boys were doing. He wondered if he would ever see them again. Not likely, he thought to himself. The last few weeks were the worst in his professional career. His prodigy, Brian Wu, had betrayed him in Hong Kong and nearly compromised MI6's network there. He had to kill one of his most trusted assets in Urumqi after she joined the assassination corps and almost killed Michael. Michael had been captured and the joint operation with CIA had failed. A lifetime of service with MI6 seemed to be over. It was not how John imagined it would be.

Alag Khairkhan Nature Preserve, Mongolia, June 27, 9:25 AM

Michael and Echo finished breakfast and began to pack up their items from the makeshift campsite they set up the night before. They were near the western base of the Alag Khairkhan nature preserve, just outside the Great Gobi B from the night before. The Mongolian government designated the landscape as a preserve in 1996. The site was approximately three hundred and sixty-four square kilometers and home to rare endemic plants and snow leopards. The elusive and endangered snow leopard was a beautiful creature, whose base color varied from a yellow tan and smoke gray with white underparts. Rosettes, mostly black round markings, were visible on the head and legs.

Michael had been awake for hours and eager to find Liu. He was a bit restless and the chip implanted in his neck remained firmly on his mind. The commander of the assassination corps had lost five men the night before and would have only a handful of remaining men, assuming his intelligence was accurate. Michael was relieved after observing how Echo maintained her composure the night before. Her acquisition skills and ability to engage targets using multiple weapon systems were impressive, he thought to himself.

"Echo, you promised last night we would resume our conversation. Now is an appropriate time," said Michael as he smiled.

"Of course. As I said last night, there are many of us who prefer a more open dialogue with your country. We are seeking a back channel. We want the ability to share information to prevent miscalculations on both sides. We want to improve relations with America, rather than remain divisive."

"What the hell makes you think I'm the right guy for this, Echo? And what makes you think I want to?"

"I don't. That's why I am asking."

"I'm a core collector, Echo. I collect information and sometimes I am required to kill people. I am not a politician and not looking to become one. I leave political matters to others."

"We are simply looking for someone to reach out to in the event our governments come to a serious misunderstanding. We are looking for reasonable individuals to contact during tense times. Consider this possibility as insurance for both our countries."

"Do you understand that I am in no position to advise policy makers? I work in the field. I'm not a bureaucrat or analyst."

"I understand. But someday you may be in such a position. If not, you may be able to offer information that clarifies an issue so there are no mistakes. I am not asking you to divulge sensitive information to me. I just want us to be able to prevent a misunderstanding. As you know, many members of your country do not trust us."

"Frankly, I don't trust you either. But I do understand what you're looking for, Echo. How many others like you share your sentiment?"

"Many. There are still a considerable number of high-ranking party officials that seek to confront the United States in the future. Some of us want to see a different approach."

"Which is?"

"We want to prevent a military conflict or strategic miscalculation."

"Echo, just how the hell do you think people like us are going to do that?"

"By ensuring our governments understand what our motives truly are when tensions rise. And they will, Michael."

"This is way above my pay grade, Echo. But I do understand what you're trying to do. Why don't we revisit this on our way back to Hami?"

"Do you want to know why we are so concerned about Liu's order in Pyongyang?"

"You have my attention," said Michael.

"The target is President Kim. That is who Liu's assassin is targeting."

"Well, that certainly changes things, Echo. There are many in my government who want to see him dead."

"If Liu is successful, we believe there will be millions of North Koreans fleeing into China. That is not an acceptable outcome."

"That sounds like your problem, Echo, not ours."

"I have been instructed by my chain of command to let you go immediately after we identify Liu's assassin. You will be free to go, Michael."

"What about John?"

"John has been moved to a prison in Beijing. We have convinced our superiors to keep him alive. He has been spying in our country for a long time and we cannot just let him go. He may be released in the future if you are willing to cooperate."

Michael leaned back and thought for a moment.

"Damn, Echo. How much more are you going to lay on me? I'm a damn collector. You say you're going to let me go? When exactly?"

"When we are satisfied that Liu has identified the asset. You may even call your agency to coordinate for an extraction inside Mongolia. You will not have to return to China."

"What about Guozhi?"

"Guozhi has already returned to his full-time military duties."

"I have to be honest, Echo. I'm not sure I want to leave John behind."

"He has done much damage to my country, Michael. You have my assurance there are some of us who will work hard to get him released in the future. You have my word."

"Your word? I don't know you well enough for that to mean anything, Echo."

Echo stood up and walked to the jeep. She removed a briefcase and carefully unlocked it.

"This is the syringe that I will use to remove the device, Michael."

"You mean now, Echo?"

"I want to earn your trust."

"How do you know I won't kill you and leave?"

"I will have access to John and so will many in my organization who think like I do. If he is not eventually released, we will arrange for his transfer to another facility where he will find a way to escape. If something happens to me then John will rot for the rest of his life or even be executed."

"You would do that for an MI6 operative who spied in your country for decades? I doubt that, Echo."

"What do your instincts say, Michael?"

"Trust is earned, Echo. I might feel differently if the chip was removed."

"The chip will remain inside your neck until you return home. However, this device will render the chip inactive. I will shut it off permanently."

"Do it," said Michael.

Echo placed the metallic syringe over the incision area. A few seconds later, an electromagnetic pulse sent a short burst of radiation toward the chip. The chip's software included instructions to deactivate itself if any radiation was detected. Michael felt nothing and the low level of radiation required to deactivate the chip was not enough to cause any damage to Michael's body.

"There, you are a free man, Michael. Have I earned your trust?"

"For now, Echo. For now. When will we arrive at Liu's hideout?"

"This evening, Michael. He is only fifteen kilometers from here. We will drive to the southern end of Bugat and move alongside the hills there."

"Okay, Echo. I'm still here. Let's do it."

Echo and Michael would spend the morning studying the geography and topography surrounding Liu's hideout. The high-quality satellite images sent to Echo's cell phone would provide the operatives an opportunity to carefully plan their approach and vantage points. The resolution was equivalent to a NIIRS rating of eight, meaning the satellite could acquire images such as windshield wipers on a car. Michael had never seen Chinese satellite imagery before and was impressed.

The satellite used to support Echo's mission in Mongolia was called a Yaogan 14. Its optical and radar reconnaissance imagery had been operational since 2011, when the Chinese used a Long March 4B rocket to hurl the spy satellite into low earth orbit approximately three hundred kilometers above the earth.

Michael became more impressed with Echo as the morning wore on. She was a deliberate planner and her capabilities as a sniper were on clear display the night before. Her selection of vantage points near Liu's compound were good, Michael thought to himself. He had no objections to her recommendations as Michael would have full operational control from this point on.

"Echo, how do you feel about allowing me to contact my agency for additional support?" asked Michael.

"That will not happen, Michael."

"Why the hell not? Is this a joint operation or am I just along for the ride?"

"What assets do you need that we do not have?"

"I'd like more eyes on the target as we make our approach to the compound."

"Such as?" asked Echo.

"I might be able to get real-time satellite imagery support. The video feeds could be sent to us directly or communicated via a cell phone."

"Michael, I have several mini-drones that will be used to support your final approach to Liu's location. We will be communicating on secure radios. Will that be sufficient?"

"How many drones do you have?"

"Three. I can control up to two at a time. The third is a backup."

"How long can they be operational?"

"The battery life is approximately twenty-five minutes," said Echo.

Michael looked at the map again. Echo's vantage point and location would be approximately four hundred meters from Liu's remote compound. The terrain did not appear too difficult and he believed he could get to Liu within ten minutes, assuming there was no resistance during his final approach. Michael concluded the drones would suffice.

"Okay, Echo. I'm comfortable with that."

"Good, are we ready to go?" asked Echo.

"One more thing, Echo."

"Yes, Michael?"

"When this is over, I want to see John."

"I cannot promise that, Michael. It may result in too many questions."

"I see John when this is over, or Liu's man in Pyongyang will remain operational."

"I will have to check with my superiors, Michael. Can I contact them on the way to Bugat?"

"Yes. Now let's get this son of a bitch and go home."

Michael and Echo began their final approach to Bugat. Michael was determined to see John one more time and assure his new friend that help was on the way.

The White House, Washington, D.C., June 27, 3:11 PM

Herb McMullen remained at his desk. The President was scheduled to visit South America in a few weeks. President Trump would visit Brazil, Chile, and Peru to improve sagging relations between the countries. The unrest and political turmoil in Venezuela would be at the top of his agenda, including anti-terrorism efforts after a recent Islamic State attack in Lima, Peru. McMullen would add intelligence sharing efforts to the agenda and brief the President on potential sales of military aircraft capable of signals intercept, like the MC-12W.

The MC-12W, first introduced by the United States Air Force in 2009, was a twin-engine turboprop aircraft, powered by Pratt and Whitney engines. Its primary mission was to provide intelligence, surveillance, and reconnaissance support to ground forces. The MC-12W was designed to support irregular warfare missions including counter-insurgency, foreign internal defense, and building partnerships. The purchase of the seventeen-million-dollar aircraft was floated months ago by the Peruvian Ambassador. McMullen thought the asset could be of value while fighting Islamic State militants popping up throughout the continent.

Then the national security advisor's phone rang.

"Herb, it's Mark. The damn North Koreans just fired another missile. Initial data suggests it was an intermediate range ballistic missile."

Admiral Mark Forsyth was the Commander of Pacific Command and had instructions to call the White House immediately upon detecting any North Korean missile launches.

"Dammit, the President is going to be furious. Where is it going?"

"On an eastern trajectory. It looks like it's going to fly right over Japan."

"President Kim is testing my patience. If he keeps doing this, the President may feel compelled to strike."

"I understand, Herb. There are no good outcomes here."

"Okay, Mark. Thanks for the update. I'll brief the President right away."

"Good luck, Herb. I know there's a lot of pressure to do something. Keep the President focused on economic and diplomatic options."

"I will, Mark."

Click.

President Trump had just returned to the oval office. An afternoon meeting with the Congressional Black Caucus was productive for both sides and the President appeared visibly happy.

"Mr. President, I have news out of North Korea."

"Come on in, Herb. It figures after a good meeting with the CBC. What is rocket man up to now?"

"The North Koreans just launched another missile. It's an intermediate range ballistic missile and its trajectory indicates it will fly over Japan."

"When did the launch occur, Herb?"

"Just a few minutes ago. Mark called me."

"Any idea on where it's headed?"

"No, sir. It's too early. I'm sure the Japanese are tracking it as well."

"Okay, Herb. I got it. Can you let the Chief of Staff know? We'll need to get a statement ready for the press."

"Will do, Mr. President. Are we still on for our meeting with the VP and your trip to South America next month?"

"We are. I'd like to get Olie up here in the next couple of days. Let's see what he thinks of the launch. I'll see you at 4:30."

"Yes, sir."

Herb McMullen returned to his office. The walls were adorned with pictures indicating a lifelong service to his country. His most prized possession, a custom Guidon he received from his soldiers after his first company command, often reminded him of the challenges and privilege associated with leading America's finest warriors in peace and war. The President's desire to have Oliver Tanner brief on North Korea's latest missile launch would challenge his values and integrity. He knew Oliver was probably right and that North Korea was probably six months away from being able to deliver a nuclear warhead onto American soil. However, another year of private negotiations with North Korean representatives might lead to an acceptable diplomatic resolution that could appease the President. Herb McMullen needed time and called a trusted associate at the Pentagon.

"Good afternoon, Lisa. It's General McMullen."

"Hey, sir. How are you today?"

"Managing. The North Koreans just fired another missile. This one is projected to fly over Japan."

"I heard. I won't have the telemetry data for several hours."

"I know, but I need you to prepare a briefing for the President."

"Sir?"

"Are you still convinced the North Koreans won't have re-entry capability for another year?"

"Not as confident as I was a few months ago, but a year is not unreasonable."

"Oliver is going to brief the President in a few days. I want you there. I want you to stress the North Koreans are another year away."

"Sir, I'm not sure I believe that anymore. The test in March challenged our numbers."

"Lisa, I want you to make the case for a year. We are secretly negotiating with the North Koreans and need a year. We won't get to any resolution within six months. You know that. I am worried the President will make a hasty decision."

"You mean a preemptive strike, sir? I understand what you're asking for but I'm not sure I believe it."

"If you agree to make the case for a year, I can assure promotion to one star. You can have whatever assignment you want when your tour is over. I'm not asking you to lie, Lisa. Rather, make the case for a year based on the data. Do you believe Oliver Tanner is right?"

"He is the best, sir. I'm not convinced its six months or one year. It's somewhere in between."

"Can I count on you to push the year narrative?"

There was a pause. Lisa Bouquet was experiencing a moral dilemma.

"Lisa?" asked Herb.

"I can push the one-year narrative, sir. I'm not convinced Olie is right. When will I need to brief the President?"

"In a few days. My executive assistant will contact you. You will be given ten minutes. Thank you, Lisa. I will remember this."

Click.

Herb McMullen sat back in his chair. He stared at his unit Guidon and wondered if what he was doing was ethical. He wondered what his former Marines would think of his decision to push the narrative and exert pressure on the ambitious Captain. He quickly reminded himself it was for the good of the nation. If a year of negotiation led to a peaceful resolution on the Korean peninsula, a minor ethical infraction would be worth it. At least that was what the career military officer and national security advisor to the President would say to himself over the coming days.

Bugat, Mongolia, June 27, 9:25 PM

"It's time, Michael. Are you ready?" asked Echo.

"I am. Let's get to it."

Echo reached into the large black case and pulled out two CH-901 mini-drones. Each portable killer drone, also known as a "kamikaze," weighed twenty pounds and included one explosive warhead. The tactical drone, fielded by Chinese military forces since 2016, was like the "switchblade" drone used by American special operators. The warhead on a "kamikaze" could take out targets including personnel and light vehicles. Tonight, it would cover Michael's approach to Liu's compound. Echo would acquire targets and relay them to Michael in real time. The two warheads would be used if Michael was unable to engage Liu's security forces.

Michael placed the electronic earpiece into his right ear. The wireless device would be linked with Echo's radio and allowed her to relay observations of Liu's compound. She would identify targets and engage them directly if Michael was unable to. Michael began walking toward Liu's compound.

"Test, test, test," whispered Echo.

Michael raised his right hand and gave Echo a thumbs up. His device was working perfectly. Time to find Liu and get him to talk, thought Michael to himself.

Michael would approach Liu's compound from the southeast. There was a ravine near the compound that would allow him to approach without detection. A few minutes later, Michael stopped along the ravine and peered toward the compound. He was approximately sixty meters away.

"Movement, along the eastern side of the building. Engaging target now," said Echo.

Michael waited patiently and turned his attention toward

the northeastern side of the building. He peered through the binoculars but saw nothing. The binocular, used by Chinese special forces and members of the Ministry of State Security, was a generation 3 model with a 50mm germanium lens.

Echo took a deep breath and placed the crosshairs on the chest of the roving guard. She gently exhaled and squeezed the trigger. The round hit the man and he fell onto the ground.

"Target is down. I see nothing else, Michael. You may move when ready."

Michael looked through his binocular and scanned the building. He saw no signs of activity and decided to carefully ascend the ravine. He was now in open terrain and vulnerable to detection. He sprinted toward the building and found himself along the southern wall.

"I see nothing, Michael. Moving the drones to the northern side of the building. Stay put."

Michael kneeled to the ground and waited as he placed the binocular on the ground. It was no longer needed.

"Two men are positioned along the northern wall, Michael. I cannot engage."

Michael stood up and walked along the southern wall of the building. He peered around the corner with his weapon drawn. Nothing. The western wall was clear as he carefully moved forward. A few moments later, Michael reached the corner.

"The two men are still there, Michael. You may engage immediately."

Michael spun around the corner and fired two rounds at each of the astonished guards. Both men fell to the ground instantly as Michael moved along the front side of the building. He reached the front door and carefully turned the knob. It was unlocked.

"Michael, I'm picking up one individual in the first

room. There is a second individual laying down in the rear room."

The drones were doing their job, thought Michael. The CH-901 hunter drone was infrared capable and allowed thermal images to be displayed on Echo's controller in real time. Chinese technology was clearly as good as Echo touted it would be. Chinese technology, much of it stolen from the United States, was saving his life. How ironic, Michael thought to himself.

Michael had to be careful. If he stormed into the building too quickly, he might kill Liu. The mission would be over and John's chances to return home were dashed. If Michael entered too cautiously, Liu or his last remaining guard could kill him. He did not know which one of the two men inside was Liu as he saw no lights emanating from inside the building.

The career intelligence officer decided to take an unorthodox approach. He simply pushed open the door and moved alongside the exterior wall. He figured if one of the men exited it would be Liu's guard.

"Michael, one of the men is approaching the front door. He appears to be holding an assault rifle."

Michael waited.

"Bai? What is it?" asked the man inside.

Silence.

"Bai. What the hell is going on? Get back to your post."

Silence.

"Michael, he is one meter from the front door," said Echo as her drones had a clear view of the interior of the building.

"Bai. What is going on?" asked the man as his finger remained on the trigger.

Silence.

The man was nearly at the front door as Michael could see the sights at the end of the rifle. The man stopped moving.

"Bai. What is going on outside? Answer me," shouted the man.

Silence.

The stranger took another step and Michael Brennan struck. He grabbed the end of the rifle and pulled the man outside. The man began firing aimlessly into the air and the surrounding terrain as his body twisted violently. Michael quickly released his right hand from the rifle and reached for his pistol. The stranger was not Liu Zhun and Michael fired three shots into the man's stomach. It was over before it started. A few seconds later the man fell to the ground screaming in agony. Michael was merciful and fired a single shot into the man's forehead.

"Liu is in the back. He appears to be crouched behind the door and holding a weapon."

Michael slowly stepped into the hideout. It was dark but he could see the hallway leading to the rear office.

"Liu Zhun. My name is Michael and I am with the CIA. You are surrounded. Give yourself up. I just want to talk with you."

"What the hell does CIA want with me?"

"We know about your man in Pyongyang. We want to assist."

"I have no idea what you are speaking of."

"You do, Liu. I am here to help. We know the Chinese are looking for you. They have Guozhi."

Silence.

"Michael, there are two vehicles approaching your location. They appear to be Mongolian military," said Echo.

Echo observed the vehicles approaching from the west

along a narrow trail originating from the small town. The mini-drones were now operating at approximately one hundred meters above the compound giving Echo an unobstructed view of the surrounding area. The contingency they rehearsed earlier was, unfortunately, coming to fruition.

"We know about the assassination corps, Liu. We want the target in North Korea eliminated as much as you do. Come out," said Michael.

Silence.

Michael turned his attention to the front entrance of the building. He approached the front door and quickly peered around the corner to get a look. Michael saw the vehicles moving at a high rate of speed and were about two hundred meters away.

"Michael, wave your right hand if you want me to engage the vehicles. I am certain they are on Liu's payroll," said Echo.

Michael waved his right arm as Echo watched the thermal image in real time on her console. The "kamikaze" drones would now do the job that Michael and Echo had planned for.

Echo pushed one of the buttons on the console and armed the first drone. It was a fire and forget warhead that allowed the operator to quickly acquire and engage their target. The lead vehicle never had a chance as the warhead slammed into the hood of the jeep. It was immediately disabled and ablaze within seconds.

The driver of the second vehicle slammed onto his brakes. There was nowhere to go as the narrow trail was surrounded by boulders. Echo took aim and armed the second drone. A few moments later, the second vehicle was ablaze and the threat to Michael was eliminated.

"Targets destroyed, Michael. I see no further activity."

"Liu, did you hear the explosions? The Chinese are here. We don't have much time. We want to support your efforts in Pyongyang," said Michael.

Silence.

"He's still behind the door, Michael. He's just sitting there," said Echo.

Michael knew Liu was assessing the situation. He was scared, his security detail was eliminated, and he had few options. Michael remained patient.

"How do I know you won't kill me?" shouted Liu a few moments later.

"You don't, but you do need to trust me, Liu. Come out. We can help."

"Who is with you?" asked Liu.

"Just me, Liu. We have a Chinese asset nearby. She will assist us."

"How will she assist us? How can I trust her?"

"She works for CIA. You can trust her."

"I am coming out."

Liu Zhun exited the room and slowly walked toward Michael. The commander of the assassination corps lowered his weapon and presented himself. It would be the worst mistake of his life.

Uyench, Khovd Province, western Mongolia, June 28, 9:50 AM

Michael Brennan awoke. The long journey from Bugat to Uyench was necessary after Echo's decision to engage Mongolian troops presumably loyal to Liu Zhun. A secure facility to house Liu and get him to talk was located near Uyench. The Enterprises Division, an agency within the Ministry of State Security, had secured the building as part of its overseas activities. The building in Uyench had been leased by the intelligence organization since 2016 and used sparingly by Chinese spies operating in Mongolia.

The six-hour drive was arduous, but allowed Michael to establish rapport with Liu before his interrogation. The commander of the assignation corps had already begun to trust Michael and assumed he was telling the truth. Liu was still bewildered how his operation was uncovered and suspected Guozhi got sloppy. Either way, he was confident that Michael's claims were genuine.

"Good morning, Liu," said Michael.

"Good morning, Michael."

"My agency is willing to relocate you immediately. But first, we need to know who your operative in Pyongyang is."

"I am not ready to give you that information. I will do so only after I am transported to a safe area."

"Where would you like to go?" asked Michael.

"Brussels. And I want a pension."

"Done. Now who is your operative and how can we assist him or her?"

"Him. I will share that information once I am safely in Brussels."

"Your demands are unreasonable, Liu. My agency will not move you unless we are sure your operative exists. How can we support him if we do not know who he is?"

"He is weeks away from executing his plan. You don't need to know who he is right now."

"We do. We want to begin our operation immediately. We want to contact him and find out what he needs. He must need some support."

"He needs nothing, Michael. I am afraid you will only put him at risk."

"Then what's the difference if you tell us now or later?"

"I'm not ready to share that information, Michael. You have not yet earned my complete trust."

"Neither have you, Liu. You don't think we're going to let you just leave and hope you tell us who the asset is, do you?"

"I am hoping you do."

"That's not the way this works. Echo and I saved your life last night. How long before Chinese intelligence suspects we are here?"

"How do I know you are not working with the Chinese? Echo could be with the Ministry of State Security. How am I supposed to know if you are telling me the truth?"

"Liu, I am a patient man. Echo is not with Chinese intelligence. I will not say it again," said Michael as he leaned toward the commander.

"I could be in Brussels this evening. I promise I will reveal the operative at that time. Until then, I will not give you his name."

Michael stood up and walked deliberately toward Liu.

"Liu, we want to see the President killed as much as you do. But for me to let you go, I've got to have a name. It's the only way this works. If not, I have orders to turn you over to the Chinese."

"And how will you do that?" scoffed Liu.

"By simply making a phone call. My boss in Langley calls his counterpart in Beijing, and you're in a Chinese prison awaiting execution. That's how I will do that."

"I would rather die than give up that information."

"I don't think so, Liu. If you were prepared to die, you would not have left that room in Bugat. You want to live. I can make sure you do. Or not, it doesn't matter to me," said Michael coldly.

Liu Zhun knew Michael was right. He did want to live, and his imprisonment left few options. He tried to stall.

"Can I provide you the information once we are airborne?" asked Liu.

"No."

"How do I know you won't kill me once I give you the operative's name?"

"You don't. You must trust me. Enough with these questions. Who is the operative and how can we reach him?"

"There is a Chinese saying that dates back thousands of years, Michael. As a man sows, so shall he reap."

"I have already provided an act of kindness, Liu. You are alive."

"My operative is Sun Boling. He is a naval officer on the ambassador's staff."

"How have you been communicating with him?" asked Michael.

"Shall I call him?"

"Yes, but use another name when Echo comes in. Do you understand?"

"Why?" asked Liu.

"You have to trust me. Use another name. Am I clear?"

Michael stood up and opened the door.

"Echo, come in. We are ready."

Michael returned to the table where Echo would join

them.

"Do it now, Zhun. Use Echo's cell."

Liu Zhun dialed Boling's number.

"Zhun, I thought we were no longer communicating?"

"Our operations have been compromised. However, the Americans have agreed to assist you."

"Huh? What has happened, Zhun? How could they do that?"

"I do not know. I had no choice. It appears Guozhi was caught and gave us up. One of their operatives would like to speak with you."

Echo reached for the phone.

"Hello. My name is Echo. We have an asset inside Nampo. He will provide whatever support you need to accomplish your mission."

"What mission is that? I want to speak with Zhun now."

"He wants to speak with you," said Echo as she turned toward Liu. She appeared confused and wondered why Liu had not provided his name.

"Zhun, what the hell is going on? How can I proceed if our operation has been compromised?"

"All I know is that Guozhi has spoken. We are not certain if all our operations have been compromised. We must remain hopeful the corps will achieve success. We have multiple operations planned. I understand your concern. The Americans were alerted and have agreed to help us. We must trust them. We have no choice."

"I must have assurances that my sacrifice will mean something, Zhun. How can you expect me to go on? Why don't we wait and look for opportunities in the future?"

"We must proceed as planned. Let the Americans help you. Someone will contact you shortly."

Click.

"I'm not sure you have the man's confidence, Zhun."

"He will do his job, Michael."

"No, Zhun. He will not."

Michael immediately reached for his pistol and pointed it squarely at Liu.

"You should not have placed your trust in me, Liu. Your operative tried to kill me in Urumqi and Wu betrayed John. I have all the information I need."

"There are others. I'm just one of many, Michael. My death does not matter," said Liu.

"I don't care."

Michael fired four rounds in Liu Zhun's chest. The commander of the assassination corps was dead.

"What the hell did you just do, Michael?" shouted Echo.

"What needed to be done. I have the operative's name. I will share that name with you after I see John."

"I told you John would be taken care of. His safety is now in jeopardy."

"Echo, I am simply buying insurance here. I do trust you. It's your chain of command and some of my people in Washington that I don't trust."

"How can I explain this to my people, Michael. We agreed you would identify the assassin and let us take care of him."

"You will, Echo. I just want to make sure I see John again. I believe your government will release John if I agree to give up Liu's man in Pyongyang. You said it yourself, Beijing cannot risk millions of refugees crossing the border. John's transgressions will be overlooked."

"I don't know, Michael. This just became complex."

"Quite the opposite, Echo. We want our governments working closer. This allows us to do that with stipulations. John gets released and Beijing sees continued stability in the north."

"That is not what we agreed to," said Echo.

"I lied, Echo. It's what we do."

Echo stared into Michael's eyes. The American spy was a good man and did what any operative would have done for his partner. She knew John could probably be released if Beijing was certain his Intel was good. After all, releasing the spy would give Beijing some much needed propaganda and good will with the west, while retaining its strategic buffer with South Korea and its American ally. Echo was now even more convinced that Michael would be a strong ally in the future. Her demeanor changed instantly.

"I did not think you would kill him so quickly, Michael. Might it not have been better to confirm who the assassin is?"

"You will have your man, Echo. The operation is over. I want to see John. Let me call Langley and then you can call your handlers in Beijing. I promise you will have your man soon."

Michael dialed Doug's cell phone.

"Michael, good to hear from you. Where the hell are you?" asked Doug enthusiastically.

"I'm in Uyench, Mongolia. We've identified Liu's man in Pyongyang. The target is President Kim."

"What? Liu was going after Kim? Do the Chinese know?"

"Yep. One of their operatives was with me."

"Christ. What the hell are the Chinese going to do?"

"I don't know, and I don't care, Doug. John has been moved to the Qincheng prison in Beijing. I will give the Chinese the assassin's name soon."

"Who is it?" asked Doug.

"In due time, Doug. My mission ended long ago with

the missile launch. My job now is to get John out."

"Michael, I'm going to have to report this to the Director. I can't promise what her response is going to be. She will likely want to see Kim killed."

"Not my problem, Doug. And what if we kill Kim? Then what? How do we know someone worse won't come to power? I don't buy the bullshit in D.C. about him being crazy. He's rational. And I doubt he will pick a fight with us."

"You know that doesn't matter, Michael. If the Director or the NSC wants him dead, they'll want you to keep the Intel from the Chinese."

"That's not going to happen, Doug. I gave my word I would assist them. John's life depends on it. I'm not going to see him rot in jail."

"God dammit, Michael. You know how to put me in a fucking box. You know I've got to give the Director an update. I can't promise what happens next."

"I know, Doug. I am going to Beijing. I will provide an update from there. Do what you have to do."

Click.

"Your boss doesn't sound happy, Michael," said Echo.

"He'll deal with it. He knows I'm right."

"You are, Michael. I wish you would trust me, but I understand your concern with my government."

"Will you have trouble convincing Beijing to let John go?" asked Michael.

"Probably. But I can be persuasive," said Echo with a smile.

Echo and Michael soon began their journey south toward the Chinese border. A flight later in the evening would take them to Beijing where the two would seek John's release and prevent a catastrophe along the Korean peninsula.

CIA HQ, Langley, Virginia, June 28, 10:15 AM

Doug Weatherbee reached for his phone. The long-time clandestine officer was relieved. Michael was safe and apparently working with the Chinese to get MI6's agent released. The news regarding President Kim was troubling. He had an obligation and duty to report to the Director despite the operation being officially over after Michael's Intel on the missile launch. A close friend of the President, she was likely to support the leader's assassination.

"Nikki, it's Doug. Can you go secure?"

"Yes, is everything okay, Doug? I'm about to give a speech."

"One of our operatives has determined who the target is in Pyongyang. You're not going to like it."

"Who is it?"

"President Kim."

"Are you kidding me? Jesus Christ. How reliable is the Intel?"

"We got it from the commander of the assassination corps. The Intel is good."

"Who else knows?"

"My operative says he was with a Chinese agent."

"What do they intend to do with the Intel?"

"Not sure, Nikki. You know they won't allow Kim's assassination. They do not know the assassin's name."

"This is unbelievable. We've never been this close. I'll have to notify the President immediately. Tell your operative he will not share the Intel with the Chinese."

"Yeah, that's a problem. He's agreed to provide the name once he releases the MI6 operative he was captured with."

"Are you serious? That's not his call. I want you to tell

him to keep the Intel until we give him instructions."

"Nikki, he's a NOC. His mission is over. He's going to Beijing."

"Do we know when this operative will strike?"

"No, but my guess is that we have time. Michael would not be traveling to Beijing if the operation was close to being executed."

"What the hell do you think the President is going to say when he finds out there is a chance that President Kim is killed?"

"He'll probably want to see him dead, Nikki. I can't promise he'll agree to do this."

"Who the hell is this guy, Doug?"

"Michael. He's my best operative and our most valuable core collector."

"You tell Michael that his tenure with this agency will be over if he shares that Intel. I'll smooth things over with SIS. They will understand."

"Nikki, you know I rarely speak of policy. What will happen if Kim is killed? How do we know the new regime won't be worse?"

"Does that matter, Doug? You know how the President feels about this."

"I'll pass your instructions to Michael when he contacts me. I can't assure you he will listen."

"He better, Doug. Thanks for the Intel. I'm going to contact the President right away. Let's discuss this again after lunch."

"You got it, Nikki."

Click.

Doug expected the Director's reaction. The President had nominated her shortly after his election where he championed a harsh approach toward the reclusive regime. But he wasn't convinced the President would want to see a regime change. Rather, Doug believed the President would want to exhaust all elements of national power before using kinetic force.

Doug promised Alex Sawers an update and quickly placed a call to "C" who was likely enjoying an afternoon tea in London.

"Alex, my operative just contacted me. I have some bad news."

Alex sat back and expected the worse. He feared his legendary operative was dead.

"I presume you have news regarding John?"

"He's been moved to the Qincheng prison in Beijing. It gets worse."

"I doubt that," said "C."

"The target in Pyongyang is President Kim. Michael knows the name of the assassin, but has not shared it with the Chinese. He thinks he can free John first."

"We can't trust the Chinese, Doug. They'll imprison him the moment he divulges the information."

"I don't agree, Alex. I trust Michael's judgment implicitly. I'm sure he has good reasons for making the deal."

"Which are?" asked Sawers.

"I don't know. All I can say is I trust him. What do you think the Chinese will do once they get a name?" asked Doug.

"That depends on who the asset is. Can we assume the assassin is Chinese?"

"It's probable. There's little chance Liu contacted someone inside North Korea. It has to be someone there on a business contract or under diplomatic protection. Hell John, he could be a member of Kim's inner circle for all we know. We're just guessing at this point."

"If that is the case, Doug, then the Chinese will arrest him and return him to the mainland. I don't believe their leadership will allow Kim to be killed. What does your Director think?"

"She wants to keep the Chinese in the dark."

"That's it?"

"That's it, Alex. I just spoke to her."

"Thank you, Doug. I'll give the Foreign Secretary an update. I'm certain our views on this will be addressed with President Trump very soon. I'd like to speak with your man when this is over."

"You got it, Alex. Talk soon my friend."

Click.

Michael Brennan held one of the most sought-after pieces of intelligence in the world. Doug knew there would be heated debates at the White House in the coming days. Would John be sacrificed by policy makers advocating for letting Liu's assassin do the job? Or would they realize that the unknown of a post-Kim presidency was too great of a risk? Would the Director pressure Michael? thought Doug to himself.

It didn't matter. Nothing could be done until contact was reestablished with Michael. For now, the non-official cover spy would keep the world waiting.

The Peninsula Hotel, Beijing, China, June 29, 10:30 AM

Michael stared out the window from his luxury suite atop the Peninsula Hotel. The five-star rated venue was one of the finest in Beijing. The walls were a beautiful cream color adorned with famous Chinese works of art. The spacious marble bathroom included a hot tub, a hands-free telephone, and a nineteen-inch TV. It was a bit much, thought the career operative. Nonetheless, he had finally earned a good night's sleep and was ready to see John at Qincheng prison, located thirty kilometers north of central Beijing.

He was not alone. Two men from the Ministry of State security remained with Michael throughout the night. Echo may have trusted Michael, but her superiors felt otherwise. He was, after all, an American spy who withheld information in exchange for the release of an MI6 operative. Beijing was none too pleased but knew his information was valuable. For now, they would approve Echo's operation and play along.

Michael considered his options. There were very few. He had to be sure John would be released after giving Chinese intelligence the information they needed. However, Echo was an operator and even her handlers at MSS headquarters could change their minds at any moment. Then there was a knock at the front door.

"Good morning, Michael. Are you ready to see John?" asked Echo.

"I am. How close are we to getting him released?"

"It's going through the normal bureaucratic process. It will take another day or two."

"If your government doesn't agree to release him, then what?" asked Michael.

Echo ordered the two men to wait outside. She immediately reached for a pen and pad of paper provided by the hotel.

"Then we'll have to consider other options, Michael. Let us wait," said Echo as she handed Michael the note.

It read............*plan b like we spoke of in Bugat.*

Echo knew the Chinese had bugged the room before Michael's arrival. It was standard procedure to place audio equipment in the rooms of prominent western businessmen and suspected spies. Michael was aware of the practice and expected Echo's response.

"We must leave now, Michael. The prison is expecting us soon. They will have John ready."

"Well, I sure hope your bosses think carefully. The assassin is nearly ready," said Michael playing along.

Echo and Michael exited the Peninsula and quickly moved into a Mercedes SUV. There were two vehicles in front of them and one in the rear. The Chinese weren't taking any chances.

Traffic along Highway G6 was minimal and the convoy soon exited onto Huaichang Road. The prison was only a few miles away. This time, however, traffic was heavier.

Michael soon found himself along a narrow road lined with white birch trees. The prison, built in 1958, was tucked away in a misty mountainside and held China's most notorious inmates and political prisoners. Its red gates were surrounded by low concrete walls. For those on the outside, Qincheng seemed like a luxury retreat rather than a maximum-security prison.

The prison's commander and senior officers were expecting Echo and the rest of the MSS team. They were not accustomed to visitors unless, of course, they were senior officials from the Communist Party. The introduction of an American spy was a serious violation of protocol and akin to treason thought many of the staff there. However, orders to allow the visit came directly from the Minister of Public Security. There must have been one hell of a good reason for this, thought the prison's commander. After all, Qincheng had many secrets to hide.

"Welcome. I am Colonel Pan. You are here to visit inmate 62007?"

"We are. This is the American. He has permission to speak with the prisoner for fifteen minutes," said Echo.

Colonel Pan reached out and shook Michael's hand. The act pained the career officer as Michael quickly noticed the reluctant gesture. But his orders were clear.

Echo would accompany Michael through the visitor's office and into John's cell. Michael would not be left alone per their earlier agreement.

John's cell was tiny by any measurable standards. It was only six feet long by three feet wide. The bed was made of wood and there were metal grills guarding the small window at the top of the rear wall. It was a hell hole, thought Michael to himself as he entered through the iron door to John's cell.

"Michael, what the hell are you doing here, old chap. I never expected this."

"Here to save your ass, John. How are you bud?"

"The food is horrible, and the company is worse. Why is Echo here?" asked John.

"We made a deal. I'll explain later. I know who the assassin is in Pyongyang."

"Who?"

"That is for another time, my friend. I've given the Chinese an ultimatum. If they let you go, I give them the name."

"I see. What makes you think they'll play along?" asked John.

"They have no choice. I'm no analyst but it doesn't take

a rocket scientist to know they want what I've got. The target is President Kim."

"Kim? Jesus Christ. Did Liu Zhun tell you the assassin's name?"

"He did."

"Where is Liu now?"

"Buried somewhere I suppose," said Michael as he turned to Echo.

"He has been disposed of," said Echo.

"You can't trust the Chinese, Michael. They will violate whatever deal you made the moment they get that Intel."

"I know. That's where Echo comes in," said Michael.

"John, I am certain they will let you go. If I am wrong, there are those of us in the MSS who will work to free you in the future," said Echo.

"Just how the hell are you going to do that?" asked John.

"Do not worry about that. For now, you are safe and we must wait for news from Beijing. This only works if Michael provides us with the information."

"Michael, what in bloody hell are you going to do?" asked John.

"Going to see you get on a plane to London. When you are safely on the ground, I will give Echo what she needs."

"I doubt they'll let me go. You are wasting your time, Michael. I wish you hadn't come."

"Do not doubt me, my friend. This will work. I'm not going to let you rot in this hell hole."

"Does London know I'm here?" asked John.

"I assume so. I called Langley and let them know you were moved here. Doug is a good man and I am sure he has passed it on to London."

"I'm afraid you may have made a mistake, Michael. I can't see how the Chinese allow this. Think about it. You are asking them to let two western operatives just leave their country. In exchange, they get the name of an assassin who may or may not be in the position to kill the North Korean President. How do we know the man can do it?"

"We don't. I thought about that John. I'm betting they don't take the risk."

"What's to prevent them from alerting Pyongyang and keeping Kim out of the public eye for a while?"

"Nothing. Next question," said Michael with a smile.

"I doubt we'll be taking that chance, John. There's too much at stake. Besides, Michael did not have much of a choice."

"She's right. Guozhi implanted a damn chip in my neck."

"You could have gone home, Michael."

"Maybe. But where is that? I belong here. You will not die in this prison, John."

"I wonder what Langley and London will think of this? They might want to see Kim dead. Can you be sure they'll agree?"

"I don't care. I made a deal and that's what we're going to do. Besides, what does killing Kim accomplish? They'll put another man in his place within hours. He may be worse."

"I cannot disagree with that. Okay, Michael. This is your show."

"Sit tight, John. I don't know how this will unfold. Just be ready to go home and see your boys."

Michael gave John a quick embrace as Echo called for the guard to open the cell's door. The two returned to the front entrance of the prison and started their journey back to the Peninsula hotel. John began thinking of his boys as Michael wondered what his next move would be. He had the Intel the Chinese needed but he couldn't help wondering how much opposition there would be to the agreement. There was much to lose on both sides.

Hami, China, June 30, 7:07 AM

Lewis MacDonald remained in his hotel, along with the rest of his team. They were following Sawers' instructions and keeping a low profile in the city. A call from London had finally come, thought Lewis to himself.

"Lewis, I have a new assignment for you. I want you to go to Beijing and await instructions. Our man has been moved to Qincheng. I believe you are familiar with the prison?" asked Alex Sawers.

"You know I am, Alex. Is this another wild goose chase?"

"It may be, but I want you there before the morning and prepared to move at a moment's notice."

"What do we need to be prepared for, Alex?"

"An execution, Lewis."

"The target?"

"An American CIA operative. He has sensitive information and reports indicate he's going to share that information with the Chinese."

"No way in bloody hell, Alex. I won't be a stooge to whatever scheme you are cooking up."

"Your compensation will be five million, Lewis. The rest of your team doesn't have to know who he really is."

"What kind of Intel do you have on him?" asked Lewis.

"None now. We're searching through Chinese closed-circuit television in the areas we know he and our man worked. This is not something I want to do, Lewis. The Prime Minister is negotiating with the Americans."

"Do they want him dead?" asked Lewis.

"Some support it. Others do not."

"What information does this man have that's so damn important, Alex?"

"You know I can't share that, Lewis. This is what we signed up for. I don't like it, but if the order comes, then I must execute it. We have our duties."

"If it's just the one man, I will do it myself. My team is going home, Alex."

"That's your call. I do not care how you get the job done."

"Okay, Alex. Contact me in the morning with an update. I want half the money in my account by then."

"Agreed."

Click.

Lewis MacDonald had not always been the most honorable man. He was an SIS operative who learned to operate in the shadows. This gray area often left operatives like Lewis struggling to determine right from wrong. It was never easy following orders from bureaucrats in London, but service to country meant getting his hands dirty from time to time. Over the years, this inner struggle weighed on the operative and many like him. There were many operations when Lewis questioned his orders, but believed their motives were justified. In time, this unquestioned devotion to duty and service became more difficult. Despite being a paid contractor, Sawers' order troubled the former spy.

Lewis exited his room and quickly informed the team of the change. They would return to London in the morning and he would wire them a percentage of the revised contract. They were, after all, a team, though Lewis would keep half for himself.

A short while later, Lewis found his way back to the hotel room. Why would they want an American operative dead? he thought to himself. If the man was betraying his country, why was MI6 involved? Why weren't the Americans handling this? Lewis brushed the questions aside for the moment. Beijing and a five-million-dollar contract would remain fresh on his mind for the foreseeable future.

Pyongyang, North Korea, June 30, 9:28 AM

Sun Boling arrived at his office. His recent conversation with Liu left the career naval officer and assassin with many doubts. Liu had ordered him to proceed with the operation despite the many apparent failures the corps had suffered after Guozhi's capture. What was the point? Boling asked himself. Liu told him long ago that each operation had to unfold nearly simultaneously to have the desired effect. Boling began to panic and seriously considered ending his efforts.

Then his phone rang.

"Boling, the ambassador wants to speak with you right away."

"On my way," said Boling.

A few minutes later, Boling arrived and entered Ambassador Li's office.

"Good morning, Sun. I'm sorry to call you in on such short notice," said Li.

"That is not a problem, Mr. Ambassador. How may I assist you?"

"Your recent presentation at Rajin naval base was well received. The North Koreans are requesting another briefing next week. Apparently, President Kim is interested in attending."

"Why would he do that? As you know, I cannot share all the technical information and any missiles they purchase will not be linked with our satellites."

"I'm sure he is aware of that by now. However, I need you to do it. We are hoping for additional contracts."

"Of course, Mr. Ambassador. I would be honored to give the presentation. What day is it scheduled for?" asked Boling.

"Next week. It appears the briefing will take place at

their Eastern Fleet headquarters in Wonson. We'll know more this afternoon. I am approving a few days of vacation prior to the brief. I want you to enjoy yourself and be well rested. A lot is riding on this, Boling."

"Thank you, sir. I will do my best."

"The commanders of the Eastern Fleet and Korean People's Navy will also be in attendance, along with a few representatives from the Workers' Party."

"This sounds like a large gathering, sir," said Boling.

"Quite the contrary, Boling. There will be less than ten in attendance. The North Koreans value their secrets as do we."

"An intimate setting is good. I will not let you down. What if there are questions I am not allowed to answer? I can't imagine President Kim approving more sales without learning more of our technical capabilities."

"That is not something you need to worry about. They will eventually find solutions to any technical limitations. They have made many such purchases in the past."

"But how would they overcome guidance issues without access to our satellites?" asked Boling.

"Not our concern, Boling. Just make them happy and let them figure it out," said Li as he smiled.

"Yes, sir."

Boling departed and returned to his office. The unexpected opportunity to brief President Kim was a gift. It would give Boling the best opportunity to carry out his mission. But Liu's plan had unraveled, and doubts had crept in. Would the assassination of President Kim really mean the fall of the Chinese government? Too many other events had to happen if the corps was to achieve its ambitious goals, he thought to himself. He decided to reach out to Liu despite his assertion that someone would be contacting him soon.

The phone rang and rang.

Boling hung up and dialed it once again.

Still nothing. Boling leaned back in his chair and looked out the window. The dark clouds hovering outside were an ominous sign, he thought to himself. But for who? Sun Boling was cut off from his commander, and unsure of what to do next.

Peninsula Hotel, Beijing, China, July 1, 02:10 AM

Michael Brennan awoke. His cell phone had buzzed, and he sluggishly turned his body toward the nightstand. His eyes began to slowly open as he struggled to focus on the five-inch screen. It was a missed call from Echo. Michael turned on the light and was prepared to return Echo's call. Then the phone rang again.

"Echo, what the hell is going on?" asked Michael groggily.

"You are in danger, Michael. Are my men with you?"

"I assume so, Echo," said Michael as he reached for his pistol.

"Go check. Be prepared for anything. I am on my way."

Michael hung up and carefully approached the bedroom door. He could hear the television and assumed one of Echo's men was probably awake. Nevertheless, he didn't take any chances. He slowly turned the doorknob and peered into the large living room.

Then suddenly two rounds were fired from across the room. The first round landed in the wall's casing just inches from Michael's head. The second round entered through the door's panel as Michael returned fire.

"Go forward. We have him," yelled one of the men as he fired several more rounds towards Michael's position.

The second man sprinted toward the sofa and crouched behind it as he fired several rounds in Michael's direction.

Michael had enough. He reached around the corner and fired the remaining rounds in his pistol toward the couch. He quickly released the magazine and slammed in another as he sprinted toward the second assailant. Michael fired two rounds toward the first shooter and then dove to the floor alongside the couch. The daring move gave Michael an opportunity to fire a single round into the man's chest as he fell to the floor. Michael noticed the body of one of Echo's men and assumed the other was dead.

"This isn't working out as planned, is it?" shouted Michael.

The second assailant fired aimlessly toward the couch.

"Who the hell are you?" shouted Michael as he peered above the couch.

The tables were now turned. The second man remained crouched behind the bar. His partner was dead, and the element of surprise was lost. Sun Tzu would be disappointed.

"There's no way out of this, man. Raise your hands slowly and stand up. I will not fire," proclaimed Michael.

"I cannot do that. I have my orders," said the assassin.

"From who?" asked Michael.

Then Echo arrived and opened the front door. The man crouched behind the bar looked as she drew her weapon and fired. Two rounds entered the assailant's chest and he fell to the floor.

"Good timing," said Michael.

"We must leave now, Michael. There may be more on the way."

"What the hell happened here, Echo? You obviously got wind of it."

"We received intelligence from a source who indicated these men were coming for you. I know nothing else, Michael."

"That's not good enough, Echo. I thought Chinese intelligence had this place secured?"

"Me too. I don't know, Michael. I'm going to take you to one of our safe houses. It's not far from here. We'll figure this out later."

"You don't have any idea who's behind this, Echo?"

asked Michael.

"I have my suspicions."

"Which are?"

"They could be operatives within the Ministry of State Security. They may not have wanted you to give us the Intel on Liu's man in Pyongyang."

"That seems like a bit of a stretch, Echo. I thought your government was prepared to do anything to keep Kim alive?"

"We are, Michael. But there are always a few who dissent on such matters. Let's get you out of here and with any luck, my government will approve John's release very soon."

"I sure as hell hope so, Echo," said Michael as he followed her out the door.

Echo reached for her cell phone.

"I need a cleaning team sent to the hotel at once. Dispose of the bodies right away and let me know when it's finished."

"Yes, ma'am," said the operator on the other end.

Michael followed Echo and exited the hotel to the vehicle parked outside. As he sat down and closed the passenger door, he wondered why the man behind the bar did not fire at Echo. Michael wanted answers, but his first concern remained the release of John Dearlove.

The two soon found themselves at a high-rise apartment complex in downtown Beijing. The massive complex was seventy stories high and housed some of Beijing's elite political leaders and business executives.

"Michael, have you considered my proposition to give us the Intel regardless of whether John is released?"

"I have."

"And your answer is?" asked Echo.

"No. I want him released and my timetable has been moved forward. I want an answer by this evening, Echo."

"I cannot guarantee that, Michael."

"You'll have to, Echo."

Michael continued the bluff. He had every intention of providing the Chinese the Intel they wanted. After all, he believed President Kim was a rational leader who would never risk his ancestral regime. He would continue being provocative and continue his enduring quest to acquire long-range missiles capable of delivering nuclear warheads. However, Michael gambled on the notion that the reclusive President was not suicidal. He hoped the bureaucrats and intelligence analysts back home had arrived at the same conclusion.

Michael would soon drift asleep. Before doing so, he wondered why the second killer at the Peninsula Hotel did not fire on Echo. In time, he hoped he would get the answer.

The Situation Room, The White House, Washington, D.C., July 1, 9:02 AM

President Trump arrived in the situation room. Awaiting him were the Vice President, National Security Advisor, Director, CIA, Director, Defense Intelligence Agency, Captain Lisa Bouquet, and Oliver Tanner. A single member of the situation room sat in the corner and was responsible for changing slides during the presentation.

"Good morning, everyone. Let's get started, okay."

"Good morning, sir. I know you asked for Olie, but I've taken the liberty to ask Captain Bouquet, a senior intelligence officer assigned to the J2, to join us. I'd like to offer you two views on North Korea's missile program."

The President did not appear pleased but deferred to his trusted national security advisor.

"Okay, let's see where this takes us," said the Commander-in-chief.

Captain Bouquet began her briefing. She focused on two key developments observed during recent North Korean missile tests. She first stated that technical data collected from the Hwasong-14, an intercontinental ballistic missile, did not indicate enough power to deliver a nuclear-armed missile to the American mainland.

"How long before the North Koreans can achieve this capability?" asked President Trump.

"It's my judgment they are approximately twelve months out, Mr. President."

"What if you are wrong? What if they already have the capability?"

"The data is clear, Mr. President. They need to conduct many more tests to generate the thrust needed to deliver a nuke."

"Okay, go on," said the President.

"The second issue is re-entry. The latest test indicates the heat shield they're using is flawed. Even if the North Koreans could solve the weight issue, they do not have the capability to protect the nuclear warhead during its terminal phase. Even at a depressed trajectory, or lower apogee, the heat shields are not enough."

"Why do we think the re-entry vehicle is flawed? How do we not know the North Koreans didn't just detonate it on the way down?"

"It's possible, sir. But they haven't tested it yet and we see no indication they will have the heat shields necessary for quite some time."

"How long is that?" asked the President.

"At least another test or two. Then they'll need to study the data and begin production. This will take at least a year, sir."

President Trump turned to the Director of the Defense Intelligence Agency.

"General Richardson, do you concur with Captain Bouquet?"

"I do not, sir. I think Olie has a different view, Mr. President."

Herb McMullen appeared visibly upset. But he figured Tanner's boss at DIA would side with the career intelligence analyst.

"Olie, what say you?" asked the President.

"Well, Mr. President, I disagree. I believe President Kim is six months away from being able to hit the mainland. I can go through the slides to show you why that is."

"That won't be necessary, Olie. I trust your analytical judgment."

"Mr. President, I think it's important to see the data.

I think Captain Bouquet's argument is compelling. I think you'll see why Olie's data may be inconclusive," said Mc-Mullen.

The President was not amused by the inference. He turned to Oliver Tanner.

"Has General McMullen seen the slides, Olie?"

"I believe the Director sent them to his office last night, Mr. President," said Tanner standing resolute.

"Herb, what is it about Olie's conclusion that you disagree with?"

"I believe the heat shields need further testing. It takes months to prepare for an ICBM test. Then the data must be studied. They'll need to do at least two more tests. I believe Olie's assertion that the heat shields will be ready in six months assumes both tests are successful."

The President sat back in his chair and stared at Tanner.

"Why are you convinced the heat shields will be ready in six months?" asked the President.

"Sir, all the North Koreans need is silicone elastomers or a ceramic based surface insulation system. The technology has been around for decades, and the North Koreans possess such materials. I don't think it's a stretch to assess they'll be able to protect the re-entry vehicle. It's simple engineering and the North Koreans have good engineers."

Then the President stunned the room.

"Olie, if we ever got the chance to kill President Kim, should we take it?"

"Mr. President, Olie is not cleared for this," said Mc-Mullen.

"Excuse me, Herb, it's a hypothetical question."

"No, sir," said Tanner emphatically.

"Why?" asked the President.

Oliver Tanner looked at his commander and looked for

a nod of approval. General Richardson gave it.

"Mr. President, Oliver is an analyst. He doesn't have the expertise to offer his opinion," chimed in the CIA director.

A cloud of tension had appeared over the gathering.

"That's okay, Nikki. I'm just curious what Olie thinks. Let him speak," said the President.

Nikki sat back and appeared visibly frustrated. This is not what she and Herb discussed at breakfast.

"Sir, President Kim is rational. I do not believe he would ever strike first and attack the United States or our allies in the region. He knows he would be killed within hours of such a move. His priority is to cling to power. If we take him out, who comes next? His replacement could be worse. I would advise against it, Mr. President."

Short and to the point. Oliver Tanner learned long ago to be brief, be bold and be gone.

"Thank you, Olie. I don't like it, but I agree with you."

Herb McMullen looked at Nikki. They had lost their bid to convince the President to let the operation in Pyongyang unfold. Oliver Tanner had once again gotten the better of Herb McMullen.

Later that evening, Oliver Tanner sat on his couch watching the evening news. He was sipping on his favorite drink, a cocktail consisting of Jack Daniels Tennessee Whiskey and coke. Two cherries helped curb the harshness of the famous American liquor produced in Moore County, Tennessee. Breaking news flashed across his screen. It read............ *National Security Advisor to the President resigns.*

Oliver Tanner smiled. Herb McMullen's days of pressuring intelligence analysts were over.

Daxing District, southern Beijing, China, July 1, 4:22 PM

Echo and Michael remained at the safe house in the southern district of Daxing. Michael was anxious and getting nervous while waiting for news from Echo's handlers in the Ministry of State Security. The district was home to nearly seven hundred thousand residents and considered a prime location for Echo's safe house. Over the years, Echo had used the location to run her assets and collect valuable intelligence. She had never envisioned using it to protect a CIA operative. Nevertheless, Beijing approved the move and would accept the risk that Michael Brennan became aware of its location. It didn't matter, as soon as the target in Pyongyang was identified, Michael would be deported, and the safe house closed.

Then Echo's cell phone rang.

"Echo, this is Han. The Director will be arriving at your location soon. Please be prepared to receive him and some of his staff."

"Why is the Director coming here?" asked Echo.

"He wants to meet the CIA operative and gain the intelligence himself."

"That is my job, Han. Why was I not informed of this earlier?"

"I am simply passing along the information as I was instructed. He should be there at five o'clock."

"Okay, Han. Has a decision about the British operative been made?"

"Yes."

"What is it, Han?"

"The Director will notify you personally."

"Why the secrecy Han?"

"Goodbye, Echo."

Click.

Echo returned to the sofa and sat next to Michael.

"Any news, Echo?" asked Michael.

"The Director of the Counter-intelligence Division will be here soon."

"Have they released John?"

"I do not know, Michael."

Echo appeared uneasy. Michael knew something was wrong.

"Why is your Director coming?" asked Michael.

"I do not know that either, Michael."

About twenty minutes later, Echo and Michael heard a knock on the door.

Kwang Zeng, the Director of the Counter-intelligence Division, along with several of his officers entered.

"Director Kwang, I am honored you are here. May I ask why?"

"To do this, Echo," said Zeng.

The man flanked to his left immediately reached into his jacket and removed a pistol. He pointed it squarely at Echo's body and fired four rounds into her chest. A few seconds later, he took three steps forward and fired another round into her forehead.

Echo was dead. Michael did not flinch.

"Michael, I am Director Kwang of the Counter-intelligence Division. I've been told you have information about an assassin in Pyongyang?" asked Kwang.

"I do. Why the hell did you shoot her?"

"I will ask the questions, Michael. Now, who is the assassin?"

"I will tell you if I know John Dearlove has been freed."

"This is not a negotiation, Michael. I will only ask one

more time. Who is the man in Pyongyang?"

Michael stared into the Director's eyes. He immediately knew he was a serious man.

"I will not speak unless I know John is free. We had a deal."

"No, Michael. You had a deal with Echo. Ding," said Kwang as he turned to the man to his right.

Ding fired a single round into Michael's left arm. The round grazed the muscle surrounding the shoulder. By all measures, it was a scratch and intended to warn Michael.

"We can do this all day. I will honor my deal with Echo when I know Dearlove is safe."

Kwang Zeng looked deeply into Michael's eyes. He too knew the CIA operative was a serious man and unlikely to give up the information. The gambit had failed. Kwang then reached into his pocket and pulled out a cell phone.

He dialed a number and handed it to Michael.

"Hello?" answered Dearlove.

"John, it's Michael. Where the hell are you."

"I'm at the Beijing International Airport. I just boarded a private jet and sitting here. Where are you, Michael."

"Not far my friend. You're going home."

Click.

The man sitting next to John Dearlove reached for the phone and hung up.

"The British spy will be in international air space soon. Now, who is the man in Pyongyang?"

"How do I know you won't just kill me and bring John back to prison?"

"Trust is earned, Michael. For now, you will have to trust me. We both know you have no choice. I want the man's name in Pyongyang. I don't care about you or the British spy. You have my word."

Michael gave in. His gut instincts told him the man was telling the truth. Even if he was wrong, he had gotten John as far as he could without the Intel. It was time to reveal the name.

"The man's name is Sun Boling."

Kwang smiled.

"Thank you, Mr. Brennan. John will be airborne in a few minutes."

"May I ask why Echo was killed?"

"Echo was a member of the assassination corps here in Beijing. She was in a different cell than Guozhi. She would have killed you the moment you revealed the assassin's name."

"Who were the shooters at the Peninsula Hotel?" asked Michael.

"Members of her cell who did not agree to keep you alive. They wanted you dead the moment you were brought here to Beijing," said Kwang.

"How many more of these bastards are in your country?" asked Michael.

"We've arrested several dozen members around the country. But we are unsure how many more there are."

It made sense. Michael had wondered why the second shooter at the Peninsula Hotel had not drawn his weapon at Echo.

"You have a problem on your hands," said Michael.

"We will identify the rest of the group in time, Mr. Brennan. My men will now take you to a hotel near the airport. Once we have Sun Boling in custody, you will be flown to a location of your choosing. Where would you like to go?"

"Jakarta."

"My government thanks you for this information. I do not want to see you in my country again, Michael. Do I make myself clear?" asked Kwang.

"Quite clear. However, I cannot promise my government will not order me to return in the future," said Michael with a slight grin on his face.

Kwang dismissed his arrogance.

"Then you will have to convince them. It would be a mistake, otherwise," said Kwang.

Michael and two of Kwang's men soon exited the safe house and began their short trip to the Hilton Beijing Capital Airport hotel. Michael would remain there until Sun Boling's capture and subsequent interrogation.

Beijing International Airport, China, July 4, 3:45 PM

Michael Brennan boarded the Air China passenger jet bound for Jakarta, Indonesia. The seven-hour flight would give him an opportunity to make some much-needed phone calls to Langley. Kwang and his men prevented Michael from making any phone calls during his stay at the Hilton. On his way to the airport, one of Kwang's men told him of Boling's execution. The man had confessed after several days of brutal interrogation.

About fifteen minutes into the flight, the captain made an announcement that it was permissible for the passengers to turn on their digital devices and use the aircraft's telephone services. Michael's cell phone had been confiscated in Hami by Guozhi, so he was forced to use the plane's unsecure line.

Michael called Doug Weatherbee, his boss at Langley.

"Doug, it's Michael. I'm on the way to Jakarta."

"Michael, great to hear from you. What happened to our man in Pyongyang?"

"Dead. How is John?"

"He's safely back in London. He asked that you call him."

"Absolutely. Have someone from Jakarta pick me up. I'll send a report in a few days."

"You got it," said Doug.

"Do I still have a job, Doug? Or did I piss off enough people in D.C. by giving the Chinese what they wanted?"

"Oh, you still have a job, Michael. In fact, I'm sending you back to Tel Aviv soon. Do you remember Aaron?"

"Of course. He worked with Elif on that job we did a few years ago in Turkey."

"Elif is alive, Michael. She never died in Hatay."

"Huh, Aaron told me she passed."

"He lied, my friend. She survived the attack."

"What about my job in Indonesia?"

"On hold for now, Michael. Aaron has asked for you and I've agreed to his request."

"When do I leave?"

"Take a few weeks off, bud. I'll send you instructions when its time."

Michael hung up and planned to call John Dearlove shortly. He and his new friend would catch up and make plans to enjoy a hearty meal in downtown London. In the meantime, he gazed out the window toward the clear blue skies and wondered what deadly mission awaited him next.

Acknowledgments

To the courageous men and women who operate in the shadows, thank you for your service to our great nation. Though most of your stories will never be told, your sacrifices make the world a safer place. To Shane, Matthew and others at Spybrary, your friendship and comradery mean everything. To my beautiful partner Laura, your wisdom, strength and love inspires me to write. Finally, thank you to "Ted", a true hero doing good work.

Author Bio

Lieutenant Colonel Michael Brady, USA, (RET), is a former career intelligence officer and Director of the Presidential Emergency Operations Center in the White House under President George W. Bush. He has performed a wide variety of tactical and strategic intelligence functions including long-range surveillance, intelligence analysis and collection management.

Please visit his website at www.michaelbradybooks.com

CPSIA information can be obtained
at www.ICGtesting.com
Printed in the USA
BVHW081124131118
532911BV00001B/21/P

9 781641 368568